DOUBLE LIFE

ASTRONOMICAL LOVE SERIES
BOOK 3

K. ILLER

First edition January 2025

Book Cover by Kim Giller

Editing and Formatting by Vanessa Mena, Dark Queens Author Services

TRIGGER WARNINGS

Brief mentions of lewd acts involving a minor (masturbating in front of minor)
Brief mentions of abuse of a minor (hitting, belt whipping, duct taped to a chair half naked)
Attempted rape of a minor
Mentions of child neglect
Mentions of drug addicted parents
Foster caregiver abuse and neglect
Theft
Hints at possible incest between father and son
Foster "siblings" romance
Bullying
Bully the bullies
Teen pregnancy
Hypervigilance
Bodily fluids (vomit, blood, spit, feces, cum)
Murder
Torture
Kidnapping
Captivity

Degradation
Human trafficking
Rape
Threats of harm to a child
Coercion
Mentions of COVID
Bruises
Piquerism
Suicidal ideation
Nicotine/Smoking
Theft
Criminal activity
Explicit language
Abuse
PTSD
Consumption of bodily fluid con and non-con (cum, feces, vomit, urine, blood)
Violence
Blood play (consensual and non-consensual)
Truancy
Hacking
Bound by restraints - rope and chains
Framed for murder
Deceased parent (murdered)
Seeing murdered parent (not MCs)
Credit card fraud
Stolen identity
Degradation
Sexual tension
Scars
CBT (cock and ball torture with rope)
Impersonation
Castration
Cutting tongue

TRIGGER WARNINGS

Eye gouging
Ear canal stabbing
Slit throat
Force fed acid

In the midst of a storm in your brain, you'll fear that the rain will drown you and the lightning will strike. Just remember that there's always beauty and light within it, even if the darkness that closes in tries to snuff it out.
Still not seeing it?
Open your eyes and you'll find that the beauty and light was you all along.

Listen to the playlist on Spotify. Scan or click below.

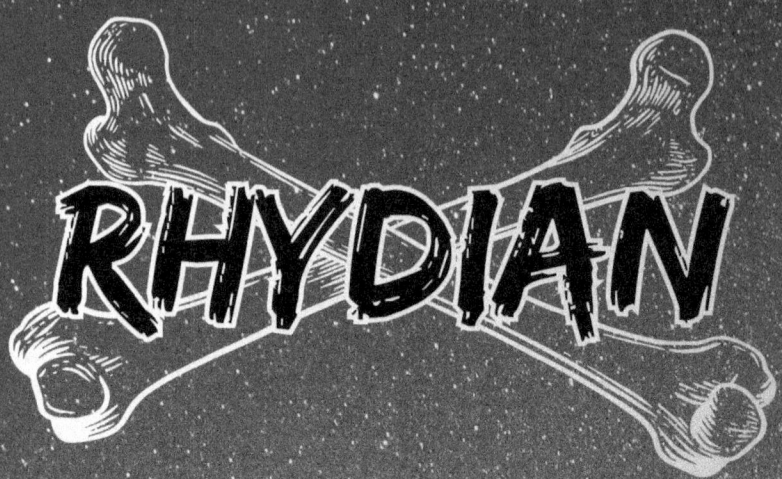

RHYDIAN

PROLOGUE

LIFELESS STARS

January 2019

Rhydian

I could almost imagine it isn't the dead of winter while we're roasting in this fucking social worker's hot box of a car. My poor excuse of a winter coat crinkles every time I wipe away the sweat from my face.

I roll my head against the frozen window and bounce my leg, trying to distract myself with the Taylor Swift song playing on the radio. Our far-too-young for this job social worker turns the volume up. Jesus Christ, the last thing I need to do is memorize the words to yet *another* Taylor Swift song. I take a deep breath in through my nose and immediately regret it. My nostrils are filled with the scent of stale cigarettes and air freshener. Speaking of cigarettes, I catch Rhyatt just as he snatches a pack of smokes out of her purse. He looks at me with a goofy ass smile and shakes it in my direction before pocketing it. I roll my eyes at his antics just as the car slides to a stop in an icy driveway.

Rhyatt and I lean our heads together as we stare out the windshield at our new home. Well, by the looks of this rundown house, it's only new to us. I'd ask if they ever scope these places out before bringing foster kids in, but years of house-hopping tells me that no, no they fucking don't.

The Slater twins have a reputation amongst the foster community. I think they're just mad because we refuse to become victims of our circumstances. We protect ourselves and those who need it. We take what we need to survive, because who the fuck else is going to provide for us? Sure as fuck won't be our deadbeat dad, or our mom who's now dust and bones six feet under. You would think people would talk more about the shit these foster parents do than about us, but what the fuck do I know. Our worker clicks the music off, unbuckles and slowly turns to face us. In sync as usual, Rhyatt and I both sit back so she's not in our space. She attempts to smile but it falls flat, ending with a heavy sigh.

"Alright, boys. I know you don't need me to remind you, but I'm going to do it anyway. This is it. You have five months until you age out, and this is the last foster home available to you. You're all out of chances. Make. This. Work."

Rhyatt looks around at the frozen tundra outside and makes a show of twirling his bangs tinted with faded blue Sharpie as he says, "Would you say that we're... on thin ice?"

"Enough," I groan at his cheesy ass joke and smack his arm. I point at the darkening sky. "It's getting dark. You know what that means."

The worker crinkles her brows in confusion. "What about the dark?"

Rhyatt and I toss our ratty backpacks on our shoulder and grab the garbage bag that holds what little belongings we have. "You don't want to know," we say in unison as we open our doors.

PROLOGUE

I throw my leg out to test how well our newly-stolen shitkickers handle the ice. My toes press tightly against the toe of the boot, doubled-up socks doing little to stop the biting cold as I pull myself out of the car. I hike my backpack strap further up my shoulder and step up beside Rhyatt. We slowly walk behind the worker, watching as she wobbles and skates across the slick driveway to the old, rickety steps. Our boots crunch against the haphazardly tossed salt on the steps and we wait as she knocks on the door. I take notice of the peeling paint on the house, making it look like a mix of puke green and brown. She raises her hand to knock again and freezes mid-motion as the door is yanked open with a squeak.

An older guy with shaggy gray hair and an unkempt anchor goatee schools his angry features. His yellowing, jacked-up teeth make me cringe as he attempts to smile, the effort making his face look awkward. The sudden transformation makes Rhyatt and I tap our elbows together. The quick change in his demeanor tells us we're heading straight into the lion's den… again. Jokes on him, though. Age doesn't define strength, and as the saying goes, there's strength in numbers. Two against one, we'll always defeat the predator that lies in wait.

The social worker clasps her mitten-covered hands to her mouth and blows into them. Stepping back, she turns so she can look at us, standing stiffly and the man hovering in the doorway who's sizing us up.

With a tight-lipped smile, she nods. "Well, you have all the information needed on the boys. Thank you so much for doing this. Feel free to call the number on the card in the packet if you need anything." She turns her back to him, fully facing us. "No more incidents. Behave."

Her gaze drops pointedly at our stolen boots, and then meets our eyes. I refrain from rolling my eyes at the 'incident' she's referring to. Rhyatt snorts and shakes his hands in the air.

"Yeah, you caught us, lady. How could we resist stealing empty beer cans and cigarette butts from the last shithole?" He scoffs and pushes past her. She doesn't reply, just skates her way back to the car as we get ready for what lies beyond the threshold. Dear old foster daddy crosses his arms and blocks the doorway. I stand next to Rhyatt as we match his stance and stare him down. A key dangling from a chain around his neck glints in the faint light and lands perfectly over his forearm. My stomach twists at the realization of what it is.

How many things are locked up to keep us out?

Or worse, keep us locked in?

A voice, smooth and sinister, slithers out from behind the old man. "Dad? Are they my new brothers?"

I bristle at his question. "No."

He steps into view with a grin and pushes his hair back from his forehead. I almost miss what he says when I notice he has a matching key around his neck. "Hi, I'm Blake," he says, all with all the fake polite charm he can muster. "I hope one day you'll both feel comfortable enough to call me brother." Rhyatt's responding snort morphs into his goofy-ass giggle.

"Enough. Blake, go find something to do." Thatcher snaps his fingers. His gaze shifts back to us "You two, follow me."

Every step he takes up the stairs is punctuated by a loud creak, the sagging steps threaten to give out under his weight. "My name is Thatcher. You can address me as such, or sir. I'm not your daddy. You will follow all of my rules without question. Home before dark. Stay fucking quiet. Meals are at the same time every day. If you aren't sitting at the table when the meal is ready, you forfeit your chance to eat. Don't even think about trying to find something for yourself, all the food is locked up.

You ungrateful little shits always act like the government gives us fat checks to babysit you. Newsflash: they don't."

At the top of the stairs he turns and brandishes the key around his neck with a devilish grin. I shove my hands in my jacket pockets and push my nails into my palm to keep from doing something stupid. Typical. Another piece-of-shit foster parent. He spins to the left and walks to a door at the end of the hall. He pulls the key over his head and it ruffles his greasy hair. We walk up behind him as he opens the door and looks back at us with a weird smile. "Play nice, boys."

Rhyatt and I look at each other in confusion. "Huh?"

Dim light spills into the hall as he slowly opens the door. With a muttered, "Behave."

I walk in first, with Rhyatt close behind me, too close. His full weight crashes into my back and we fall to the floor, a tangle of limbs, backpacks and garbage bags.

"WHAT THE FUCK?!" We shout simultaneously. The door slams shut behind us, followed by the clink of the lock turning in place.

A soft whimper catches my attention. I jerk my head up, searching for the source of the sound. In the corner of the room, shaking legs come into view covered in baggy sweats and balled up fists next to them. I suck in a sharp breath and my heart races when I see her face.

It's her.

Beautiful Ophelia.

I can't believe she's here. Her brown hair is thrown up in a messy bun, with stray hairs falling around her face. Full, pink lips tremble and hazel eyes reach mine. Her left eye is framed by a nasty bruise which instantly has me pissed. I stomp towards her, fists clenched, ready to ask if the piece of shit Thatcher did that to her. She lunges forward, eyes wide in panic, throwing haymakers.

"Don't touch me! I can't believe you! I thought you guys were different!"

Different? I step back with my palms up in surrender, ready to block the hits. "Whoa, whoa! I wasn't going to touch you. I was just going to ask if Thatcher did that to you." She immediately freezes mid-swing, hair falling from the hair tie as her chest heaves.

"What?" She croaks.

I put my palm over my heart, "I'm Rhydian-"

"I know who you are," she rolls her eyes with a huff. "Everyone does. You're the protectors at the school."

Feisty little thing.

"We protect those who need protecting, yes. Which means we will *never* hurt you. I understand that trust isn't something freely given, but I promise we'll keep you safe." I rub my finger around my eye and point towards hers. "That shit is done. Go get some sleep, we'll stay by the door."

She bites her lip and searches my face before taking a step back. "Okay," she whispers. She drops onto the small mattress on the floor and gasps, "Oh." She quietly slides the closet door that's next to the mattress open and crawls in. I watch as she pushes a box aside and a giant hole in the wall is revealed. She pulls out a big, black garbage bag that looks far worse than ours and tosses it on her mattress. She pushes the box back into place and crawls out of the closet, closing it behind her. I watch as she takes slow steps towards us with the bag. "We only have one bed. If you're sleeping by the door, it'll be really uncomfortable. This should help."

I take the bag from her outstretched hands and find pillows and sleeping bags inside. Rhyatt yanks the bag out of my hands and laughs. "Right on, mystery girl, thanks."

She nods, taking a cautious step backwards. "I'm Ophelia by the way."

I quietly hum *Ophelia* by *The Lumineers* with a smile on my face. A blush forms on her cheeks and she ducks away. My amusement is short-lived as a pillow smacks my face, blocking my view of her. My eyes water from the fabric trying to become one with my eyeballs.

I throw a hand out and blindly swing at Rhyatt. "Bitch."

"Jerk," he responds, before dropping to the floor and getting comfortable in the sleeping bag. I roll out my sleeping bag and crawl inside, pushing my feet against the door.

"Don't forget to have-"

"One boot on the edge and one in the middle, yeah I know, Rhyd. Try to remember you're only four minutes older, not years, bossy pants."

I close my eyes and sigh. I can't believe she knows who I am. Turning my head in Ophelia's direction, I smile when she quickly shuts her eyes.

Caught you, pretty girl.

"Every predator is a prey, and every prey has a predator."
   -B.U.K.O.L.A.

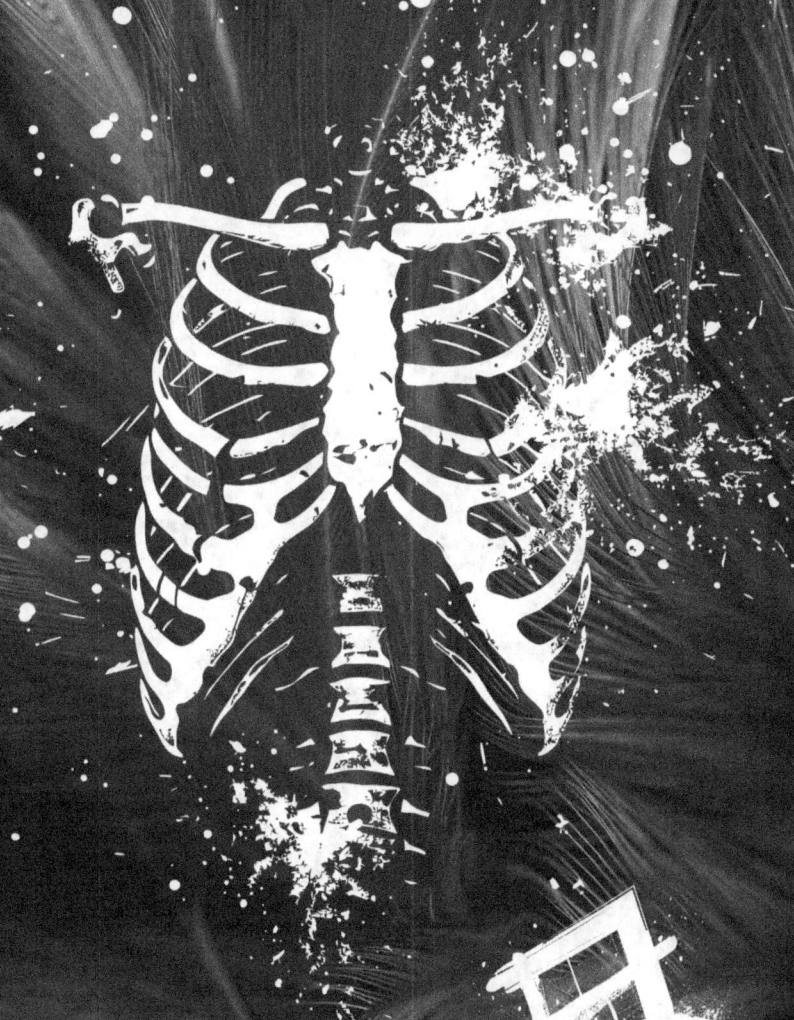

♪ PART 1

CHAPTER ONE

GIVE

February 14, 2019

Ophelia

I briefly awaken to the faint sound of whispers behind me. Sleep sucks me in again and the last thing I hear is a low murmur.

"Just keep her safe, bitch."

"Sure thing, jerk."

I want to laugh at their antics. Maybe I did, but I finally feel somewhat safe enough to let the darkness creep in again and I'm out.

I feel as if my body is bouncing on a trampoline. My eyes shoot open and I try to get my bearings. My heart races at the thought of what I could be waking up to. I *knew* I shouldn't have allowed myself to get too comfortable. Thatcher is here for me again. I sigh in relief when I hear Rhyatt's goofy laugh. The tension in my body melts away as my vision clears and I see him twirling his bangs, which are now colored with red Sharpie. I need to convince him to steal actual dye to get more variety. I know it's easier to steal Sharpies, but doesn't he get tired of only using a few different colors? There's so much fun to be had with real hair dye.

"Good morning, Ophie girl. Get your booty up and get ready. Let's blow this popsicle stand before Creepy McCreeperson wakes up for the day."

I stretch my arms out to the sides, my face scrunches in confusion when my hand falls on something that feels like a row of smooth rocks. My fingers close around it and bring it closer, sucking in a breath when I see what it is. A bracelet with rock beads. A smile breaks on my face when I realize where it came from. My favorite twin. I run my finger across each bead before sliding it on my wrist. Did he remember what I told him while rambling on about my obsession with ravens?

Embarrassment floods me as I recall gushing about everything I've learned about ravens, and how my last name started it all. I spilled my guts about how my hunt for my birth parents turned into discovering John Lennon and The Beatles. I told him how I fell in love with their song *Blackbird* and how that song and ravens became my new identity. For once, something was mine, and I held onto that like a lifeline.

That conversation is where I learned about Rhydian's ability to memorize the words to a song after only hearing it once. My cheeks burn when I realize the other twin is standing above me, watching my expression with a smirk. I clear my throat and shuffle off the small tattered mattress on the floor. I'm still half asleep and forget that we have the mattress close to the door. My feet get caught in the boys' blankets and I careen towards the closed door. Rhyatt yanks me back by the hood of my oversized sweatshirt. "Sorry!" he says, letting go as I regain my balance. "Knew I should've picked those up before you woke up. My bad, Ophie."

I shake my head and step away from his hold. "No, it's fine. You can do that while I go get dressed in the closet. When I'm done, you can toss me all of it so I can put it in there."

I shake my head and chuckle as Rhyatt gives me a goofy ass salute. "Yes, ma'am!"

We tip-toe down the stairs. I've mapped out every spot that makes the steps creak and carefully avoid each one, Rhyatt close behind. I grab the door handle just as my stomach rumbles loudly. I quickly slap my hand over my stomach, willing it to shut the fuck up. I look over my shoulder in a panic and Rhyatt is searching the space as well. When we don't hear Thatcher, we rush out the front door, closing it softly behind us. I speed-walk to the sidewalk, Rhyatt falling into step next to me. I release the breath I was holding with a shaky laugh.

"Fuck, I hate it here."

"You and me both, sister," he says as he nudges me.

We both pull out our travel toothbrushes and toothpaste, brushing our teeth quickly. Rhyatt spits his toothpaste out in the road, while I spit in someone's bushes.

I roll the sleeves of my hoodie up and pull my backpack in front of me to grab my sweet pineapple and honey melon lotion. I wouldn't dare wear that shit while in the house with nasty Thatcher, but I'd like to at least smell somewhat decent at school... for Rhydian. I rub the lotion along my arms, neck, hair and wipe the excess around my hoodie and jeans. I toss the lotion in my bag, zip it up and toss it over my shoulder, hearing an, "Oomph."

I freeze in place and slowly look over my shoulder. *Be nice, Ophelia; don't make yourself a target again.* I give a small wave. "Hi, Blake," my voice shakes despite my best efforts.

He adjusts the cuffs of his button-up shirt. A smile creeps on his face. "Hello, *sister*," he drags out the word and slowly turns his head towards Rhyatt. "Hello, *brother*." I shiver at the sick thrill in his voice when he calls us brother and sister. It's almost as if it turns him on to call us his siblings. "I wish you guys would have waited for me. Where's our other brother?"

Rhyatt drops his arm over my shoulder protectively and steers me back towards the school. I look up at him and notice the clench in his jaw and his narrowed eyes. "*My* brother is already at school. He had shit to take care of."

Ever since the twins moved in last month, I've always wondered if they had some sort of sixth sense for good and evil. It's like they know what truly lies within a person, no matter how they present themselves. I've never breathed a word of what I've endured in Thatcher's house of horrors. Before they moved in, I spent many days and nights with Thatcher and Blake hovering over me while thrusting their hands down their pants and touching themselves.

A shudder racks my body at the memory, and I swallow back the bile that creeps up. As if that wasn't bad enough, Thatcher thoroughly enjoyed hitting me or whipping me with his belt. He would always use the same phrase, 'You know why,' when in reality, no, no I fucking didn't.

Blake remains quiet the rest of the walk, pretending to sulk at Rhyatt's continued dismissal of siblinghood. As soon as we walk through the front doors of the school, Blake rushes past us. Rhyatt suddenly stops mid-step and grips my shoulder tight, making me stumble. I look at him, confused. "What's wrong?"

I pull away from his hold and follow the direction he's looking, since he didn't seem to hear me. Ah, yes. Lore Wolfe. I swear he's in love with her, but he'll never admit it. He turns towards me with a nervous smile. "Uh, are you good here? I - uh-"

I laugh and shoo him away. "I'm good, Rhyatt. Go get your girl."

The color drains from his face and he quickly looks around. "No. No, she's not, we're not... it's not like that, Ophie." I slap my hand over my mouth, shaking with silent laughter and walk away.

At my locker, I spin the dial a few times, before stopping on *0*. My backpack slips from my shoulder as I spin my combination, *1 - 24 - 6*. I take a deep breath and hope I did it right. Don't ask me why, but these fucking locks give me hell. The locker opens without fight and I mutter, "Fuck yeah," under my breath.

I grab my backpack and reach in to pull my lotion out. My fingers brush against something soft, and I carefully pull it out. Fuck butterflies fluttering in my stomach, a flock of ravens are up in this bitch. There's a single raven feather, and the light shines perfectly on its darkness as I twirl it in my fingers. The first warning bell goes off and I snap out of my trance. I put the feather in my locker and notice another gift. Tiny bones laid out in the shape of a heart.

What is he up to?

Everyone jumps to leave when the lunch bell rings. Chairs squeak across the linoleum, backpacks smack against desks and murmured voices increase in volume. I hastily shove my history book in my backpack and zip it, rushing past everyone to my locker.

I jump and turn when a hand appears in front of my face with a wooden box. My hair whips around and smacks Rhydian in the face. His head jerks back, and face scrunches at the assault. "Sorry," I giggle.

He doesn't say anything at first, just stands there frozen with the box still in his hand. "What's this for?"

"It's f-or," he clears his throat and speaks up. "It's for your treasure."

I look closer at the box and see that the handles are made from carefully entwined twigs and on top, *Ophelia* is engraved. Coins, pebbles and beads are glued to the top surrounding my name. My whole body feels as if it's buzzing.

I carefully take the box from his hand. "Thank you so much, Bones."

His smile grows. "What was that?"

"What was what?"

"You called me Bones."

I look down at my shoes, suddenly fascinated by every scuff. *Maybe if I stay quiet, he'll drop it.* Gently, he tilts my head to look at him. His smile makes my chest tighten and I blow out the breath I was holding.

"Ravens collect bones for their nests," I explain, my voice soft. "As a foundation. You remind me of a safe shelter with a strong foundation. And you're very protective. I think you probably have or will break bones while protecting people."

I laugh at how silly it sounds and shake my head, his hand falls from my chin and immediately miss his touch. "Anyways, why did you get me all these gifts? I feel awful, I have nothing for you.".

"Just being you is enough. Happy Valentine's Day, little raven." The nickname makes heat rush to my cheeks. Unsure of what to say, I put the bones and feather inside the box, clasping it shut with the little hook lock. I slide the box and my lotion in my backpack and zip it up, slamming my locker shut harder than I meant to. I spin around and before I can overthink it, I skip over to him and place a lingering kiss on his cheek.

A zap tingles on my lips and I pull back with a gasp, pressing my fingertips to my lips. He says nothing as he stares at me in shock, a blush tinting his cheeks.

I have nothing tangible to give him in return, but I can gift him a piece of myself that I've never imagined sharing with anyone. "Can I show you something?"

Without a word, he holds his hand out to me. I swallow my nerves down and grasp his hand. Interlacing our fingers, he leads us out the front doors of the school.

We walk in silence for a while as I lead the way. Having his hand in mine makes me feel safer than I've ever felt my entire life. I stop when we reach the train tracks, the gravel beneath our feet crunching. The sun peeks through the clouds rolling in and he uses his hand as a visor to look around.

"Now what? I've seen train tracks before, pretty girl."

The familiar buzz takes over my body again. If he keeps calling me *little raven* and *pretty girl*, I'm afraid I'm going to turn into a personal vibrator for all eternity. Great, now that image is in my head. I can't hold back the laughter that bubbles up at the image and Rhydian looks at me. A breathtaking smile breaks across his face and it steals my laughter away. I'd give anything to see that smile forever.

"You're beautiful," we both whisper.

We fall together in a fit of laughter, our bodies leaning into each other is the only thing keeping us from crashing to the ground. Regaining our composure, our gazes clash and I realize how close we are.

What is happening?

It's like someone turned the knob to infinity and I can feel and see everything at max intensity. His shirt beneath my fingertips feels buttery soft, the breeze on my skin feels like a deep caress. The last rays of sunshine kiss the tips of his hair, and the shadows of the clouds coming in wrap around us like a cocoon. His heartbeat pounds against my hand and I rub small circles over his chest, as if to soothe his racing heart.

Is this what home is? Happiness? Safety?

I don't have much, but I'd give it all up to keep this feeling. To keep him. I must have closed my eyes at some point, because I don't see it coming when I feel his lips brush against mine in a feather light touch. My breath hitches when the familiar zap hits our lips. Only this time, I welcome it. I refuse to pull away from him. I feel his fingers run through my hair, until both hands are cradling my head, holding me in place against him. Cold rain-drops fall between us, breaking the kiss. We barely pull back, breathing each other in. The sky opens up and rain pours down over us, drenching our clothes. Thunder rolls in as if the back-ground music to this moment.

"Dance with me."

His hands fall from me and he shakes his head, regret filling his eyes. "I-I can't."

Disappointment fills me and I step back. "Oh. Um... I understand."

He rushes forward, shaking his head. "No. No, you don't. I mean, I literally can't. I want to. I just don't know how."

I take slow, measured steps towards him, as if at any moment he'll turn and run. I grab hold of his hands and place them on my hips. "Hold me here," I say softly while guiding his hands to hold my back. "Or here. Whichever feels more comfortable." I settle his hands back to my hips, giving him the chance to decide. I place my right hand on his shoulder and let my left caress the side of his neck and then place it on the back of his head. "This is where I hold. Sing to me. Anything. Get lost in the words, in the feel of my body and the sound of the thunder. I'll do the rest."

Something I've said has triggered his brain, and it's almost as if his brain is shuffling through his playlist of songs. He starts to hum a tune that seems familiar but I can't quite place. Slowly, I move my feet and he follows suit, gripping my hips tight. He melts into me, his nerves washing away as he slides his arms around my back and pulls me closer. His hums become words and I realize he's singing *Existentialism On Prom Night by Straylight Run.*

Lightning streaks the sky above us, illuminating his face. Raindrops cling to his lashes and slowly glide down his face. A few land on his lips and I can't stop staring at his mouth. The words fall from his mouth, every movement and raindrop that glistens on his lips has me transfixed. I wish there was a way to add this memory to my box of treasures. I never want to forget this moment.

"When storm clouds gather and the skies grow dark, I know you will be my shelter and keep me safe from harm." -Unknown

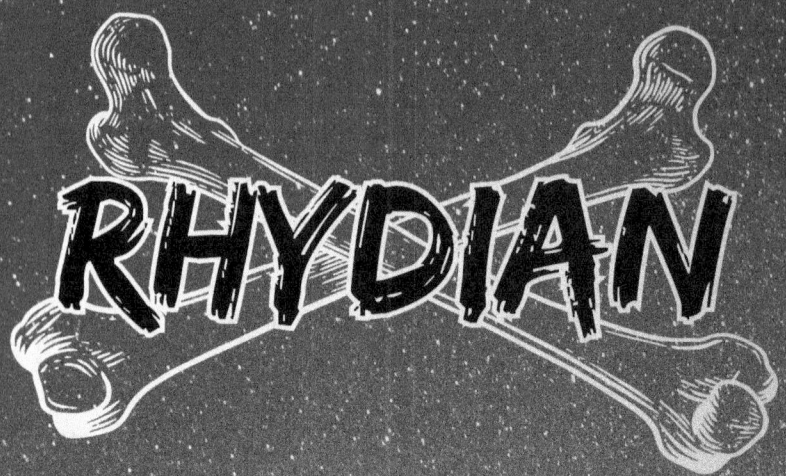

CHAPTER TWO

WONDERING

May 21, 2019

Rhydian

I listen to the quiet shuffling sounds of Ophelia as she gets ready for bed in the closet. Rhyatt sits to the left of me on the edge of the mattress while we brace our boots against the bedroom door.

"Come on, man. Rock, paper, scissors to see who is on watch first," Rhyatt whines.

I'm already shaking my head before he even finishes his sentence. "No. I want Ophelia to fall asleep in my arms. She can't exactly do that if I take first watch."

Rhyatt groans and moves away from me. He presses his back to the door and rests his arms over his legs. "You could have her wake up in your arms if you keep an eye out now."

"Stop whining like a child, Rhyatt."

He flicks his bangs back and sticks his tongue out. "Am not."

I kick my boots off towards him and he smacks them away. He gasps and braces his hands over his heart. "I'm hurt, brother."

"You're about to be if you don't shut the fuck up. If it'll get you to stop bitching, then tonight you can go first and tomorrow night, I will." I watch as he plays with the laces on his boots, refusing to answer me. I kick my foot out and tap his shin. "Okay?"

He returns my kick while yanking his shirt off and slapping it over his pillow. Punching it a few times, he lays down and wraps the blanket over himself, grumbling. "Fine."

An ache builds in my chest, sharp and insistent, and I rub my hand over my heart. Shit. The bittersweet thing about being a twin is knowing when something's up with them, at least feeling-wise. It's like an itch you can't scratch, or like when you know the name of something but can't quite place it, the word longing to spill past your lips. You know if something is wrong or right, but you can't pinpoint exactly what it is. I look towards the closet, wondering what's taking my girl so long. I find her head peeking out with a sad smile on her face. I tilt my head in question and she flicks her head towards Rhyatt. I mouth, 'thank you,' with a nod and sit as close to him as I can.

He grunts as soon as I'm braced against him, but I ignore it and whisper, "Pinky promise." He mumbles something against his pillow and I nudge him again. "Come on, Rhyatt. Pinky promise." He rolls to his back with his eyes squeezed shut and pulls his arm from under the blanket. With his pinky held up in the air, I hook mine around it. "What's going on, Rhy-Rhy?"

His eyes shoot open and he glares at me. "Don't call me that... *Rhydi*," he pouts. Ophelia's soft voice behind me catches our attention. "Is it because of me, Rhyatt?"

His head is torn between nodding yes and shaking no, stuttering, "Y-n-yes. NO." He sits up abruptly, and waves his hands in her direction, tears filling his eyes. That incessant ache in my chest hits again.

"It's just always been me and Rhydian. With the life we've had, I've always worried about the day that something or someone takes him away from me and then I'll be all on my own. Don't get me wrong. I'm so happy he found you, but I feel like this is it. We're moving forward, and you guys will take one path, and I'll be left behind. I just need you to know, I'm glad it's you. I-I love you, Ophie."

His eyes widen and she gasps as I growl, "What the fuck?!"

He throws his hand out towards me in defense. "Not like that. I swear. *I swear.* I mean it like family. Not in the way you love her, Rhyd. Promise."

I feel like I just swallowed my tongue at his words. I haven't even had a chance to tell her yet. I punch him in the shoulder and he winces, rubbing at the sore spot. "Oww, bro."

I grit my teeth. "Thanks a lot. Told her before I even did," I grumble under my breath.

Ophelia jumps on Rhyatt, knocking the air out of him as she holds him tight. With a kiss to the side of his head, she says, "I love you, too, Rhyatt."

She ruffles his hair and laughs as he playfully pushes her towards me, which I take advantage of to bring her against my chest. I feel her breath against my ear and I shiver, gripping her tighter.

"I love you, Bones."

I smile at the nickname as if it's the first time I'm hearing it all over. The mattress jolts next to my leg and I glare down at my pain-in-the-ass brother. "What, bitch?"

"I'll take first watch... jerk."

Ophelia

I can't even bring myself to eat, so I just push my plastic fork around the food on my tray. My stomach is in knots with a strange mix of hunger and nausea, but there's no way I'm going to eat whatever this mystery sloppy joe mix is. I'll throw up for sure.

I look up at the sound of scraping against the cafeteria's linoleum floors. Rhyatt sits across from me and takes the fork from my hand.

"Thanks, Ophie."

My response is cut off when I'm lifted from my chair and brought down on Rhydian's lap, wrapped in his warm embrace. I melt against him with a sigh. "Hi, Bones."

He brings his nose to my hair. "Hi, little bird."

I narrow my eyes at him. "Raven. Not just any ol' bird."

He chuckles in my ear, sending a shiver down my spine. "You'll always be my little raven, but it always gets you to look at me when I say bird instead."

I scoff as he places his large hands over my stomach and I barely hold back a flinch. Soon.

Across the table, Rhyatt freezes mid-bite and looks up. His eyes slowly scan the back of the cafeteria and I turn to see what has his attention. I bite my lip, hoping my laughter doesn't bubble up. Of course it's Lore. I love watching the two of them. I wish they would both grow a pair and just get together. If she's not

looking, he's watching her every move, and when he's not looking, she does the same in return.

Rhydian presses his lips to my cheek and the familiar zap is
there, followed by warmth spreading through me. I lean into his
kiss and practically whine when he pulls away.

"Rhyatt and I have to go do something, but we'll see you at the
house tonight." I spin the best I can in his hold and look back at
him, panic immediately tightening my chest.

"W-what? Can I go with you? Please?"

He looks past me and I'm sure he and Rhyatt are talking in twin
telepathy. *Assholes.* His eyes find mine and he shakes his head
slowly. "Not this time, pretty girl. Just something we have to do.
Make sure you put everything you can against the door to keep
Thatcher and Blake out until we get home, okay?"

Bile rises in my throat at the reminder. I got too comfortable
having the twins around. I haven't been alone with those sick
fucks for awhile. His pinky waves in front of my face to get my
attention. "Pinky promise?"

As worried as I am, I smile at the small gesture that they've let
me be a part of. It's always been their thing, but they let me join
in and it feels… special. Important. I lift my hand and wrap my
pinky around his. "Pinky promise."

He leans forward and pecks my nose. "That's my girl. We'll try to
be back as soon as possible." I keep my pinky wrapped around
his, as if it will provide me the courage I need to speak up. He
pulls his pinky from mine and puts me back in my seat, breaking
our connection. I look up and close my eyes as he leans down to
kiss me. They slowly flutter open when he pulls away and pushes
his chair in. I reach out like my lifeline is about to be severed.

"Can we talk when you get home? It's… it's important."

I watch as his eyes narrow and can practically see the wheels spinning in his brain. He opens his mouth and whatever question he had is cut off by a growl across the table and the loud squeal of a chair before it crashes to the floor.

I feel like my neck is going to break with how fast I whip my head to watch Rhyatt as he charges across the cafeteria. He looks like a fucking predator on the prowl with the way his body moves, and his normally goofy expression morphs to steely anger. Veins protrude from his hands, arms and temples. That can't be healthy. He ignores Rhydian's attempts to rein him in, which isn't an easy feat since they're both stacked with muscles. I stand and see that he's heading towards the king of bullies, who has stupidly chosen Lore to be his new target. The asshole is stabbing at the keys on her laptop. In an act of bravery, she slams it shut on his hand and he snatches it back, rubbing at the biting pain.

"YOU BITCH!" He screeches.

He raises his hand and I can't tell if he's going to hit her or the laptop. Rhyatt is there within seconds, with a guttural war cry tearing from his throat, "MOTHERFUCKER!". He rears back his fist and slams it into the guy's face.

I watch as blood sprays from his nose, followed by a steady flow over his lips and teeth as he shouts in pain. The cafeteria erupts in squealing chairs and chants from students, "Fight, fight, fight."

Lore's stare remains on Rhyatt, her mouth partially open. There's no fear in her eyes, only admiration. As quick as it was there, it's gone in an instant when Rhyatt returns her look. With a roll of her eyes and a shake of her head, she shoves the laptop into her messenger bag. I never realized reading lips would come in handy until this very moment. She curls her lip in disgust as she throws the strap of her bag over her shoulder. *'Don't call me that!"*

She shoulder-checks him as she walks past and he slowly spins in her direction with the classic Rhyatt smirk. Rhydian grips his shoulder and talks in his ear.

He rolls his eyes. 'Fine'.

I absentmindedly rub my stomach and watch as they run out of the cafeteria doors that lead to the courtyard. The school's resource officer runs in through the other doors to assess the situation shortly after.

Too late, buddy. Too late.

"I am there, waiting, watching, keeping to the shadows. But when you need me...I will step out of the shadows and protect what's mine."
-Unknown

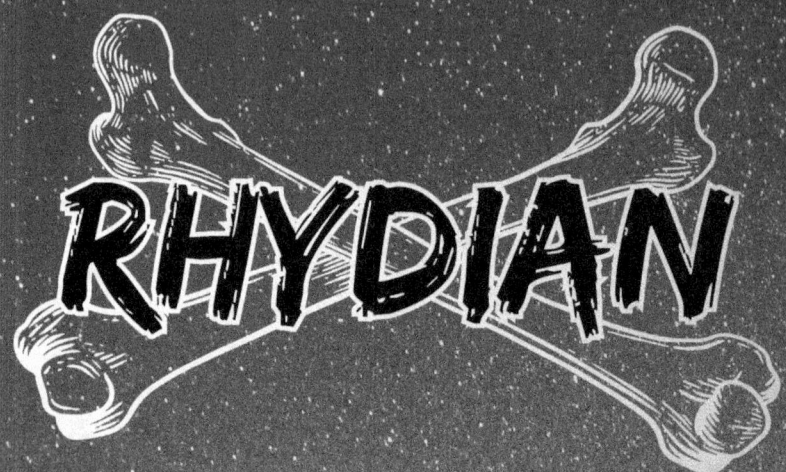

CHAPTER THREE

ONLY LOVE CAN HURT LIKE THIS

Rhydian

I hold on to Rhyatt's hoodie as we run out of the school, our boots pounding against the ground echoing around us. The city bus nears the bus stop and I frantically wave at it to let them know we want on. The bus stops with a squeal and a hiss of the doors as they slide open. I pull my wallet out of my back pocket as I walk up the steps, breathing heavily as I swipe my transport card. Rhyatt follows suit behind me with an excited, "Thanks, man."

I hold my breath as I walk past an old lady sitting in the front seat, who clutches her purse when she sees us. *Jesus, grandma, we won't steal from you. Worry about that perfume choice instead.* Rhyatt and I toss our backpacks on the floor and drop down on the back seat of the bus. He nudges me with his elbow. "So where do we want to check first? Their apartment or walk around downtown?"

I look out the window and watch the school disappear behind us. As difficult as it is, I need to push Ophelia to the back of my mind so I can focus. "Downtown. I doubt we'd find much at the apartment at this time."

"Agreed. If all else fails, we really need to go to the library and get some more books on constellations. Probably be best to do some research on better ways to spy on someone, cuz this guessing game shit just ain't cutting it."

I throw my head back against the seat with a sigh. "Yeah."

With practiced ease, we pull baseball caps from our backpacks and put them on, pushing the bill down below our eyes. I grab the stop cord and pull it down. The ding echoes throughout the bus and the lights brighten in response. Grimacing at the sticky feeling of the cord, I wipe my hand against my jeans. The bus lurches forward as it brakes to a stop. We throw our backpacks on as we stand and wave to the driver before stepping down onto the sidewalk.

Wasteland, Baby by Hozier floats in the air and I hum along, the words playing like a movie in my head. The song pulls my gaze to a giant banner that announces, '*GRAND OPENING* '. Beneath it, the store front reads *Swan & Scribe*.

Through the windows, I watch as people shuffle in and out of the store and endless amounts of bookshelves and tables inside. Beside me, Rhyatt shouts, "DUDE, BINGO! If this isn't a sign, I don't know what is."

He grins, waiting for me to catch on. "Get it? Sign?"

"Yeah, got it," I mutter, shaking my head.

"Yeesh. Maybe we should've let Ophie come with us. You're a lot grumpier without her."

The door above us jingles as we open it, and immediately the warm smell of coffee and books greet us. At the checkout desk, a lady with long, black curly hair stands. She glances up and greets us with a smile. "Hi! Welcome to *Swan & Scribe*, can I help you find anything?"

"Yeah, we were just wondering if we were allowed to read the books here? Or do we have to purchase them first?" Rhyatt asks. He shuffles back and forth and looks down at his feet. *Oh, fuck, please don't do it.* He slowly raises his head, his once bright eyes now shine with tears. *Fuck, he's gonna do it.* With a sniffle, he quietly says, "We're just a couple of foster kids. We don't have the money to buy anything. I really wish we could, though."

She crosses her arms over her chest and narrows her eyes. "Nice performance, kid. Wasn't necessary, though. You're allowed to read the books here without purchase. We have many tables for you to sit and read, a section where people can play games, a café and upstairs we have private book nooks. Just don't fucking steal from me or you'll find yourself with a chancla up the ass. Got it?"

Rhyatt and I look at each other in shock and then back at her. I snort and Rhyatt busts up laughing, hunching over to grab his knees. He slowly stands and takes deep breaths, giggles bubbling up between each one. "You got it, spicy lady. Yeesh." She tilts her head to the side, effectively dismissing us.

I scan the pages of a book on various constellations and the history behind their names. "Rhyd, how cool is it that we're Geminis and the symbol for that constellation is twins?"

"Super cool, Rhy," I mumble in response.

"Why do you think he's so fascinated by the stars? I mean, don't get me wrong, stars are beautiful and mysterious, but what started it all?"

"Your guess is as good as mine."

The window in front of us shows that the sun is just starting to set, painting the store in warm gold. Shit. I look around for a clock and spot one saying 5:29PM.

I slam the book shut. "Dude, we have to go. We're about to miss the last bus out of town. Shit, shit, shit."

We each grab a stack of books and then notice the bus pulling up. "No time, drop them. Let's go, let's go."

We run for the door, waving at the owner. "We're sorry, so sorry, we have to go."

A flash of lightning illuminates the sky, followed by the angry grumble of thunder and pouring rain. We jump on the bus and adjust our hats so they're backwards and the raindrops aren't falling on our faces. The chipper bus driver peers through the windshield. "Just in time. Looks like we got a storm on our hands, boys."

Ophelia

Please come home.

Please come home.

Please come home.

I never made it to our room. As soon as I walked in the house, I was grabbed by my hair and yanked back.

"Hello, *sister*."

Now I'm in the living room, my sweat-slicked legs stick to the chair I'm bound to with duct tape. Fucking freak took my clothes and left me in my bra and panties. The duct tape cuts into my skin with every desperate twist and turn I make trying to get free. Blake stands behind me, his fingers holding a chunk of my hair as he leans down to sniff it. "You smell so good all the time, *sister*. Fucking delicious."

I gag as bile rises up my throat, barely swallowing it down. I inhale deeply through my nose and cringe when the scent of beer, body odor and cigarettes fills my nostrils. Thatcher.

"Alright, Blake, we're going to try this your way first. If she doesn't give us the answers I'm looking for, then I take over."

He stands in front of me, his sardonic smile showcasing his decaying teeth. My skin crawls when I feel Blake's rough fingers slide along my shoulders. He pushes my bra straps down, letting them fall beside my upper arms. He starts whistling and trails his nails down my arm as he walks by. He stands next to his dad and smiles, reaching his hands out towards Thatcher. He gestures downward and Thatcher thrusts his hips towards him, his erection obvious in his jeans.

What the fuck?

Blake grabs Thatcher's belt and starts undoing it. I feel a hot flash takeover as my stomach churns violently. Tears fill my eyes, blurring my vision and drool pools in my mouth and I'm unable to stop my hiccup from turning into retches. Vomit expels from my mouth and down the front of me. The sour taste of my vomit, tears and snot floods my mouth and makes me dry heave.

Thatcher sighs in exasperation, as if I'm the fucking problem here. He slaps Blake's hands away, to which he pouts and steps back. Thatcher yanks his belt from his pants with a snap. My panic seems to tamper down my nausea as I breathe heavily, bracing myself for the first hit. He folds the belt in half and slaps it against his hand, prowling towards me. The chair squeaks beneath me as I continue to thrash around and twist my wrists and ankles, trying to get loose.

He brings his arm back and swings the belt down over my legs. The burning sting has me howling in pain.

"Where are your brothers?"

I cringe at his words. I'll claim Rhyatt as my brother, but Rhydian? Fuck no. I glare at him, baring my teeth like a fucking animal.

He meets my challenge with his fist. My head snaps back from the force of his punch to my nose. Pain explodes in my head, and I feel the warmth of the blood pouring from my nose and my head spins. *Don't pass out. Anything can happen if you're passed out. Fight.*

"Tell me where the fuck they are or this will get so much fucking worse for you. Stop protecting them, you little whore," his face turns bright red as his anger increases. "Fuck this. You got nothing to say to me? Maybe a good fuckin' will get that mouth of yours movin'."

I shake my head frantically as he nods with a grin. He lifts his leg and kicks me square in the chest. Air leaves my lungs in a scream as the chair flies backward. I crash against the floor, the impact making the chair splinter to pieces below me.

My head bounces off the floor as my wrists are smashed between the broken chair pieces and the floor. Thatcher kicks the broken pieces of the chair away from me while unbuttoning his pants. Blake walks up beside him, his hand already down his pants and stroking. I start to dry heave again and only small amounts of bile flow from my mouth.

"Do you really think your puke is going to stop me, little girl?"

As he gets closer, I kick my legs the best I can with the chair legs still taped to my ankles. He laughs as I scream, "GET THE FUCK BACK YOU SICK FUCK!" He grabs the chair legs connected to my ankles to control my kicks. I continue to strain against his hold as he tries to push his body closer to me.

"FUCK YOU! FUCK YOU! HE'LL FUCKING KILL YOU, YOU SICK SON OF A BITCH!"

"Funny, cuz I don't see anyone here to save y-"

The front door swings open and smacks the wall with a bang. While he's distracted by the door, I kick again and connect one with the side of his leg, causing him to crash to the floor with a shout. The twins walk in, matching expressions of murderous rage. I sigh in relief when I see them.

My boys. My Bones.

Their eyes soften briefly as they land on me, and harden once more when they zero in on their targets. Blake stands there frozen with his hand still down his pants, mouth agape. Thatcher is still down on the floor holding his knee, muttering curse words.

Rhyatt doesn't hesitate and quickly shuts the door. He makes his way over to Blake, who attempts to back away from Rhyatt, but stumbles back. Rhyatt grabs Blake's head and slams his knee into his face. Blake crumples to the floor, knocked out .

Rhydian grabs his hood and pulls his hoodie off, tossing it over to Rhyatt. He curls his lip in disgust as he stares down at Thatcher. Refusing to look away from the piece of shit, he asks, "Are you okay, little raven?"

I'm frozen. Why can't I get the words out? Shit, am I okay? Rhyatt drops to his knees and pulls the duct tape off me. I hiss every time a piece is pulled from my raw skin.

"I'm sorry, I'm sorry, Ophie."

Rhydian walks up to Thatcher and kicks his head like it's a fucking football. Spit, blood and chipped teeth fly from his mouth as he crashes to the floor. I sit up as Rhyatt puts Rhydian's hoodie over my head. I wrap my arms around myself and breathe in his scent, letting it envelop me.

He makes sure Thatcher is knocked out before running over to me. His knees slide across the floor as he reaches out and places his hands on my face and down my body.

"Are you okay? How bad are you hurt?" His voice cracks. "What did he do to you? I'm so sorry I didn't get here sooner. I'm so sorry. I'm supposed to protect you."

I slam my lips to him to stop his frantic words and then quickly pull back holding my hand over my mouth, remembering that I smell like vomit. I look down at his hoodie and a fresh wave of shame comes over me when I see his hoodie is also covered in my vomit.

I start crying again, "I have puke all over your hoodie."

He chuckles at my words. "That's what you're worried about right now?"

I throw my arms out to the sides. "Well, yeahhh. Now your hoodie is fucking disgusting cuz of me."

"I don't fucking care, Ophelia. All I care about is that you're okay. Are you?"

I shake my head and the only answer I have falls from my lips in a whisper, "I don't know."

He drops a kiss to my forehead. "Rhy and I have something we need to do. I need you to close your eyes for me, little raven."

"Are you gonna kill him?"

Without hesitation, he nods. "Yes."

I nod in return. "Good. But I'm not closing my eyes. I want to watch that disgusting piece of shit take his last breath."

Rhyatt wiggles around in a dance while laughing. "Fuck yeah! Ophie's a badass!"

I watch as they both stand and it's almost breathtaking to watch them morph into the dark beasts they need to be for this moment. The storm continues outside and at this moment I can't tell which is emitting more rage, the twins or the storm. They pull knives from their pockets and flick them open with a click.

"We don't have time to make it perfect," Rhyatt says.

"We just have to be sure," Rhydian agrees.

I watch them kneel down and take turns plunging the knife into Thatcher's stomach. His body jolts and he awakes with a gasping scream. Rhyatt flips the knife around in his fist and slams it into Thatcher's throat.

"Shut the fuck up."

His scream turns to a wet gurgle as blood spurts around the blade of the knife. Rhydian doesn't stop, he continues puncturing his stomach in seemingly random spots. When the gurgling noises stop, Rhyatt yanks the knife from Thatcher's throat. A weak spurt follows the blade and then slowly trickles down his throat. He brings the knife down to follow along with Rhydian's random stabs.

Panic hits all over again when I realize what this means. They can't stay here. They have to go. I slowly get up and feel the pain from everything Thatcher did to me. There's no time to think about that now. I grab their backpacks and hobble up the stairs to our room. I go to the closet and yank out the garbage bag filled with blankets and pillows.

Tingles spread throughout my body and it's as if the pain is washed away. With precise movements, I quickly and methodically gather their clothes and put them in their backpacks. I zip up the backpacks and watch as they step into the room calling for me. We all freeze and stare at each other. There's a question in their eyes as they look at the backpacks in my hands and I stare at them with blood covering their faces, hands and clothes. I look down and pull at the hoodie I'm wearing. He can't take this, it's covered in vomit. I turn and yank down one of my over-sized hoodies. I walk up to him and put it on his head.

He pulls it all the way on and tilts his head, "What are you doing, little raven?"

Tears fall down my cheeks and I take a deep breath. "Saving you like you saved me."

I hand them their backpacks and then grab the garbage bag on the floor and hold it out to Rhyatt. I look at Rhydian and try to memorize everything. Every strand of hair, which has various shades of brown and almost blonde. The curve of his brows and nose. The curl in his lips. The way his eyes sparkle in the light with shades of brown, gold and green. I fall into his arms and he grips me tight. I inhale his scent and try to hold on to the warmth of his body and the beat of his heart.

"I love you, Bones, but you have to go."

He pulls back just enough to look in my eyes. "I know, but you're coming with us."

"I can't."

His hands grip the hoodie I'm wearing. "What do you mean? You can't stay here, you have to come with us."

"Not yet, Rhydian. I have to make sure the cops believe some-body else did this. An intruder or something. I have to keep them away from you guys. If I'm going to be away from you, I'd rather you be free. I will find you, I promise. When it's safe, I will find you."

There's a break in the sounds of the storm and sirens can be heard in the distance. My heart beats frantically, with every beat a piece splinters away. I press my lips to his, savoring the feel and taste.

"I love you so much. Please. Do this for me. You have to go. Now."

"She's right, Rhyd. Come on."

Rhydian kisses me again on the lips, then my nose, cheeks and forehead.

"If you don't come find us, we'll come find you, pretty girl. I promise." I stifle a sob as I pull away from him and nod.

Rhyatt swoops in and squeezes me tight. "I love you, Ophie. Stay safe."

"You too, Rhy. Take care of each other, please."

Rhydian keeps staring at me as Rhyatt pulls him out of the room. I fall to my knees and sob.

I place one hand over my heart and one over my stomach. "Don't worry, baby. We'll be with Daddy soon, I promise."

"If I never see you again I will always carry you inside, outside; on my fingertips and at brain edges and in centers, centers of what I am, of what remains."
—Charles Bukowski

CHAPTER FOUR

FAR FROM HOME

Ophelia

The last of my sobs die down and all I'm left with is silent tears that continue to fall. I wipe my face with the sleeve of Rhydian's hoodie and wince at the sting of my tears leaving my face raw.

Blake's sudden wailing startles me, making my heart race. Fuck, he's awake. There's a loud bang and then Blake shouts, "HELP! THEY DID IT! LOOK WHAT THEY DID TO MY DAD!"

I stand on shaky legs, realizing the police are here and it's time to weave a believable tale of tonight's events. I make my way down the stairs and cringe at his hysterics. He sounds like he's completely lost his mind, repeating himself over and over. When I reach the bottom of the stairs, the sight before me makes me freeze—this isn't the police.

There are two tall, dark-haired men standing in the living room. Their backs are facing me as they look down at Blake and Thatcher. I put my hand over my stomach and take a step back.

"Make the call, fratello. Take care of the police and make sure it's known who did this. Then make arrangements for a trip to the hospital in Damascus," one of them said in a grating tone.

The more docile looking man nods and presses a phone to his ear. He steps around Blake while speaking in Italian. Blake looks up and his eyes narrow when he sees me. He jabs his finger in my direction and I frantically shake my head.

"YOU BITCH! YOU'LL FUCKING PAY FOR THIS! YOU EVIL BITCH! I'LL FUCKING KILL YOU!"

The men quickly turn in my direction. The man with the phone ends his call and pockets it. He kicks Blake in the back of the head so hard, his eyes roll to the back of his head before slumping over Thatcher's dead body. The other man looks at me with a calculating smirk and a feeling of unease washes over me. His eyes are cold and sharp, and even though they were dressed in crisp button-down shirts, he couldn't hide the cruelty in his eyes. Something tells me that as bad as things were with Thatcher, this man can show me a worse fate than the house of horrors. I look towards the front door. I have to try.

"Don't even think about it," he demands as he takes a menacing step forward.

I yelp as I run towards the door. I'm just steps away from the front door when a sharp, stinging pain shoots through my scalp, my eyes blurring with tears as I'm yanked backward by my hair. My hands are thrown above me, but I quickly bring them down over my stomach.

"No, no, no. Please. I'm pregnant, please don't hurt me." A shiver wracks my body at his cruel laughter.

"Even better. You'll be perfect. Can't get a puttana double pregnant."

What?! "Please don't do this. Just let me go. I won't tell anyone anything, I swear."

How do I get out of this? I need to get to Rhydian. "Now why would I let you go when you're the one I'm here for, piccolo prigioniero?"

I furrow my brow wondering what he means by being here for me and the Italian he spoke. "What does that mean?" I whisper. I feel a prick to

42

the side of my neck and hiss, "Wha-" My head spins and my vision blurs.

A distorted, distant voice whispers in my ear, "It means little captive."

MAY 2020

Aria

I'm not sure when it happened, but I learned that Thatcher made a deal and I was the price. Little did I know, I would be making a deal with the devil myself. I never realized the true cost until I spent my first night writhing in pain, with blood and sweat gluing me to the leather seats in the back of a car. I tried to focus on the music he kept on repeat during the assault until he told me what it was called.

'I picked this song just for you, piccolo prigioniero. It's called Remember Me by Jurrivh. Beautiful song, isn't it? I want you to remember me in everything you do. Any moment you find peace or hope, you'll remember me. In your final moments, your last breath... remember me.' He's played it every night since.

I learned the devil goes by the name of Aldo. Of course he gets to keep his name while everything is taken from me, including my first name. Despite all of the pain, I endure and after losing my sweet Bones, I refuse to give up. I push through every excruciating moment, because within the darkness is my rainbow after the storm. Rhayvin Grace.

If it wasn't for her, I would've killed myself after that first night. She's five months old now and I swear, she looks more and more like her daddy every day. Every moment has been bittersweet. It breaks my heart that he missed watching her grow in my belly and now all these beautiful baby stages. Not only do I carry him in my heart, but she's a piece of him I get to cherish, always. She will never go a day without me telling her all about him. Sadly, I'll have to teach her that he is a secret that only we can talk about, and never in front of Aldo.

I will never compromise Rhydian's safety, and in turn Rhyatt's, by speaking of them. It's a struggle to not shout for them to save me whenever Aldo and his friends touch and hurt me for their pleasure. A tear slips down at the flash of assaults over the last year. I quickly swipe it away when I hear Rhayvin's coos as she wakes up from her nap. I wince when my finger brushes against the bruise blooming beneath my eye.

This pool house is a prison and the closest access I'm allowed to the internet is watching online videos. I've always used them for music and learning how to be a good mom. I need Rhayvin close to me always and I can't stand when she's out of my sight. One thing I learned was how to make my own baby carrier so I can cradle her closer to me and rock her.

One of the things the videos taught me is that our children can feel our emotions and in turn it can affect theirs. Now that she's waking up, I know it is not the time for me to think about those disgusting pigs or how much I miss Rhydian. With one hand holding her close to me, I use the other to pick up the remote and turn on our music. I play all kinds of music for her but her favorites seem to be *The Beatles* and *Taylor Swift*.

Never Grow Up by *Taylor Swift* starts to play and I sing along. I wish I would've found a way to record Rhydian singing to me so I could share his voice with her. I walk over to the sliding glass door where I can see the main house, pool and a beautiful flower maze.

Theia steps out of the main house, arms crossed and a scowl on her face. Poor girl is as trapped as I am. I wave at her in the hopes that she'll stop by for a visit. She's so kind to me and loves holding Rhayvin. She even paints beautiful pictures and takes pictures of them on her phone to show me. Her eyes flick towards the window and she subtly shakes her head at my wave. Shit. That can only mean one thing.

My heart starts to race and my stomach knots at what's to come. I look back at the main house and watch as Aldo and his brother Alonzo step outside. Aldo snaps his fingers at his brother and then points towards Theia. Alonzo nods and walks after her as Aldo makes his way towards the pool house. Just as the videos say, Rhayvin feels my overwhelming panic, making her stir and fuss. I quickly step away and rock her. "Shh, shh, shh. It's okay, mommy's got you."

The door swings open and bangs against the wall, startling me with a gasp. Aldo looks around and his darkened stare falls on me. He steps aside as a maid comes running in, panting with strands of hair sticking to her face. Leaving no room for argument, he demands, "Give her the baby and go straight to the room, piccolo prigioniero."

I bite my tongue to hold back a scathing response at his barked orders. *For Rhayvin. You're doing this for Rhayvin.* I shakily remove the makeshift carrier from around me and hand her over to the maid. She refuses to look at me and quickly scurries off to Rhayvin's room.

I stand and watch until the door is shut and then make my way to the devil's playroom.

My own personal hell.

"Being a mother is learning about strengths you didn't know you had, and dealing with fears you never knew existed."
-Linda Wooten

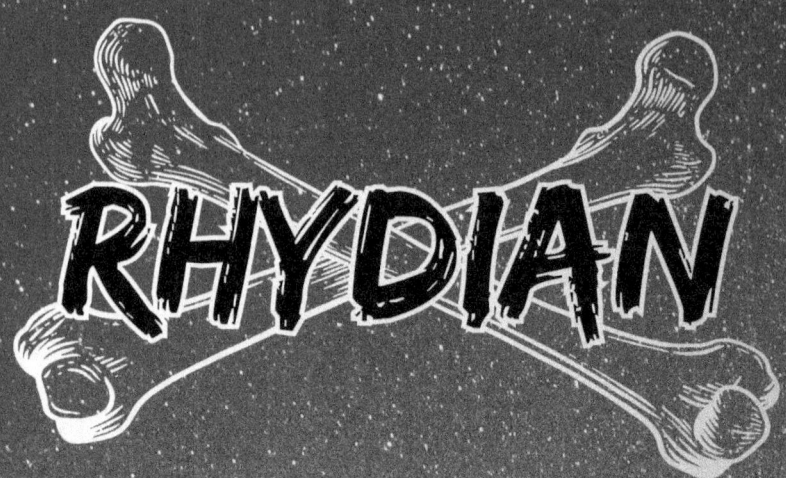

RHYDIAN

CHAPTER FIVE

THE KID I USED TO KNOW

Rhydian

Even over the booming thunder, I swear I can hear my heart shattering as we run outside. I can't see the flashing lights yet but I can hear the sirens in the distance. Everything inside me is screaming that this is wrong. We were all supposed to get out, my little raven included. I slam into Rhyatt when he grinds to a halt.

"Oomph. What are you doing, Rhy?"

I step around him to see what made him stop. A blur of movement crashes into him. I have to wipe away the rain clouding my vision before I realize that the sobbing blur is Lore.

"I'm so glad you're here. Please help me. I need to get the fuck out of here."

"Whoa, whoa, whoa. What's going on, little succubus? Are you hurt?"

She squeezes him tighter, I can see her whole body shaking. As if my heart wasn't hurting enough, I can now feel the ache of Rhyatt's heart while he figures out what's wrong with her. She's important to him. She's always been important to him, even if she fights him every step of the way. He keeps a tight hold on her but pulls back enough to look at her. "Lore, I need you to talk to me. I need to know if you're hurt, or if someone is after you."

She slowly lifts her head and sniffles with a shuddered breath. "M-my mom. She's dead and… I'm not safe here. My piece-of-shit dad met up with some people and sold me to them or something. I think they're coming for me tonight. For all I know, they're already here. Please. You guys are carrying a lot, I know you're leaving. Please take me with you. I'm begging you."

He looks back at me, the question in his eyes. I can't make him suffer just because I can't bring my girl with me. I nod in response and he leans down and kisses her forehead. "Of course you can, baby girl. We need to hit the side roads before we're seen. Let's go."

I glance back towards the house as we walk away. I take a step forward, the need to be back with Ophelia more than I can take. There's a squeeze to my shoulder, Rhyatt doing his best to comfort and guide me in the direction I have to go.

How do you keep moving when your heart is no longer with you?

MAY 2020

I take deep breaths in between every push up. Sweat drips down my face and blurs my vision. Rhyatt and Lore's old-married-couple bickering fades into the background. Two-hundred and one. *Ophelia.* Two-hundred and two. *Little raven.* Two-hundred and three. *Where are you?* Two-hundred and four. *Why didn't you wait for me?*

I jolt at the feel of fluff smacking me in the face. I drop back on my knees and glare over at my pain-in-the-ass brother who's giggling and waving. I catch the look of pity on Lore's face and quickly ignore it. I wish she would stop fucking staring at me like that. Hell, I even catch Rhyatt doing it when his attempts to joke around with me don't work. They never work. I have no sense of humor now that I don't have my girl by my side.

I have no clue where she is or if she's okay. Did something happen? Did she give up on us? Move on? The lyrics of the remix for *Ain't No Sunshine* by *Bill Withers and Lido* play inside my head. I tear my shirt over my head and wipe the sweat from my face, neck and arms. I drop to my ass and lean against one of the beds and notice that Lore is no longer looking and Rhyatt's smile has dropped.

"What?" I snap.

With a sad smile, he tilts his head towards Lore. "She has something for us."

I put my hand on the bed behind me and push myself up to stand, tossing my shirt on the bed. Rhyatt grabs the trash can from under the desk and sets it between his legs. He pulls his wallet out of his pocket and one of our stolen credit cards. He holds it up before snapping it in half.

"She says it's time to start using the next ones."

I turn towards the nightstand between the two beds and pull my wallet out of it to destroy my own card.

"I can't believe this whole setup you got from that show is working. You think we could pull off using cards that say Winchester? Run around telling people we're the Winchester brothers?" Rhyatt laughs.

Lore scoffs. "You guys will never be as badass as them... or as hot." Her shoulders shake with silent laughter as Rhyatt leans into her space to gawk at her. He pulls his knife out of his back pocket and flicks it open before stabbing it into the desk next to her laptop. "If you're going to wound me, baby girl, at least make it count."

I grit my teeth in annoyance at them and myself. A part of me hates that they get to have these moments together, while I'm left all alone without Ophelia. Then I hate myself for feeling that way because I should be happy for Rhyatt. What's worse is all I've been doing is hurting him and I can't stop it. I constantly catch him glancing my way and trying to rub away the ache in his chest.

"Shut your face, Rhyatt. Just go get dinner, it's your turn to go," Lore says in exasperation while rubbing her temples. He leans down with puckered lips and she slaps a mask over his mouth. He laughs and slaps his hand over hers briefly before she yanks her hand away.

"I knew you cared about me. Or do you just think I look like a sexy superhero with it on?"

"More like I'm more concerned for my own health. If you get sick, I get sick. Fuck that."

My heart rate spikes at the thought of him catching this Corona shit. The information is scary. Who knows what's true and what's not, but it doesn't look good at all. "RHYATT ARES! Stop fucking around. Get out there, keep your hood and mask on and get dinner."

He snaps his mask over his face and narrows his eyes. "Sure thing, *Rhydian Apollo*," he grumbles. That familiar twinge in my chest hits as I watch him angrily shove his hoodie on and stomp towards the door.

"Fucking jerk," he mumbles as he slams the door behind him.

I sigh and head to the bathroom. I shut it and lean back whispering, "I know, bitch."

"Who am I really? Am I still the same person if I'm not even technically a person anymore? Does being stronger make me different? Will it?"
—Carrie Jones

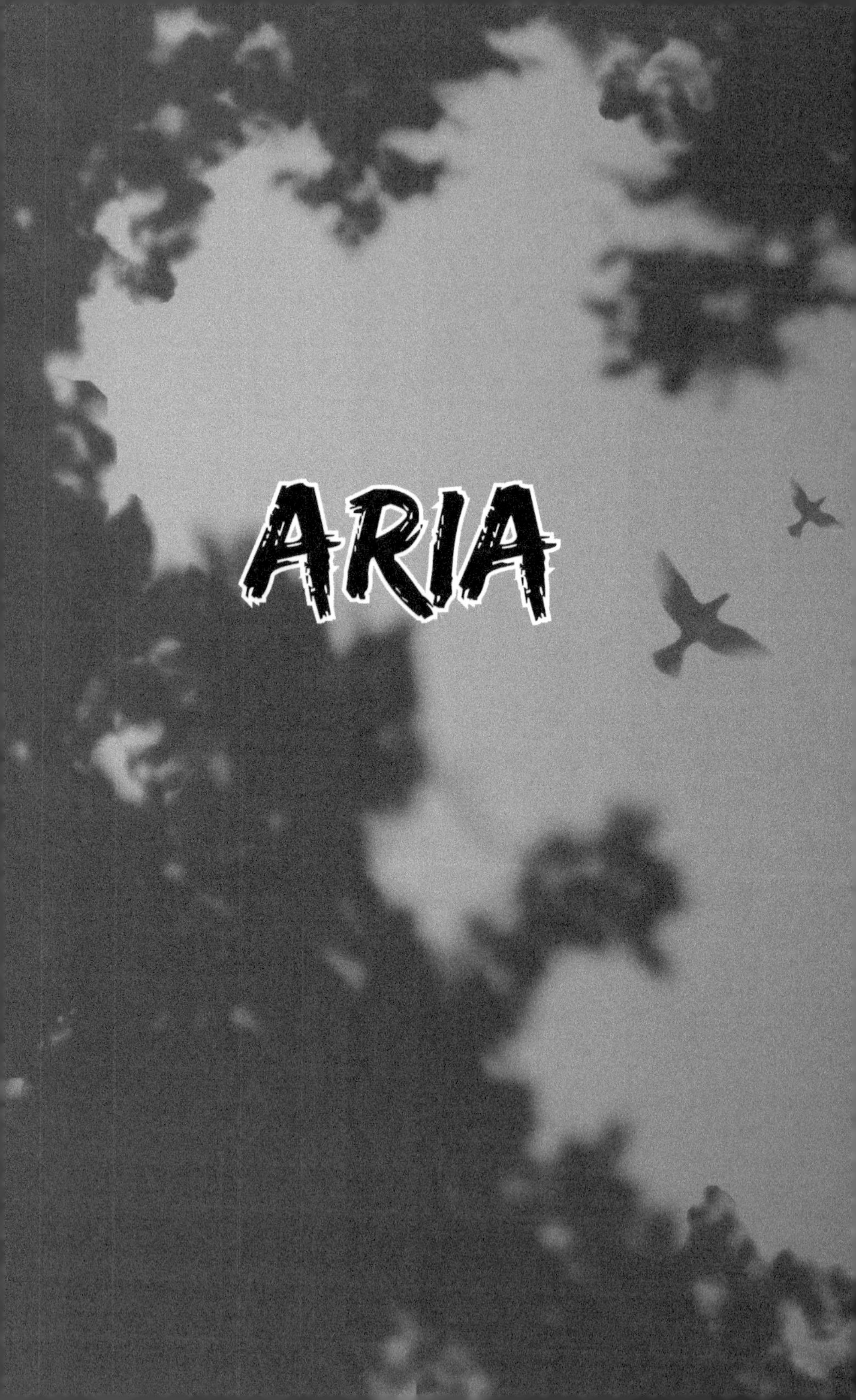
ARIA

CHAPTER SIX

I CAN'T BREATHE

JULY 2021

Aria

My whole body tenses when I feel Aldo stirring behind me. I force myself to steady my breathing and pretend to sleep. It takes everything in me not to move or hiss at the pain of him squeezing my freshly bruised hip as he hovers above me.

"Mmm, I'll see you tonight, piccolo prigioniero," he whispers gruffly, his hot breath fanning my hair against my face. He thrusts his morning wood against my back to emphasize the meaning behind his statement. I refuse to move until I hear him leave and shut the front door.

My heart races as hot and cold flashes wrack my body. I fling the covers back and run to the bathroom, crashing to my knees. My stomach lurches violently and I pull my hair back just in time to throw up in the toilet. My throat burns as bile comes out and I dry heave until I'm empty. Shaking, I wipe the drool from my chin and stand to flush the toilet. I rinse my mouth out with water and find myself staring at my reflection. The all-too-familiar feeling of darkness suffocates me.

Instead of just standing there, I imagine myself smashing the mirror in a million pieces with my fist. Instead of regret, I welcome the feeling of my flesh tearing with every piece of glass in my knuckles. Without thought, I grab the biggest shard of glass and stare at my reflection, knowing what I need to do. I'll earn my wings and fly far away from here. I bring it to my throat and grit my teeth.

"Fuck you, Aldo," I whisper as I slice cross my throat. Blood pours down my throat and I can hear gurgled breaths morph into a gasp when I hear Rhayvin's cries.

I grip the counter, breathing hard and shaking my head. I look at the mirror once more and realize it was all just an ideation. My eyes well with tears when I realize that I let the darkness way too close. I can't let it win, my Rhayvin needs her mama. Her light will help me fight the darkness. Everything will be okay.

I take a deep breath and wipe away the tears before walking to her room. I open her door with a bright smile on my face. "Good morning, my little birdy."

My smile falls when I see her gripping the crib railing, looking flushed. Tears cascade down her round cheeks. I pick her up and she quickly nestles her face into my neck, trying to snuggle closer. Her forehead feels warm against my neck. I rock her back and forth and coo, "Is my little birdy sick? Shh, shh, it's okay."

I get her changed and then head to the kitchen with her still cradled in my arms. I attempt to put her in the high chair so I can make her breakfast but her cries grow louder and she grips me tighter. Shit. "Okay, okay. Mommy won't let you go."

I pull the eggs out of the fridge and sausage links from the freezer. I grab a skillet and stop when I hear Theia singing Rhayvin's song over the intercom. It's our code that it's just her and it's safe to open the door. I rush over and open it, just like my smile fell earlier, Theia's falls at the sight of us. I step aside to let her in, and she turns towards me and holds her arms out. "Give me that sweet bird. Are you guys okay?"

I hand Rhayvin over and sigh as I throw my hair up in a messy bun, kicking the door shut. "That motherfucker," Theia mumbles as her eyes narrow.

"What?"

She nods towards me. "He's left marks on you again. Fuck, I can't wait for our plan to all come together and get the fuck out of here. I'm so sorry, Aria. I'm really trying, I promise."

My nose burns and my eyes water at the thought of leaving here. To be free. For Rhayvin to be safe. To find Rhydian. I clear my throat and move past them to the kitchen. "I know you are, Theia. Thank you. Also, be careful, I think Rhayvin is coming down with something."

"That won't stop me from hanging out with this sweet girl. You make breakfast while me and my bestie listen to some music."

"Thank you, Theia. You're a lifesaver."

She winks at me. "You think I'm great now, just wait til you see my surprise," she says in a sing-song voice.

I finish cooking breakfast and get Rhayvin set up in her high chair to eat. I laugh watching her pick the sausage links over the bananas or eggs. Total Bones move. I unlock the wheels on the high chair and move her around so she can be seated with us in the living room. Theia holds her bag tight with a big smile on her face, practically vibrating in her seat when I sit next to her on the couch.

"Are you ready? Are you ready? Are you ready? I'm so excited to show you this." She reaches inside her bag and pulls out a pile of what looks like pictures and clutches them to her chest, turning towards me. "The one good thing about the internet is people post everything. I did some digging and discovered that somebody posted all of your school's yearbook photos for the people who couldn't get one."

I furrow my brow. "My school's yearbook?"

She smiles and nods quickly. "From your senior year. Look what I found."

She hands over the pictures and I gasp at the first one, unable to stop the tears this time. It's a picture of me and the twins. I'm in Rhydian's lap and Rhyatt is sitting next to us. We're all making faces, Rhydian and I flip off the camera as Rhyatt throws up the rock on sign. Laughter leaves my lips at the memory. The next photo shows them leaning against the wall with their arms crossed, stern expressions, as they watch over everyone like the protectors they are. The last three are our own senior photos. I cradle them to my chest and leap towards Theia to hug her.

"Whoa." She squeals and laughs. "I take it you like them?"

"I love them so much. Thank you. This means the world to me. Now I have pictures to show Rhayvin. I always tell her about her daddy and uncle but now she can see them. This is so kind of you."

A sound alert goes off and she pulls her phone out of her pocket. She frowns down at her phone and rolls her eyes. "Alright, go find a safe place to hide those before I go."

She shakes her phone towards me and I read the text from her father. Shit. I look at the pictures once more, run to put them inside of one of Rhayvin's books and hide it in the bookshelf. "I hate to ask... but could you try and stall them as long as possible?"

She walks over to Rhayvin and kisses her cheek. "I love you, little bird."

Theia glances back at me as she leaves. "I'll do my best."

Whatever Theia did seemed to work, because Aldo hasn't shown up yet and now it's time to get Rhayvin ready for bed. I drain her bath and wrap her up in a soft towel. I hum her *Blackbird* song and head to the kitchen to give her some medicine. I change her into fuzzy pajamas and rock her back and forth as she cries and fights her sleep.

I almost jump out of my skin when the door slams, followed by, "ARIA?!"

My steps are unsteady as I walk out to the main area. His normally slicked-back hair is disheveled and jaw clenched.

"I'm just trying to get her to sleep, she's not feeling well."

From behind him, the maid steps forward and quietly says, "I'll watch over her, miss."

I protectively hold her and turn away from them as her cries grow louder. "She needs her mother, she's not feeling well."

"Look at me, piccolo prigioniero," he snaps. I take a deep breath through my nose. *Stay calm. Stay calm.* He lifts a brow and smirks. Apparently, I'm not hiding the look of hatred on my face very well. "Do you really want to argue this? You can either hand her over to the maid and get in our room, or," his eyes darken as he pauses, "she can be a gift to the men that used to play with you."

Fear and desperation spike through me. "No. Please, no. I'm sorry."

I kiss the side of her head and whisper, "I love you, Rhayvin Grace. I love you so much."

I hand her to the maid and she scurries off to her room with a wailing Rhayvin. I clutch my stomach as nausea takes over thinking about the disgusting threat he's made. It's his favorite one to keep me in line.

"Move, Aria. Clothes off and lay on the bed."

With every piece of clothing I shed, I replace it with a wall in my mind. The only way I can get through this is to pretend I'm not here. I lay on my back and my eyes brim with tears as I hear Rhayvin's cries. I squeeze my eyes shut and block her out as well. This is for her. I have to keep her safe from all the monsters.

Fuck. I can't breathe.

I feel the first strike off Aldo's belt against my bruised hip bone and hiss from the pain. He wraps my legs around him and lines himself up. I bite my tongue to keep from screaming as he thrusts forward and forces himself inside of me. I'm dry as a fucking desert so I can feel every stretch, burn and tear of the intrusion. I feel myself floating away as I remember the photos Theia brought me and focus on the memories created in those moments.

I can't be here anymore.

Rhydian.

Rhydian.

Rhydian.

> *"The only real treasure is in your head. Memories are better than diamonds and nobody can steal them from you."*
> *-Rodman Philbrick*

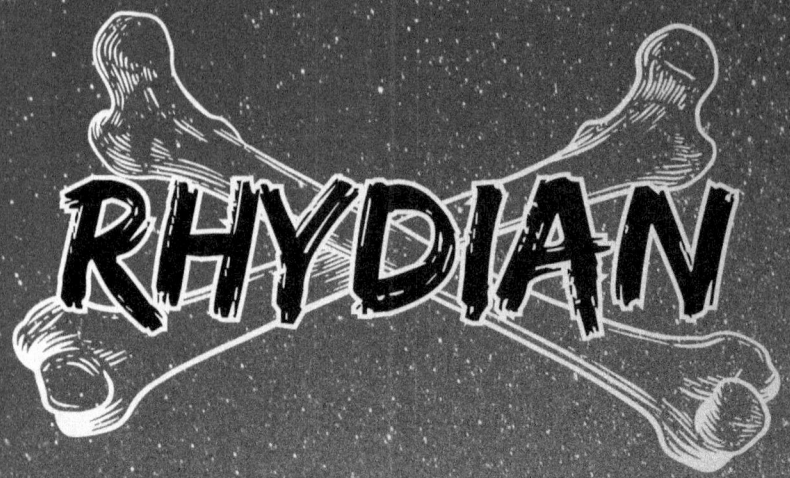

CHAPTER SEVEN

ANIMAL I HAVE BECOME

JULY 2022

Rhydian

My mind is on overdrive. I'm consumed with thoughts of Ophelia, nothing new there. She's been gone without a trace for three years. I feel so much anger about all of it, I use it as fuel for every workout and kill.

Along with thoughts of my little raven, my mind is on our current target, Joey Weyland. We found an in with this Cifarelli fucker and we're sure as fuck going to take it. It almost feels like we found this little bitch too easily. Any other time, I'd say it smells like a fucking trap, but Lore has been keeping an eye on everything she possibly can for us. She hacks into all activity and cameras involving this guy, while Rhyatt and I have been keeping an eye on him. It's easy enough, the dude is a gym rat through and through.

So while I get to work through my issues pumping iron, we're also gaining every bit of intel we can. I quickly wipe my eyes with the bottom of my shirt when the flood of sweat damn near blinds me. Rhyatt is at the end of the gym closest to the locker room and I'm on the opposite side while Joey rock climbs with some chick. The music blaring in here isn't loud enough to drown out the sounds of him groaning and grunting. If I wasn't seeing it for myself, I'd swear the dude was getting fucked in the ass with those noises.

"Shut the fuck up," I mumble. I've never rock climbed before, but I don't think it's hard enough to elicit those kinds of noises.

The girl presses her hand against her stomach and winces. "Climb to the top and back down, it's time," she shouts up at him.

The fuck? I look at Rhyatt and he's wearing the same expression on his face, but shakes his head and walks towards the locker room. When they're not paying attention I follow after him. Rhyatt is already pulling an 'OUT OF ORDER' sign from his locker and slapping it on one of the stalls. I follow behind and lock it, turning to see Rhyatt squatting on one side of the toilet with his back to the stall wall. I climb up on the other side, grunting at the tight fit.

The door slams against the wall, letting us know we're not alone. Their voices get closer.

"Lay on the bench," the woman says in a strained voice.

I peek through the crack in the door and can see the sweat dripping down her pained face from here. Joey rips off his shirt first before laying down and uses it as a pillow, his ink on full display. The girl yanks his shorts down revealing more ink and… what. the. fuck.

The dude has rope tied around his cock and balls. I put my hand over my own cock, grimacing at the idea of how painful that is. I look at Rhyatt and instead of being freaked out by the sight, he makes a 'hmmm' face. Is this motherfucker actually contemplating trying that shit out?

I look back through the crack in the stall when she asks, "Do you want me to untie you? Pick fast, I'm not gonna last long."

He writhes on the bench, panting. "Just untie it enough so you can hold on to one of the ends. I want you to tug on it while I feast."

"Gotcha." She deftly gets a piece of the rope untied and yanks her leggings down and off her feet. She places her legs on either side of his head, her chest heaving. "You ready?"

He grips her hips, yanking her down to his face. "Less talk, more feeding me."

I hope this fuck is a god at eating pussy and gets this shit done sooner rather than later. Someone's stomach gurgles, echoing throughout the space. Rhyatt and I both look at each other, hoping it wasn't one of us. We both shake our heads and look back at them.

Wait, why isn't her pussy on his face?

Great, he's not a god at pussy eating. Wrong hole, you fucking idiot.

The girl yanks the rope as she groans and... oh fuck, I'm gonna be sick. Rhyatt and I press our hands over our mouths as we watch... and hear this bitch shit in the motherfucker's mouth. He refuses to let any of it escape his mouth and slurps away like it's the best goddamn dessert ever presented to him. She moans, a sound caught between the pleasure of the act and the pain of her stomach churning. His hips thrust up with every tug of the rope she does. Their moans intermingle and he shoots a geyser of cum all over himself, the bench and floor.

Jesus, I thought we needed therapy before. This guarantees it.

"Lick it clean, bitch," she pants. She shuffles around him and grabs her leggings. Pulling them on, she snaps the waistband and without a backwards glance, asks, "Same time next week, sewer boy?"

He moans at the degrading name and nods enthusiastically, as if she can see him. "Y-yes."

He slowly gets up and licks his cum from the bench and floor. Okay, totally glad we're killing this guy. I can't with good conscience allow this sewer hoover hound to walk the Earth. While he showers, we grab our backpacks and sneak out. We make our way to his rundown, extended-stay motel, which conveniently enough, is just around the corner.

We stick to the shadows as Rhyatt calls Lore. "Hey, little succubus-"

"So feisty. We're out of there. Can you hack into the cameras and wipe us?"

We both shudder at the word wipe. We must have the same thought. *Wipe. Ass. Shit. Fucking gross.*

"Thank you... Yeah, we're on our way to the next location... Oh, baby girl, you don't even wanna know what happened in there... well maybe one thing. Be glad there's no camera footage for you to... delete in there... Okay... Mhmm... Yes, ma'am."

He yanks the phone from his ear when she starts shouting at him. He ends the call and shoves the phone in his pocket, smirking. "She loves me."

"Focus," I grunt. With a heavy sigh, he nods and leans against the wall. It's dark enough against the wall that we can't be seen but we can see out there.

We hear his whistles before we see him make his way to his room. As soon as he unlocks and shuts his door behind him, we make our way to our white utility van, the town's gas company logo on its side. I quietly unlock the barn doors of the van and open them a crack. The shit soup image assaults my brain as I grab some extra supplies from the van. I put them in my backpack, Rhyatt and I exchange a look and whisper, "Ready?"

He stumbles onto the door first and starts giggling like an idiot while knocking a random beat. The guy opens the door and his proper tone and accent completely throws me off. "Yes, hello. How may I help you two?"

Rhyatt laughs some more and sways. "Hey, man. We were told the party is here. Wooo," he throws his hands up like fake guns and points them in his direction. "Pew pew."

Joey lifts a brow and I nudge Rhyatt. "The code."

"Oh yeah. The code is 'say rawr and you'll see stars.'"

Joey tilts his head in confusion.

"Right? I swear they said it was that," Rhyatt adds nonchalantly.

Rhyatt barrels past Joey into the room and looks around. "Where is everyone?"

"Umm, excuse me. You can't just walk into someone's room. I'm going to have to ask you to please leave."

Damn, this guy is good. The way he talks makes it look like he's fucking normal and decent. That couldn't be further from the truth. The whole reason Cifarelli wants him gone is because he's a snake. Which, in the mafia world, is a big fucking no-no.

This guy has been running around playing all teams in the drug world. Which, in theory, is the least of our concerns. But after a little digging, Lore found an endless amount of protection orders against this guy. Starts off with verbal abuse and then turns into a sadistic fuck in the bedroom. Which, to each their own as long as both parties consent. They did not. It was more of a coercion act to get them to comply. That chick from earlier was lucky she complied to his brown soup request or she'd end up like the others.

The guy turns to plead with me and I block the doorway, swinging the door shut behind me and locking it. He looks between Rhyatt and I, now visibly nervous. "Listen, guys, I don't want any problems. Please leave."

I cross my arms and tilt my head as I watch him squirm. "I wonder if you'd be this polite if we were women?"

I take a menacing step forward and he step backwards, stumbling into Rhyatt. Joey jolts, but before he can regain his footing, I headbutt him. His glasses break and fall between us quicker than his own descent to the floor. I shake my head until my vision clears and wipe away the drip of blood falling down my forehead. The hiss of duct tape being extended and torn breaks the fogginess in my head.

I look at Rhyatt as he hands me a piece and points to my forehead. "Cover that before it drips on the floor."

I nod and slap it to my forehead. "Good call."

Rhyatt slaps a piece of duct tape over Joey's mouth and yanks his wrists together, wrapping the duct tape around them in layer after layer. He tosses me the duct tape and I crouch, doing the same to his ankles. Joey's feet are heavy in my hands, as Rhyatt pulls a knife from his back pocket before gripping him under the armpits. I pull a garbage bag out of my backpack and force it open, the plastic catching on my sweaty hands. Rhyatt slices through Joey's clothes like it's nothing, peeling them off and tossing the scraps into the bag.

"We've seen this guy's cock too many times today."

I shake my head, annoyed by it, and pull my knife out. "Grab his junk so I can cut it off, Rhy."

He whips his head in my direction, curling his lip. "The fuck I will."

He pulls out a pair of heavy-duty kitchen shears and hands them to me. "Use those, I'm not touching his junk, Rhyd," he scoffs.

I roll my eyes and lean down, slicing his cock off. Blood spurts about the same time that Joey's eyes shoot open and he thrashes around, screaming against the duct tape. Rhyatt looks at him with a big smile and waves. "Morning!"

He attempts to fight against his restraints and I tap his face with the scissors. "Shut the fuck up. You're making too much noise." His eyes widen when Rhyatt pulls out a handheld saw.

"Leave it for last," I shake my head.

He inspects the saw then looks at Joey's bound hands and nods. "You right, you right."

I grab our sharpened metal dowels and hand one over to Rhyatt. We both kneel beside the tub and begin puncturing his abdomen with our Gemini constellation signature. He wriggles around harder, almost fucking up our work and I slap him in the face.

"You're fucking it up. Sit. Still."

Blood pools beneath the dowels and pours in different patterns across his abdomen. They remind me of streaks of lightning. My last night with Ophelia flashes behind my eyes and I shake my head. Not now.

I nudge Rhyatt when we finish the constellation. "Switch spots with me." He moves around me and crouches, the knife glinting as he makes little cuts that remind me of shooting stars. I grip Joey's hair and notice he's passed out. I carve 'snake' on his forehead and then rip the duct tape off his mouth, handing it to Rhy to put in the garbage bag. I grip his chin, pull his mouth open and cut small nicks across his tongue. The dowel gets tossed in my backpack, Rhyatt following suit. I pull out the jar of sulfuric acid and his eyes widen.

"I'm so glad Lore saw that he uses this. I think if he knew, he'd be proud."

I grunt and nod. Everything we do is for him. "Rip me off another piece of duct tape and cut a small slit in it." I put the acid next to my leg and slide on the heavy duty gloves. "Oh, get me the funnel, too."

He nods and gets to work, handing me the duct tape first. I slap the duct tape over his mouth and keep doing it until he wakes up. His eyes shoot open, frantically looking around as he gasps for air. I shove the funnel in a slit in the tape, grab the jar of acid and carefully unscrew the top.

"Don't worry, bud, just a little water for ya."

I pour a little in at a time to make sure it doesn't shoot out of the funnel with him blowing air back into it. He convulses violently as it hits his tongue, a muffled wail rising from the funnel. I can hear the sizzles in his mouth, a mix of blood and bubbles mixing with the acid at the bottom of the funnel. I pour until the jar is empty, his chest moving with barely-there breaths. Gurgling noises fill the air from his mouth and throat. I put everything away and look at Rhyatt.

"Go ahead and use the saw now, I'm gonna go clear his room."

"Call Lore and tell her to take care of the cameras there. Then she needs to put in a call to *Amissa Stella* to say that Cifarelli has an incoming delivery behind the building."

I focus on the road and occasionally check the rearview mirror, as if Joey is going to come back to life. Not possible. He ends the call and I look over at him briefly. "Don't forget our new names. Even if you have to sit here and repeat it over and over until it sticks. Got it?"

He crosses his arms and pouts. "I won't forget."

I pinch the bridge of my nose. "What are our names?"

"I'm not a child, *Lyric*. Happy?"

"Not really, *Slayer*," I grumble. I pull up to the back of the so-called asylum and park. There's already men holding assault rifles waiting under a single light. I turn off the van and we get out with our hands up, walking slowly over. We stop with a good bit of space between us and Rhyatt starts with his fucking antics.

"Some welcoming party this is. We even brought a gift and everything."

One of the men, Aldo, if I recall from intel, steps forward. He aims his gun at us and then gestures towards the van. "Show us."

His brother, Alonzo, follows behind so they each have a gun at our backs. I open the barn doors wide and step aside so they can look.

"Santa merda," they both say when they see Joey.

I spin towards them. "So, where's Cifarelli? We want in."

Aldo chuckles darkly. "You hear that, fratello? They want in."

Alonzo forces a laugh and looks at Aldo like a lost puppy. *Interesting.* The last thing I see is them lifting their guns and slamming the butt of them into our heads.

"Anger is like gasoline. If you have it around and someone lights a match, you've got an inferno."
-Scilia Elworthy

ARIA

CHAPTER EIGHT

THE CONTORTIONIST

Aria

I lay in bed staring at the ceiling, waiting to make sure Aldo is really gone. The room is silent other than the occasional breath I let out when I realize I've been holding it for too long. It's been ten minutes since he's left. I push myself up, wincing as pain ripples through every bruise and overstretched limb — souvenirs of Aldo's handiwork.

Each ache pulls me back to the memory of his hands, twisting and bending, finding new ways to hurt me for his pleasure. I realize I've memorized every squeaky floorboard here just as I did in Thatcher's house. I grab one of Rhayvin's books and bring it back to the room, smiling at the secret pictures within. Tears blur my vision immediately.

I lay them out before me and caress Rhydian's face as if he's in front of me again. With a wobbly laugh, I look at the picture of him and Rhyatt against the wall, watching over things, and it brings me back to the first day I ever saw him.

I open my locker and the sounds of students shouting and laughing dies down. A shiver runs up my spine. What's going on? I peek over my shoulder and watch as the students are all walking alongside the wall, whispering to each other and staring at the other side of the hall.

I follow their line of sight and see two boys standing on the wall. Twins. They're both standing against the wall with their arms crossed and a foot perched against the wall behind them. The only discernible difference between the two is one has longer, dyed bangs, and while he's glaring, he also has a goofy smile on his face. The other one has shorter hair and his jaw is clenched. If looks could kill, every student passing by would perish to dust in front of him. He turns his head and my breath hitches. Is it possible for a boy to be so rough around the edges yet breathtakingly beautiful? Tall, muscled, a jawline made by the gods, with brown hair and greenish hazel eyes.

I swear his demeanor softens when he sees me, but that could just be wishful thinking. His brother elbows him and the connection is broken. I can breathe again. I can't look away as they stare at one of the school bullies shoving a kid in one of the lower lockers.

The poor kid is crying, begging for mercy, while the bully laughs. In almost synchronized movements, the twins uncross their arms and push off the wall. Every student they pass gasps. Murmurs ripple through the crowd: 'oh shit,' 'oh fuck,' 'he's gonna die'.

I watch as the beautiful twin sneaks up behind the bully and wraps his arm around his throat, pulling him away. The bully kicks and screeches while the twin with the goofy smile kneels down and kindly speaks to the freshman in the locker. And just like that, the chaos fades. They're protectors.

I'm pulled from the memory when I hear the crackle of the baby monitor and Rhayvin's coos and cute little voice trying to say, "Muh-muh." I smile at the sound of her voice and wipe away my tears. I drop the pictures in the book and close it before I run to the bathroom and splash my face with cold water. I pick up the book, dramatically open the door and start singing. "Gooooood morninggggg, little birdie! Flap your wings and fly to mommyyyyy!"

She giggles and jumps, flapping her little arms like me. "Fwy muh-muh, fwy!"

She notices the book in my outstretched hand and points to it. "Ooo."

I smile at her and walk over. "Mama has something to show you, baby bird."

I pick her up and she wraps her arms around me, hugging me tight. "Bestest hugger ever." I kiss her all over her face. She giggles and pushes at my face. "Alright, alright. Sit with Mama." I take a seat with her in my lap and open the book. With one arm wrapped around her, I point at the first picture, at Rhydian first.

"Dada," I say, pointing again, "Dada, that's your dada."

She points her chubby little finger, smudging his face in the picture. "Duh-duh."

I choke back a sob and laugh. "Yes, Dada. And that is Uncle Rhyatt. Can you say Rhy-Rhy?"

She giggles and I can't help but notice the similarities between her goofy smile and Rhyatt's. "Why-why!"

I sniffle and laugh with her. "Yes, that's your Uncle Rhy-Rhy. And there's Mama sitting with Dada."

We go through the pictures and saying their names. I close the pictures in the book and give her the reminder I hate the most. My voice drops to a whisper. "Dada is a secret." My finger presses to my lips. "Shhh, secret. We can't talk about Dada or

Uncle Rhy-Rhy in front of Mr. Aldo." I tap the book again, "Shhh."

I've never seen such an adorable serious expression until just now, as she mimics me. "Shhhh, sicket."

I kiss her chubby cheek and nuzzle her. "That's right, baby. Secret. Let's go get you breakfast and then have a... DANCE PARTY!"

I scoop her up and spin, dancing around as she squeals and bounces. "YAY!"

I lay Rhayvin down in her toddler bed and sit next to it, running my fingers through her hair. I softly sing *Over The Rainbow* to her as I watch the rise and fall of her chest. I finish the song and drop a kiss on her forehead and whisper, "Everything."

I turn on her night light, which illuminates the room with flying birds as it spins in circles, and shut the overhead light off. I smile up at the flying birds, knowing that she loves them. My smile falls when I remember all the things I endured just so Aldo would order one for her. I quietly shut the door and press my hand against my stomach as it rolls with nausea from the memory.

I walk over to the bookshelf and pull her book out, looking down at the pictures again. I run my finger along the edges as if they're a magic lamp I can rub and conjure up my Bones. The door creaks open and my stomach plummets. My heart races realizing Aldo will catch me with these pictures if I'm not care-ful. I quietly shut the book and put it back on the shelf. I start pulling out random books and putting them back, acting like I'm picking something to read. I jolt when he wraps his arms around me, nuzzling my neck.

I bite my tongue, forcing myself not to audibly gag at his scent and the feel of him touching me. He kisses my neck, murmuring, "Mmm, my, piccolo prigioniero. I feel so inspired. You're the only one that can know the beauty I discovered today." He caresses my stomach as if I'm a cat to soothe. He rubs his nose along my neck. "Get naked and lay on the bed for me, I'm going to take you to the stars," he whispers.

I put the book back on the shelf as he steps back. Keeping my movements steady, I make my way to the room, my hands trembling as I remove my clothes. Once undressed, I crawl on the bed and lay on my back, trying to conjure up images in my mind to take me away from here. I jump at the feel of his calloused fingers running up my calf. I watch, frozen, as he grabs the rope connected to the bed and ties it to my ankle.

His usually dark eyes are bright and he can't stop smiling. I'm not sure which Aldo is more terrifying; the one that's dark and angry or the one before me now who's all smiles and humming a happy tune. He finishes tying up my ankles and walks along the side of the bed, trailing his fingers up my leg and side. He ties one wrist and looks down, his smile never faltering. "I know it's been awhile since I've had to tie you down, but I really need you to stay still for this. I'll be very unhappy if you move and ruin my fun."

He finishes the last knot and when he turns away, I attempt to move to gauge how much give there is. None. I can already feel the aches in my joints. One wrong move and I'm sure I will end up with something dislocated. Sweat beads on my skin in anticipation of what's to come.

He shrugs his suit jacket off and turns as he undoes his tie. He tosses it on the bed next to me and begins unbuttoning his dress shirt. He slides out of his shirt and drops it to the floor with his suit jacket. Each move is slow, deliberate, as if he is enjoying the moment.

He crawls on the bed, straddling my legs and reaches into his pocket. My whole body tenses at the unmistakable click of a knife opening. The ropes creak with the tension and I feel the burn of my body stretching. I shiver when my shallow breaths flutter over my own skin and goosebumps cover my chest.

"Nobody else can know how much joy this has brought me. True inspiration. Keep still, Aria. Do you understand?"

I nod in understanding, not realizing my mistake until the sting blooms across my breast from his harsh slap.

"Words," he barks.

"Yes, I understand, Aldo." He pulls his phone out of his pocket and scrolls. He places the phone beside me, but I can't tell what he's looking at. I swear I can see the wheel turning in his tiny fucking brain trying to figure something out. He points the knife at his phone and then over at my stomach and nods. I feel the cold tip of the blade before the searing pain starts. My body aches from the sheer willpower to keep from fighting, but the scream falls from my lips before I can stop it. The warm blood dripping down my side tickles. Tears slide from my eyes on the same path.

Aldo picks up his tie and shoves it into my mouth, slapping his palm over the top. "Shut. Up."

I lie there, enduring every stab. My focus is on the baby monitor. I watch my sweet Rhayvin sleep and hope that this isn't the end. I can't leave her. Not with these monsters. They'll pluck her beautiful wings and leave her to a world of pain and torment.

Eighteen stabs later, he finally pauses. I breathe in through my nose and out through the tie in my mouth, preparing for the next one. It never comes.

"Bellissima," he says in awe. He runs his fingers through the blood on my stomach, swirling it around and muttering, "Bellissimi Gemelli." I brace myself for what I'll find and look down. Blood is smeared across my stomach and I see the eighteen stabs, unsure of what he was going for. The flash of his phone goes off continuously as he takes pictures. He tosses the phone down, fumbling with the button and zipper on his pants. He pulls his cock out and groans as he rubs it around the blood on my stomach. Swiping his hand around on my stomach, he brings his bloody hand to his cock and strokes it above me. He grits his teeth, jerks faster and thrusts his hips. I attempt to count in my head in order to make the time pass easier. His grunts interrupt my counting, his cum spurts and covers my bloodstained stomach. He leans over to mix the blood and cum, humming again.

I grimace when he runs the hand with the mix through his hair. With a sigh of relief, he stands and unties the rope from my wrists and ankles. I start rubbing my wrists and ankles, unsure of which ones need the most attention. Smiling down at his phone, he nods to the door and absentmindedly mutters, "Go clean up."

I run to the bathroom and shut the door. For a moment, I freeze standing next to the bathroom counter. I need to see. I'm terrified to see. I slowly turn, taking a deep breath. I stare down at the sink and hype myself up. I bounce on my toes and shake my hands out. "One, two, three. Go, bitch, go," I whisper to myself.

I look up and I tilt my head side to side, trying to figure out what I'm looking at. The pieces come together, the memory of a conversation about birthdays and stars plays in my head. A tear slips down my cheek as what I'm seeing fully sinks in. I should be horrified. Disgusted. Broken over the scars that will form.

Instead, I smile at the beauty a monster has created. I wince in pain as I caress the punctures. Aldo doesn't even realize his torture is actually a gift to me. He's left me with the mark of a Gemini constellation. The mark of my Bones.

"There was love in her broken pieces, beauty in all her scars."
  -Dhiman

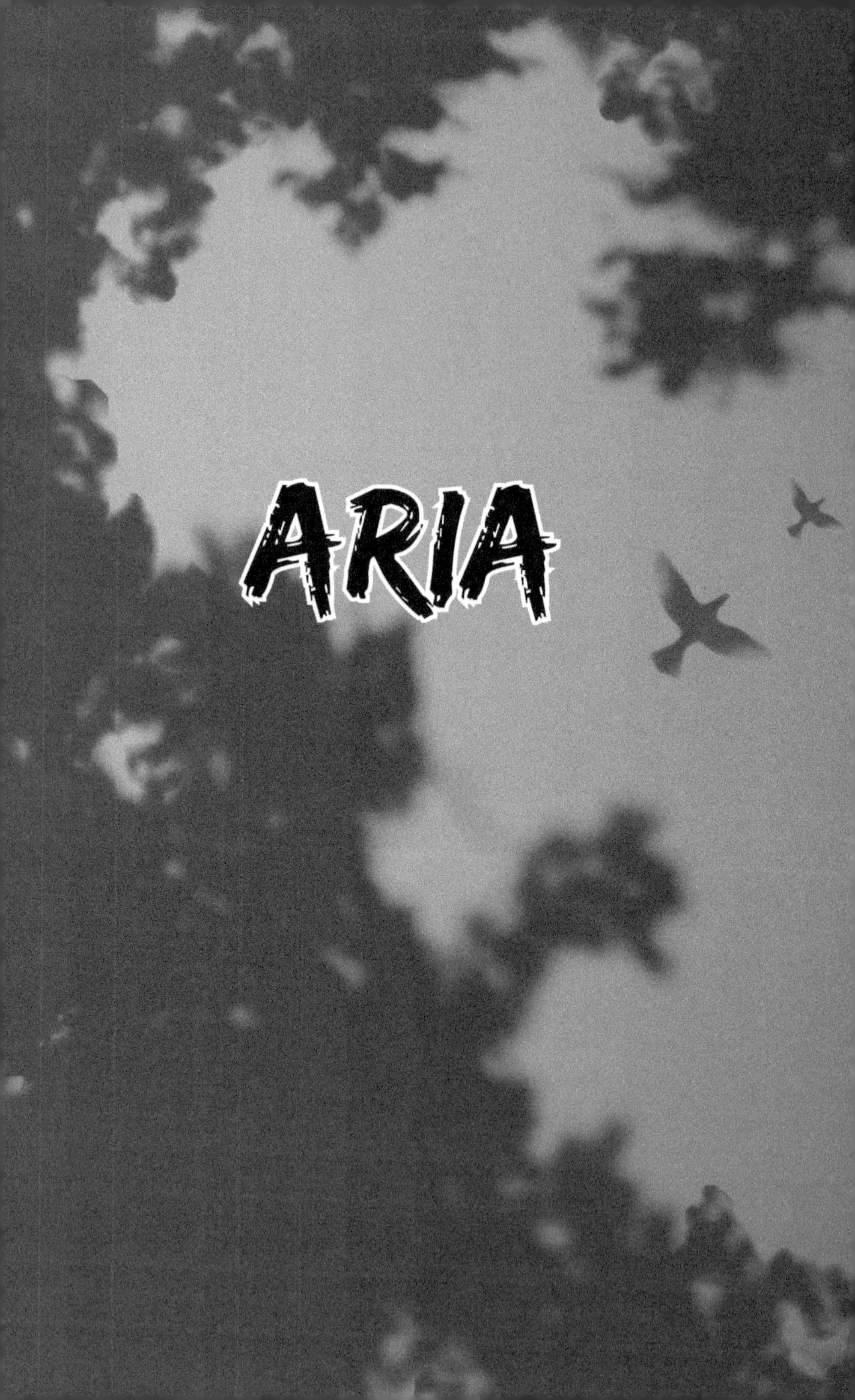
ARIA

CHAPTER NINE
NEVER FORGET YOU

DECEMBER 2023

Aria

I watch Rhayvin wiggle and huff while she tries to put on her polar bear onesie. I step forward and stop her frantic movements. "Let me help you, baby bird."

She steps back, putting her hands on her hips. "I big gool, I do it," she pouts.

I put my hands up and step back. "Okay, but can you take a deep breath for Mama and be patient?" I take a deep breath in, showing her, and then slowly push it out.

She copies it and then slowly puts it on the right way, now fidgeting with the zipper. Once it zips to the top, she looks up at me with a bright smile and puts the hood with ears on. "Grr, I powah bea."

I put my hands up to my mouth, gasping. "Oh, you are so scary! Please don't eat me!"

She claps her hands and giggles. I walk over to her bed, pulling back the sheets. "Crawl into your cave, ferocious bear."

She hops on her bed and lays down, smiling up at me. I cover her up and sit next to her bed, pulling the secret pictures out of my pajama pants pocket. I wave them in her direction. "Okay, we're going to play our learning game, and then we can look at pictures, okay?"

Her eyes light up and she bounces a little. "Okay, Mama."

"Alright, ready?" She nods and claps her bear paw covered hands.

"What's your name?"

"My name Wayvin Gwace."

I nod, and focus on teaching her how to say her r's. "That's right, your name is Ruh-ruh-Rhayvin Grrrr-ace."

"How old are you?"

She giggles and gets that mischievous glint in her eye which matches her Uncle Rhyatt's perfectly. "I fo yeas ode."

I bite my lip, trying not to laugh and shake my head. "No, baby. You are three, still. You'll be four at the end of this month."

She giggles again. "Noooo, I fo, I fo!"

"Baby, why do you always say you're four?"

She shrugs her tiny shoulders. "Cuz I wan-be." I chuckle at her no-nonsense answer.

"Okay, next question, silly girl." I lean in like I'm going to share a secret. "Are you ready to look at the pictures?"

She squeals and frantically nods. "Yes! Yes! Pwease!"

"What's the rule with the pictures and what we talk about?"

"Dey seekit, and we neva talk bout Daddy and Unca Why-Why awound Mistuh Addo. No scawy men."

"That's right. You're so smart. Do you know that?"

She rolls her eyes at me. "Well, duh."

I narrow my eyes at her playfully. "Sassy little thing. Okay, picture time."

We stare at the pictures over and over as I share more memories of Rhydian and Rhyatt. Her eyes droop on her final question and she falls asleep. I watch the steady rise and fall of her chest, sweep her hair away from her face and kiss her forehead.

I carefully stand, making sure not to bend the pictures, and switch her night light on. After shutting the door behind me, I walk to the bathroom and close it softly. Lifting my shirt, I stare at the scars on my stomach. My fingertips trace each one gently, and I imagine them connecting to form the Gemini constellation.

At the time, I thought Aldo had been stabbing me, but really they were each small punctures. Enough to leave a scar, but not enough to cause serious damage. Every movement cracked open the freshly scabbed-over wounds, and worse, Aldo would reopen them himself, prolonging the pain to ensure they would scar. I put the picture of the three of us next to my scars and smile in the mirror, imagining we're all together again. A sudden pounding on the door jolts me from my reverie. I drop my shirt and shove the pictures in my pocket frantically. The room spins, my heart racing at what's to come.

The intercom crackles to life and I hear Theia's terrified, breathless voice. "No time for the song, open the door, open the door! Please, please open the door, Aria!"

I quickly run to the door and rip it open. Theia is standing there, panting and looking behind her. "Theia?! What's wrong, what's going on?"

She continues to look behind her and back at me. "Inside, we need to get inside right now."

I pull her in and slam the door shut, locking it. I drag her to the couch and push her shoulders to make her sit. She grips her knees and takes a deep breath trying to get the words out. "We. Have. To. Go."

My brow furrows. "What do you mean? What happened, Theia?"

Rhayvin's covered feet make a soft shuffling sound as she walks out. She rubs her eyes and crawls into Theia's waiting arms. "Auntie?"

Theia rocks her back and forth, staring at me with wide-eyed, teary eyes as the words pour out. "Something is happening. I don't know where Atlas is, but I have to get you guys out of here. Aldo and Alonzo were in Papa's office. I ran down the stairs to check on him, when I heard all this crashing and screaming. Atlas' people took down something of Papa's and he's losing his mind. But then Aldo started talking about betrayal and retribution. How he's going to kill Atlas and his people. Papa. Me. I don't know what that means for you two, but I have to get you out of here."

I jump when the door swings open, slamming against the wall, revealing Aldo and Alonzo.

Fuck.

My heart pounds against my chest as they both step inside. "Well, well, well. Guess you weren't quick enough, sorella. Such a shame," Aldo says to Theia. She stands abruptly and hands Rhayvin to me, placing herself directly in front of us, as if she can block us from their wrath. I focus on Rhayvin as she starts to cry, pressing her face to my chest and shielding her from them as I rock her back and forth. Aldo stomps over and pulls a gun out, pointing it at Theia's face. I try to contain my emotions so as to not scare Rhayvin further.

"Aria, please take Rhayvin to the room," Theia says without looking at me.

I turn to run to the room but freeze at the sound of metal clicking. I slowly turn and look at Aldo as he tsks. "I don't think so. Don't think I won't kill you, Aria. You wouldn't be the first mother I've killed."

I gasp at his threat, and he looks at Theia with a twisted smile. "Oh, no, no. That honor goes to *Isabelle.*"

I tremble as I hold onto Rhayvin, whispering to her, "Shh, shh. It's okay, Mama has you. I won't let anything happen to you. I love you so much." I scream as cold metal presses to my temple and I see that Aldo is holding his gun to my head. I hold Rhayvin tight, shielding her the best I can as she sobs against my chest. My head spins and my body buzzes.

I have to save her. How do I save her?

I squeeze my eyes shut, trying not to upset Aldo by moving when he shouts, "NOW, ALONZO!"

He glares down at me and over to Theia. "The two of you are going to walk outside. You're going to listen to everything I say, and you're not going to do anything stupid." He moves the gun from my temple and then points it at the back of Rhayvin's head. I shakily grab at her head as if I can stop a bullet.

Theia and I both sob, "NO!"

"I will kill her if you do."

He barks at us to move and we start walking. Theia puts one arm around me and one around Rhayvin as we shuffle outside. I can't believe it, this is the end. My chest constricts at the thought that my sweet girl will never see the age of four. She'll never meet her daddy or Uncle Rhyatt. She'll never experience friends, school, stupid boys, love, heartbreak, anything. I'm pulled from drowning in my thoughts when I feel Rhayvin shivering in my arms. Theia and I both rub her back, trying to keep her as warm as possible in the chilly winter air. Our panted breaths surround us in a fog. I watch as Theia is shoved and stumbles, snapping at Aldo as she walks over to the lounge chairs. Alonzo walks out with blankets and Rhayvin's puffy purple coat. They start arguing as he puts her coat over her shoulders.

"Here you go, little one."

Aldo sneers at us. "I'll allow you both this one kindness. Rhayvin, give your mama a hug. Not all of us are allowed to hug our mamas goodbye."

I gently put Rhayvin down and help her into her coat, zipping it up. I wrap my arms tightly around her and cry, rocking her back and forth, humming her song. Her cries grow louder. "Shh, shh. It's okay, my baby bird. Mommy loves you so much. You are the best parts of me and your daddy. You listen to whatever Mr. Aldo tells you, okay? You be a big, strong girl for mommy."

Rhayvin cries, hugging me tight. "I wuv you, mommy."

"That's enough," Aldo growls.

He yanks Rhayvin away from me and I fall back as she screams. "Go get in the other chair, Aria."

I stumble forward, my legs barely holding me up and walk to the other chair, continuously looking back at Rhayvin. Alonzo follows me and places a blanket over each of us, whispering to Theia. I can't seem to catch my breath as I sit in the chair and watch Aldo grab a fistful of Rhayvin's jacket. I gasp as he roughly handles her and drags her along with him. He walks over to the storage closet and opens the door, grabbing one of her giant unicorn floaties. He drops it in the pool and places his foot on it, holding it in place. "Do it now, fratello." I can't look away from Rhayvin and don't realize what Alonzo is doing until I feel a pinch in my neck. I hiss from the pain and slap my hand over it. Even the irritation can't make me look away from my baby. Aldo smiles at us and then looks down at her. "Climb on."

Everything starts to spin as she looks up at him and whimpers, "B-but, I can't swim, Mistuh Addo."

"Then you better not fall off, huh? Get on there."

I sniffle and my tongue feels heavy in my mouth as my vision blurs, "Remember w-hat m-mommy said, baby."

Rhayvin looks at me and nods, "Otay, mommy."

I keep blinking my eyes to push away the blur and watch as she climbs on the float and sits in the middle of it, shaking. Aldo kicks it away from the edge of the pool and it wobbles, making Rhayvin scream and grip the handles on the sides tightly.

My baby. Oh, I love you.

My eyes feel heavy and slowly shut. I can't seem to open my eyes again and everything sounds like I'm under water. *No. No. Rhayvin. Bones. I'll never forget you.*

"Tell me darling, who were you before they stole your moon and left you with only the dimly lit stars?" -Lorelai Ellsworth

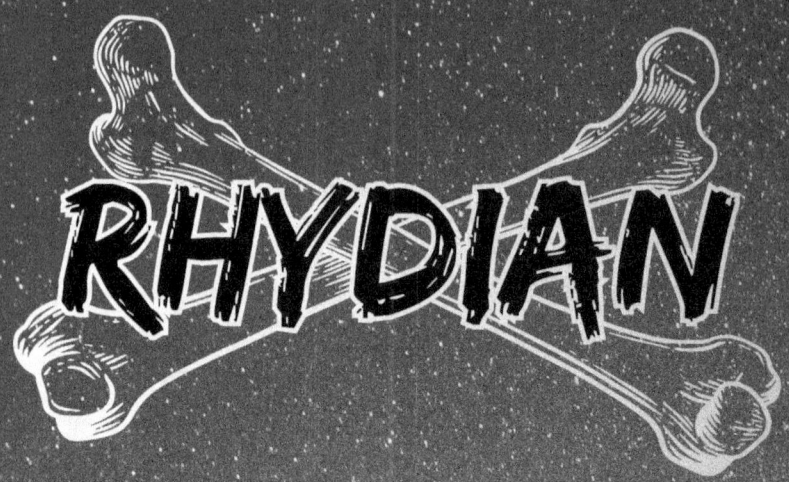

CHAPTER TEN

BODIES

Rhydian

I drive the truck on the backroads, searching for a good section of the marsh to dump Cifarelli's most recent body. Rhyatt bounces in his seat, slapping his thighs to the beat of the music. I glance at Rhyatt when a thought comes to mind.

"I think I know a good spot. Might be risky, but I think it would be a good nod to Rhys."

Rhyatt smiles at me brightly. "You mean that one spot he grabbed a target at when we were following him?!"

I nod in response and drive up the turn-off, slowly drifting to the gravel road. I take the first turn that winds around and stop when we don't see anybody else parked there. In synchronized movements, we slide our hoods on and open the door, hopping out. The dust beneath us billows around my boots, gravel crunching with every step.

Rhyatt and I each grab a handle on the barn doors of the van and open it up. Bending down, we each grab an ankle and start dragging the body out of the van. I grab under his arms while Rhyatt grabs his ankles and we carry him to the edge of the hill that looks over the marsh. The closer we get to the edge, the more we start to slip on the gravel.

"Shit. Okay, we're just going to have to swing and toss him. If we get any closer, we're all going down."

Rhyatt nods as we start to swing the body. The phone in my pocket buzzes once with an incoming text, which I ignore. I almost freeze when the buzz starts a second time, and Rhyatt meets my gaze. I'm guessing he's getting the notifications as well, which means we're one away from the text we've been waiting for. The third notification comes through just as we toss the body. We both stare at one another, quickly shoving our hand in our pocket to pull our burner phones out. My phone vibrates once more and I quickly open the notifications.

LORE: !

LORE: !

LORE: !

LORE: P.O. Box 143

"Let's go. Shoot Atlas a text and let him know it's showtime." He jumps in the van as I slam the barn doors shut, making my way to the driver side. Rocks kick back and dust flies as I stomp the gas to get going.

Without looking up from his phone, Rhyatt reminds me in a nonchalant tone, "Curve." I ease off the gas a bit, taking the turn with ease. I turn the knob up on the stereo and blast the music. I can practically see the lyrics displayed in front of me on the road as we head to the post office.

I pull up to Cifarelli's mansion and we both take a deep breath. We both move like machines. Rhyatt's usual goofy smiles are replaced with a blank mask. He almost looks like a shell of himself, but it's necessary for survival. Side by side, we walk into the mansion and head to the door to the training floor. I push the door open and Rhyatt shuts it behind him. The creaks of the old stairs are drowned out by *Bodies* blaring down below. We reach the bottom of the steps and the first target walks straight into a trap. I swiftly stab my knife in his throat and his brief gasp turns into a gurgle with the blood spilling around my knife. I place him on the ground and quickly stab out the constellation. Luckily, we've done this enough times that we don't even have to think about it anymore.

The time it takes to make eighteen stabs has been cut in half with ease. I watch as Rhyatt prowls over to two men hitting the punching bags. He pulls out his knives, one for each hand and steps between the two of them. He strikes sideways and gets both of them in the side of the neck. They drop to the floor with their hand over the stabs as if they can stop their impending death. Idiots.

I shake my head and make my way towards two men grappling on the mats. Inspired by Rhyatt using two knives, I pull another from my pocket and sneak up behind them. I wait for them to fall to the side and stab each of them in the back of the neck. They throw their heads back screaming, pushing the knives further in. They eventually both go limp when the knife severs their spinal cord. I roll them on their backs and kneel between them, plunging into their chests and stomachs, marking them with the constellation.

The music stops and I whip my head around, finding Rhyatt turning it off. I wipe the sweat from my brow and take a breath, thankful it was him and not an ambush. He meets me at the door that leads down to the cells. Once open, we come face-to-face with someone who must have been guarding Atlas. His eyes widen seeing us covered in blood and I slit his throat with no hesitation, dragging the knife down his chest before he has a chance to get a word out.

The sound of creaking boards, dirt and debris sprinkling to the floor below serve as the background beats to our mission as we run down the stairs. I shove the door open to Atlas' cell and find it empty. Rhyatt and I spin in a circle, as if we'll find the answer to where he's at.

"ATLAS?!" I shout while checking the cell across from his.

Rhyatt takes off to search another one. "DUDE, ATLAS, WHERE ARE YOU?!"

The sound of cell doors slamming against walls echoes around us. I hear Rhyatt further down. "DUDE! RHYDIAN, I FOUND HIM!"

I run towards his voice and find him in there trying to help Atlas out of his restraints. "What the fuck have you two been up to?" Atlas asks.

I look down at myself and up at Atlas, shrugging. "Just clearing a path."

Free from his restraints, he stands up and sways. Rhyatt jumps up and catches him. "Whoa, whoa. You good?"

He takes a deep breath. "Yeah, yeah, I'm fine. Let's go."

Leaving the cell, we climb the stairs, stepping over the last guy we killed. At the top, we pass the bodies scattered across the training room floor, the ones we took down just minutes ago. Rhyatt moves beside me, but Atlas's footsteps falter behind us. His mouth opens, then closes again before he finally forces out, "I... you..."

He points around at the bodies and then over to us. "Holy shit! You guys are the Gemini serial killers, aren't you?!"

Rhyatt's goofy ass smile is back and I shrug with a smirk. At the same time we say, "Guilty."

Atlas walks past us and shakes his head. "Jesus, how many secrets do you guys have? First, I find out you're Rhys' brothers and now this?!"

Rhyatt and I look at each other and shrug, following him as he stomps up the stairs to the main house. We get halfway up the stairs before Atlas looks over his shoulder with his shirt over his face.

"Cover your face! The place is on fire!"

I bring my shirt over my face and yell, "We have to check Cifarelli's office, we're supposed to bring him and the two dumbasses to Rhys."

We follow Atlas into Cifarelli's office. We all look down and find Cifarelli dead surrounded by the destruction of the whole room. "One down, two to go," Atlas says. He runs past us out of the room shouting, "Theia?!"

Flames in the kitchen build up as he runs towards the stairs to her. "Atlas! Wait! We have to get the fuck out of here!" I shout.

"NOT WITHOUT THEIA AND THE GIRLS!"

I check the rest of the top floor while Rhyatt goes after Atlas. Over the sound of flames and things breaking, I hear him shout, "NO! GET THE FUCK OFF OF ME! I HAVE TO GET THEIA!"

"Holy fucking shit!" Rhyatt yells. I scan the stairs and go with the quickest route.

I slide down the left banister and turn towards Atlas and Rhyatt. "HURRY!" Breathing and seeing is getting more difficult by the second and my heart races. I need to get them the fuck out of here, even if I don't make it. Rhyatt holds Atlas practically dragging him down the stairs, coughing and gasping for air.

"This would be a lot easier if you'd stop fighting me, Atlas. We have to fucking go!"

"Fuck. You," he shouts back, coughing from all the smoke.

Part of me hurts for him, knowing what it's like to lose the love of your life, but he's also pissing me the fuck off putting Rhyatt in danger. My hands are fisted at my sides and I grit my teeth muttering, "Come on, come on."

Atlas keeps fighting Rhyatt. "LEAVE ME! JUST FUCKING GO! I'M NOT LEAVING WITHOUT HER! JUST FUCKING LET ME GO!"

"ENOUGH! I KNOW IT'S FUCKING HARD! BELIEVE ME! BUT YOU'RE PUTTING MY FUCKING BROTHER IN DANGER WITH YOUR BULLSHIT SO MOVE. YOUR. ASS!"

My words seem to spur him on, but he's still torn. One part of him doesn't want any harm to come to us so he walks with Rhyatt, but the other side of him wants to run so he continues to flail around. Once we're finally getting out of our own personal crematorium, we hear, "Rhydian?! Rhyatt?! Is that you?!"

My heart races. There he is. "Yeah, it's us!" I shout over the sounds of the raging fire.

"Did you guys get one of them?! Throw him in the van, we got the girls and they're already on their way to the warehouse! Let's go!" He shouts back. Atlas finally stops fighting Rhyatt and pulls away, going to Rhys.

Rhyatt and I stand there trying to give them their moment, all while we're practically vibrating in place. *He's here. We're here.* We've been waiting for this moment for so long. Atlas gets clobbered by a woman and Rhys turns towards us. "I'll be honest, I don't know if I should hit you fuckers, or hug you."

Rhyatt nervously laughs, "You could always do both, that's cool."

I roll my eyes and elbow Rhyatt in the side, making him, "Oomph."

"Rhyatt, ease him into your bullshit."

Atlas runs over to us. "Can we go see them now? I need to see Theia, please."

We rush to the warehouse and watch as Theia runs to Atlas. She looks over his shoulder at us. Rhys steps forward first with a smile on his face.

"Hi, I'm Rhys."

"Hi, Rhys. Nice to finally meet you."

"Geesh, what are we, chopped liver? Not like we saved your man or anything." Rhyatt pouts.

She smirks at him. "Sorry, Slayer. Hi. Thank you, both."

I groan at his antics and elbow him for the second time tonight. "Don't be a dick."

I grunt when the little shit elbows me back. "Stop. Elbowing. Me."

Simultaneously, we grab one another in headlocks and start wrestling in the hall, slamming against the walls. I forgot how strong he's gotten.

"Truce?" I ask.

"Neverrr."

He whines at first and then relents, loosening his grip. "Okay, truce."

"Bitch," I throw back as I let go and start walking.

He giggles and says, "Jerk."

Reaching the door, we see Atlas getting shit for his attempt at a beard. Rhyatt and I can't help but chuckle. There's a gasp somewhere in the room as we step further in. I look and everything stops.

Is it supposed to hurt when your heart slowly puts all its shattered pieces back together? I suck in air, finally able to breathe again. A little girl is wrapped around her leg and she holds her tight against her. She looks at me like she's seeing a ghost. "Rhydian."

I step forward, terrified to say her name as if it will wake me from this dream. "Ophelia?"

The little girl in her arms squeals, pulling away and looking at me and then Ophelia. "DADDY?!"

My heart feels like it will beat out of my chest. *What*? I look at Ophelia, furrowing my brow. "Daddy?"

Ophelia holds a hand over her mouth, crying and then she nods to answer. My heart warms and settles, knowing that dream or not, this is where I always want to be. The little girl... my daughter... holy shit! My daughter pulls away from Ophelia and runs to me. I drop to my knees with my arms open for her. She jumps into my arms and squeezes me tight. "Daddy! Daddy! I, Wayvin!"

With a watery laugh, I hold her and notice how much she looks like the Slater brothers. Same light brown hair, same hazel eyes. I'm a father. I have a daughter. A beautiful daughter. Ophelia slowly walks over and drops behind her, smiling while crying. "Hi, Bones. Meet your daughter, Rhayvin."

I shake my head, smiling at her, knowing her love for ravens gave our daughter her name. I look down at her. My daughter. "Hi, Rhayvin."

She giggles, sounding just like her Uncle Rhyatt and looks up at me. "Hi, Daddy. I been waitin' tuh meet you foweva."

Rhyatt gasps. "DUDE! I've been upgraded to uncle! Somebody get me a crown!"

I shake my head at his antics and gently slide Rhayvin to my left thigh and open my right arm to Ophelia, pulling her closer. I nuzzle into her hair, breathing her in. I pull back a bit to look at her beautiful face. Her eyes close as I say, "I've been looking for you everywhere, Ophelia. I can't believe you were so close this whole time. I'm so sorry I didn't find you sooner, little bird."

She opens her eyes, trying to glare at me. There's my girl. "I'm not just any ol' bird, Bones. I'm your little raven."

I press my forehead to hers. "You'll always be my little raven, but little bird always gets you to look at me."

Rhyatt starts to laugh, breaking the moment. "This is the craziest family reunion I've ever seen." Everyone looks around at each other and we all break into laughter with him.

"Family is like music, some high notes, some low notes, but always a beautiful song."
-Jesse Joseph

PART 2

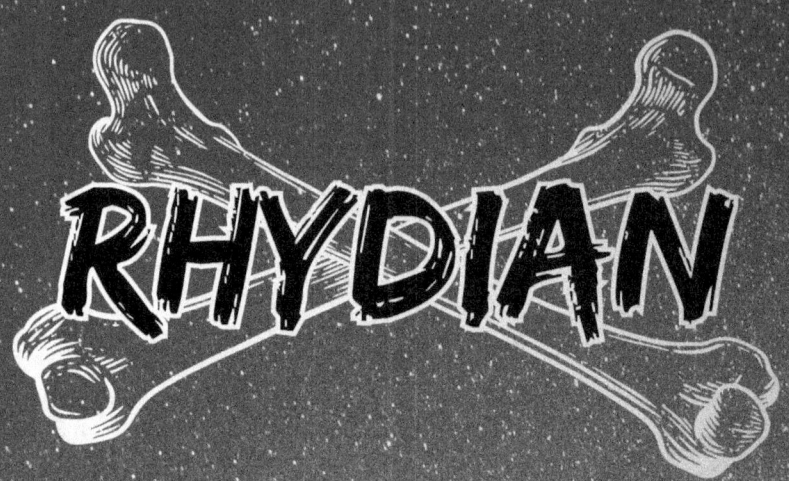

RHYDIAN

CHAPTER ELEVEN
THREE LITTLE BIRDS

June 2024

Rhydian

I look around the conference room at everyone laughing and smiling. I look down at my new little family and my heart feels full. Not all happiness can last, though. I learned that the hard way. My heart twinges as I think about all the time I lost with Ophelia and Rhayvin. It kills me that I missed all of Rhayvin's biggest milestones. I hate myself for not finding Ophelia sooner. It's my fault they went through what they did.

I know she's been through a lot, and I've tried giving her the time and space to come to me on her own to talk about it. I think I've been patient long enough, though. The unknown has been tearing me apart. I try to hide it the best I can, but Ophelia knows me well. I see it every time she looks at me a little longer and a flicker of sorrow crosses her face. I brush a piece of hair behind her ear and kiss her cheek. "Little raven?"

She looks at me, smiling. "Yeah?"

I rub my thumb along her cheekbone. "I tried waiting, but we really need to talk about what happened during our time apart."

She pulls away from me and looks down at Rhayvin and then around the room at everyone. "I know. But..."

"No. No buts, Ophelia. We need to talk about this. I know it's hard, but I'll be here, I promise. I know I wasn't before, and I'm so sorry. You don't know how sorry I am. I hate myself that you endured so much while I was gone. I promise I'll make up for it."

She looks up at me with watery eyes and grabs my hands. "Oh, Bones. I don't blame you. That's not why I haven't talked about it. It's just... It's a lot. I was just going to say, I'm ready to tell you everything, but can we do it another day? It's just too sad of a story to tell on such a happy day."

I hold my hand up and extend my pinky. "Pinky promise?"

She sniffles with a big smile on her face, lifting her hand up and wraps her pinky around mine. "Pinky promise."

Rhayvin squeals and wraps her little pinky the best she can around ours, "PINKY PROMISE!"

I laugh at her excitement to join us. "Well, look at that."

Rhys and Nova walk over hand-in-hand, smiling. He takes a seat at our table and pulls her into his lap, wrapping his arms around her and dropping his chin on her shoulder. Genetics are a funny thing. We didn't grow up with Rhys, but we share certain facial expressions. Like right now, it's like staring at Rhyatt's goofy smile. "Hello, love birds. Ha, see what I did there?"

Ophelia's shoulders shake in laughter, while Rhayvin giggles and I roll my eyes. "So original, big brother."

"You have to be nice to me, it's my big day. Anyways. I have to say you're really slacking, baby brother. I really thought you two would have beat us to the altar after finally finding each other again." Nova slaps his thigh and he exaggeratedly pouts. "Ouch, wife."

"Be nice, *husband*. They can get married if and whenever they want. "

"Thank you, Nova," Ophelia whispers, smiling.

I smile big at them. "We want... we did."

Their eyes both go wide and mouths drop. I chuckle at their expressions, breathing on my fingertips and pretending to dust them off on my chest. "That's right, big brother. We have you beat."

He looks up with a confused expression, scratching his head and then looking back at me. "Huh? When?"

"Eighteen days ago. You guys needed happy memories to replace bad ones by choosing this day. We did the same."

Rhys jumps up with Nova still in his arms, shaking her around as he bounces. "OH MY GOD!"

Nova laughs along and then smiles lovingly at him as he puts her down and yanks me out of my chair. "Oomph."

He squeezes me tight and claps my back. "Congrats, baby brother. Does Rhy know?"

Speak of the devil, Rhyatt's giggles surround us. "Tell me what?"

Rhayvin mimics his giggle and runs up to him, bouncing on her toes with her arms up. "Up, Unca Why-Why, up!" He scoops her up and bounces her in his hold. "Dey talkin' bout Mommy and Daddy. Dey mewweed."

Like the troublemaking asshat that he is, Rhyatt pretends to gasp. "They are?!"

Ophelia walks over to him and lightly smacks the back of his head. "Knock it off, Rhy."

"Ooo, ouchie. Your mommy got me, Rhay-Rhay," he winces.

Bringing her small hand up, she pats the back of his head. "Der, der. Is okay, Unca Why-Why."

He grins at Ophelia. "Sorry, Ophie. Love you," kissing her cheek before running with Rhayvin. "Come on, Rhay-Rhay. Auntie Lore needs to kiss my boo-boos. Help me convince her?"

I can't hear her, but watch as she nods and high-fives him. I shake my head laughing and look at Rhys. "His horrible performance probably gave it away, but yes, he knows. He was there when the bad shit happened, so it seemed fitting he would be there for us to erase the moment. We really did want you there, but didn't want to outshine your day. We were just waiting to tell you until after. Sorry."

Ophelia hugs me tight with a sad smile. "I hope we didn't hurt your feelings or made you feel left out. I know you guys have a lot of time to make up for, and want to be there for big moments after missing so much... but..." She looks down, holding me tighter.

Rhys shrugs as if it's no big deal. "It's cool."

His nonchalant attitude hurts more than I'd like to admit. I obviously don't want to hurt him, but I really expected him to at least be a little torn up about it. Hell, I'd even take him being pissed. Nova's biting tone catches my attention. "So help me, ghoulie, if you don't use your words right now, you're banished from sex with your wife for the foreseeable future."

His face morphs to shock and horror. "No wife sex?! You can't take that from me!"

"Watch me! Use your words and tell your brother how you feel." She turns towards us and smiles. "I am so happy for you guys. I completely understand why you did it the way that you did. As long as the day was perfect for you two and you're happy, that's all that matters. Of course we would have loved to be there, but I get it. Really. Ophelia, let's go find the girls. You can show us the amazing photos I know you have saved on your phone."

Ophelia kisses my cheek and lets go, following Nova. I watch Ophelia go and slowly look at Rhys. I realize we're mirrored images, hands in pockets, shoulders slumped. I'm sure even our solemn faces match. We both scratch our heads and say, "Soooo," drifting off with a chuckle.

"We really didn't mean to hurt you, Rhys."

"I'm not hurt," he responds, shaking his head. "Not hurt. I don't think. Listen man, I'm not one for chick flick moments. I'm happy for you guys. Congrats. I'm not mad or hurt. I do wish I could've been there since I've missed so much of your lives, like Nova said. That's all. Sooo.. we good?"

I nod. "Yeah, man, we're good."

He blows out a breath twisting side-to-side. "Oh thank fuck. Let's go grab a fucking beer or something with the guys. That was painful."

We walk over to the guys and grab a beer. Dorian looks at us and smiles bright, his eyes shining. I'm glad he got his smile back. He earned it. "GUYS! GUYS! I have something for you!"

He leans over the back of one of the log chairs and turns with flower crowns in his hands, slightly swaying. *Ohhhh. Hello, drunk Dori.* I look at the crowns and up at him with a furrowed brow. "For?"

His smile turns mischievous.

"There's no way this man is not a Slater brother with a look like that," I say to Rhys and Rhyatt.

Rhys takes a sip of his beer and with a proud smirk says, "I taught him everything I know."

Dorian just laughs and shakes his head, handing us the flower crowns. "No complaints! Required attire. All parties shall be crowned." I open my mouth to refuse and he stumbles up to me, with a finger in my face brushing against my nose. "Hey! I said no complaints Mr. Cum- eww, no. Curm. Cum-on-in. Gross. CURMUDGEON! MR. CURMUDGEON!"

His finger continues to swipe at my nose as if his finger is a sword. I swat him away. "Fine, just keep swimming on over that way, Dori. Better yet. Where's Theia?"

His head whips around and he trips as he goes in search of her. "SUNSHINE?!"

Rhyatt steps between us and wraps his arms around us. "So, which brother do you think will get hitched next?"

Unable to stop it, Rhys and I both start laughing. He looks between us over and over. "What's so funny? I'm serious."

We both pat his stomach. "It'll be Dori and Theia, dude. You only have your eye on Lore, and she can't stand you. Good luck, brother."

He scoffs. "JERKS!"

Rhys and I look at each other and then him. "BITCH!"

"TWO AGAINST ONE IS NOT FAIR!" He pulls his arms off of us and crosses them, pouting. We walk over to the girls and Rhys grabs Nova, spinning her around. I stay back and watch Rhyatt approach Lore.

"Can I have this dance, little succubus?"

She bites back a smile before turning to glare at him. "Not in this life or any other, heathen." She walks away and he follows like a kicked dog needing their owner's approval.

I walk up behind Ophelia and wrap my arms around her, whispering, "Hi, little raven."

She melts against me. "Hi, Bones."

"Birds sing after a storm; why shouldn't people feel as free to delight in whatever sunlight remains to them?" -Rose Kennedy

CHAPTER TWELVE

THE WAY THAT YOU WERE

Ophelia

Change carries a multitude of possibilities. It can leave you with beautiful memories or tarnished ones. Minor or life altering. One significant change is the Vega Altair warehouse. I thought I'd seen it all while exploring this place, but I was wrong. After we were rescued, Viking immediately got to work with add-ons.

Everyone agreed we needed a place for everyone to crash on long nights. After a few too many incidents with noisy couples, Viking installed soundproofing materials on everyone's walls. Talk about awkward. We also needed a place where the twins, Rhayvin and I could all stay so we weren't crashing at everyone's places. Being somewhere new was a big enough change for Rhayvin and we knew long term we couldn't keep bouncing her around. Our little dorm was the first to be completed so we could move in and get her settled. It's obviously not a permanent solution, but it's good for now.

I never have to worry about safety again being surrounded by The Horde. The beautiful change? Our family has grown significantly. There's been love, laughter and wedding bells. But even in the midst of light, there will always be a creeping darkness. Now that we're out of there, I realize we're not as free as I thought we were. At least, I'm not.

For a moment I was caught up in believing we were finally free, but I was wrong. The things I went through growing up and the years with Aldo tarnished me. I've learned a lot about trauma talking with Nova and Theia. They've told me I can always talk to them, or they can help me find an online professional to speak with. Theia knows enough based on the injuries she saw or helped me clean up when visiting, but I've never told the girls everything. I'm not ready. I also need to talk to Rhydian about it all like I promised tonight.

How do you tell the love of your life that you're broken and dirty? That every moment alone you thought of killing yourself? Every moment of torture and rape you wished you were dead, but you fought to stay so your child wasn't left behind and in danger.

To make matters worse, I know my Bones. He'll blame himself for every awful thing that happened. I close my eyes and grip the bathroom counter, my knuckles turning white. The girls told me deep breaths are helpful in these moments. After a few deep breaths, I focus on the tap, tap, tap on the counter. I look down and smile at the wedding ring on my finger.

I hated not wearing it every time we left our dorm, but I would've been devastated if our secret wedding overshadowed Nova's big day. Rhyatt's smartass may have pretended not to know about the day, but he was a huge part of it. Lore went online and filled out what she needed in order to be ordained and marry us. Rhayvin was our beautiful flower girl and Rhyatt walked me down the provisional aisle, which was basically the walkway from the bathroom to our makeshift living room. I cradle my hand to my chest, spinning the ring. You can do this, Ophelia. You *have* to do this.

I open the bathroom door and find Rhydian sitting on the floor in front of the door. The love and adoration in his eyes is so palpable when he looks up at me. To most, he's grumpy, withdrawn and calculating but all I see is a fierce protector who loves hard. "You ready, little raven?"

I take a deep breath, wisps of hair fluttering around my face as I exhale. "No, but I made a promise and I intend to keep it."

He stands and cradles my face in his hands, thumbs caressing my cheeks. "You're so strong. Do you know that?" I look down and shrug. "Eyes, pretty girl." I meet his eyes with a blush, his sweet words still making my heart race and my pussy throb. It's such a foreign sensation to feel again, and honestly, it's terrifying.

"Where did you just go, little raven? Something's wrong."

With a sad smile, I kiss his cheek. "I'll explain afterwards, it'll make more sense that way."

He nods and places his hand on the small of my back. "Couch or bed?"

I take a moment to think about it. "Bed. The living room is too close to Rhayvin's room, and if I cry, I don't want her to hear me."

He kisses my temple and guides me to our bed. He sits and leans against the headboard, spreading his legs and patting the space between. I crawl on the bed and sit between his legs, melting into his embrace. I recant every horrific moment, from the first night until the last. He tenses and growls throughout it all.

I can hear how monotone my voice is, as if I'm reciting a grocery list rather than flaying myself wide open and spilling every dirty secret. Will he see me differently now? Will he ever want to touch me again?

Sex has already been difficult enough these last six months and I feel awful about it. Sometimes I feel as if there's black handprints on every inch of my body. Does he see them now? Does he see how tainted I've become? How disgusting? The vibrations of his chest pull me from focusing on my racing heart and thoughts. I realize he's singing to me like he used to. I look at him and smile as I listen to the words of *I'll Be Your Mirror by The Velvet Underground*. I'm lost staring at the way his lips move, as if each word falling past them is a healing balm for my soul. His lips stop moving and he gently tips my chin with a finger. "There she is."

His eyes fall to my torso. "That's why you hide your stomach from me. All this time, I thought you were hiding your badges of honor from carrying our baby bird." Instinctively, my hands go to my stomach in a panic, as if they can shield the scars from him. They may have been a beautiful reminder I held on to while we were apart, but I never wanted him to see them. To witness the look of disgust at my marred abdomen. "Will you let me see?"

No, he can't see this. I didn't realize I had been pulling away until I feel his hands gripping my hips. His hold is tight, but his thumbs gently caress the skin beneath my shirt. I squeeze my eyes shut and grab the hem of my shirt, slowly lifting it up and off. I clench my fists tightly at my sides, my breath coming out in harsh bursts.

"Lay back for me."

I do as he says, gripping the cozy comforter beneath me. I focus on the feel of it between my fingers as he lightly traces the scars. I shiver as his lips kiss each one and he counts aloud. The pain of the memory is immediate, but pleasure collides with each kiss. As if it will wash it away. Will this be what cleanses my skin? Will love be enough to snuff out my demons? He pulls away and my eyes shoot open from the loss. Our eyes collide and fear of what I'll find in his eyes vanishes. All I find is love and… desire.

"Do you trust me, little raven?"

"With my life," falls from my lips without pause. He nods and turns away, opening the drawer of our night stand. He pulls out a red Sharpie and pulls the cap off with his teeth, spitting it onto the bed. He straddles my hips and brings it down to my stomach. I giggle when the tip of the marker tickles me.

He quickly pulls back, tsking. "I can't play connect the dots with you giggling like that, ya know?"

"It tickles, Bones."

"Be a good girl and stay still for me."

My breath hitches when he calls me a good girl. Why is that so hot? My eyes widen in horror when he responds to what I thought was a silent question. "Cuz you love it when I praise you, pretty girl."

I clench my thighs, hoping it will stifle the ache between them. He smirks when he feels the movement and begins connecting the scars, revealing the Gemini constellation. He puts the cap on the marker and tosses it off the bed, murmuring, "Beautiful."

He continues tracing the lines with his fingertips while lost in thought. He lifts his head and asks, "Would you do something for me?"

I prop myself up on my elbows and nod. "Anything."

Without another word, he gets off the bed and opens our closet. I watch as he pulls one of his kill bags down from the top shelf and kneels down on the floor opening it. He pulls out two bundles of thin, nylon rope and one of his big hunting knives.

"Rhydian?"

As if he didn't hear me, he walks over to the bed and starts tying one end of the rope to the bed. He lifts it until it's slightly above the bed and cuts it in one swift motion. The pieces fall into place and I scramble off the bed. The movement catches his attention and he looks up. My body trembles in fear, the memory playing on a loop in my mind. "Why are you doing this, Rhydian?"

He puts the knife on the bed and drops the rope. "It's not what you think, I swear. I just have an idea that I'm hoping might help you heal. I'll set it all up and if you still don't want to, just say the word and I'll leave it alone. Okay?"

My mouth has gone dry and I suck my lip into my mouth, biting it. He slowly walks towards me and caresses my bottom lip, pulling it free. "Don't hurt yourself, pretty girl." He gently kisses me and walks back to the bed, adding the next rope. He does the same with the headboard but cuts those ropes shorter.

My mouth is no longer dry as he reaches behind and pulls his shirt off. I can't find a place I want to look at more. His bulging muscles, his washboard abs or the beautiful tattoos that now cover his skin. I hear his chuckle and flip him off while I continue to stare. "Mind your business."

His chuckle grows husky. "Mind my business? Isn't my body my business?"

I'm already shaking my head before he finishes his sentence. "Not with me. With me, that work of art is mine."

He runs his hand down his chest and proudly says, "Yes, it is." He slowly drops his joggers, stepping out of them and kicking them away. His boxer briefs are all that's left and I can't decide which I prefer more. The sight of him with them on and his cock bulging through the material, or without them. He crawls on the bed and I'm captivated by the way his muscles contract and lengthen with every move. He lays on his back and puts his arms above his head.

"Tie me up, Ophelia."

My eyes widen and I look down at myself when his words have my pussy soaked. "Don't be embarrassed by what your body does. It knows what it wants. Let it guide you."

I walk to the end of the bed and grab the rope, bringing it to his ankle. There's just enough length to wrap around his ankle and knot it. There's a tremble in my fingers—half anticipation, half hesitation. His gaze burns into me, steady and unyielding.

"Tighter, Ophelia. Make it hurt."

My head shoots up. "Wh-what? I don't want to hurt you."

"That's exactly what you're going to do. The difference is, there's love in this. Pain can bring pleasure if done correctly. Everything will be okay."

"How do you know?"

"Because, as difficult as this will be for you, it will be healing. You're safe, Ophelia. You can do this."

I take a deep breath and finish tying his other ankle and wrists. He's tied to the bed the exact same way I was when Aldo scarred me. "Climb up here, Ophelia."

I drop my knee to the bed and crawl over his body, dropping onto his thighs. My hands shake in my lap. "Now what?"

"I know you have those scars memorized. Pick up the knife and give me the honor of carrying them like you do."

"Rhydian, please. Don't make me hurt you. I can't."

"Yes you can. You can cut as little or as much as you want. Let me take the pain for you." My hand trembles as I tentatively reach out for the knife beside him. I pick it up by the handle and it's heavier than I expected, cold to the touch. My fingers slide over the grooves and I look at his torso. Before my eyes, my scars appear on his stomach as a guide and I bring the tip of the knife down and push slowly. The first bead of blood pools around the tip of the knife and I'm not sure if I hiss or he does. I watch the blood drip down his side and then continue making more. I count each puncture in my head until I reach eighteen.

During the last one, I realize I'm panting and grinding against him as he grunts and grits his teeth, his cock rock hard. I toss the knife to the side and look up at him. His pupils are blown and he's breathing through his nose, a small growl spills from his lips. "You did so well. You know what's next. Look at you. Even your body knows."

I'm painfully aware of my nipples brushing against my bra with every breath, and how my panties cling to my pussy. "Help? I don't know how to start. What am I allowed to do, Bones?"

"This is your moment. Do you want to put those delicate fingers of yours inside your tight pussy? Grind your soaked lips against my throbbing cock? Or sink down on it and take flight? Those wings of yours aren't clipped anymore, little raven."

I unclasp my bra at the front, my breasts fall free and I slide the straps down. Rhydian groans at the sight and it's the push I need to continue. After all this, he still wants me. Has it always just been in my head how I see myself? If he could see it, too, he wouldn't still want me, right? I sit up and pull my panties down, lifting each leg to remove them. He's right, my body does know what it wants, and it knows that my fingers aren't enough.

I slide his underwear down and his hard cock slaps against his stomach, "Fuck," he groans. I bring my pussy down over his cock and we both moan. I watch as his hard cock slides perfectly between my lips. I grip his cock, sliding against it, riding faster. My mouth falls open when the tip hits my clit rhythmically. I can feel it throbbing the more I grind against him. Unable to stop, I lift up and bring his cock to my entrance with a barely there touch. Our heavy breaths fill the room as I slowly sink down and his cock stretches me.

"Fuck, you're so big, Bones."

His eyes are squeezed shut and the veins in his arms and neck are protruding. "Jesus Christ, Ophelia, that goddamn pussy is gripping me perfectly. I might die trying to restrain myself here."

I clench around him and he moans loud. "Sure, just bring me closer to the grave there, pretty girl. No big deal, I'm fine."

I can't help but giggle and bounce faster. My hands slide around the slick blood on his stomach, unable to get a good hold. My heart races and my stomach swoops. I can feel my thighs trembling with every bounce. "I'm so close, Bones."

"Oh thank fuck. Me too," he exhales loudly. He turns his head into the pillow and bites it, grunting and growling. With one hand, I squeeze my breast, rubbing my clit in quick circles with the other one. "Oh, fuck." I pinch my nipple, while the hand on my clit strums harder. My hips slide up, slam back down and I shatter.

Our thighs are soaked and the room spins as I drop across his chest, trembling and spent. The crash has my emotions haywire and I laugh, the ecstasy from my release flowing through me. I replay the moment in my head and I feel like a weight has been lifted. The euphoria morphs into relief and my laughs turn into tears.

"There it is. That's my girl. Let it out, baby."

Tears fall as I sit up and grab the knife, cutting his hands free from the rope. He immediately wraps his arms around me, pulling me closer. I nuzzle his neck as he continues rubbing my back and telling me how well I did and how much he loves me. I think he was right. Even in the midst of pain, you can find pleasure. I hear him whisper, "Caught you, pretty girl," as I drift off to sleep.

"You fit inside my heart like a bird. I just don't know if my heart is a cage or a nest for you."

-Unknown

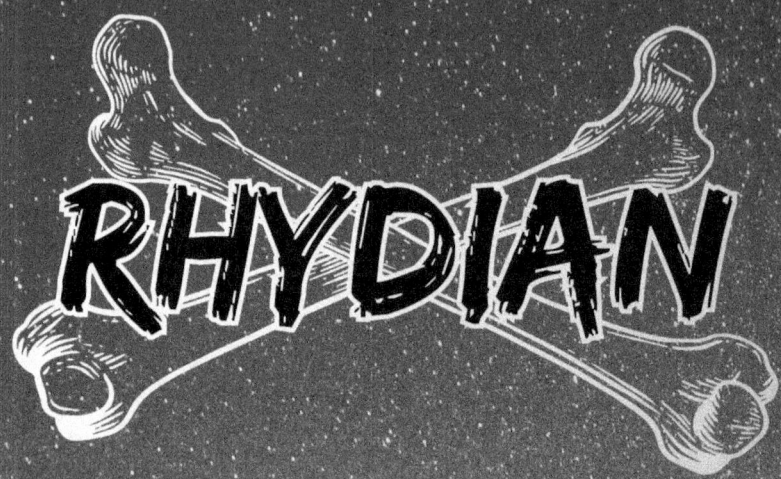

RHYDIAN

CHAPTER THIRTEEN

RAIN

JULY 2024

Rhydian

Ophelia and I are sitting on the couch, watching Rhayvin play with her toys on the floor. I kiss the top of Ophelia's head. "Go ahead and take your shower. I'll get her bedtime routine started."

"Are you sure?" She whispers, looking up at me.

I smile down at her. "We'll be fine. Join us for story time when you're done." She kisses my cheek. "Thank you."

My heart warms at the small gesture of affection. I'll never get enough of my little raven. A wave of sadness comes over me as I watch Rhayvin play a little longer. I hate that I missed so much of her life. So many firsts that I didn't get to be a part of and it kills me. I knew I shouldn't have left that night. Ophelia never would have endured what she did, and we could have been a family from the beginning. I could've watched Rhayvin grow in her belly, and get her whatever she needed. I could've held her hand and kissed her as she gave birth.

She gave up so much to keep our little girl safe. My woman is a goddamn warrior. She sacrificed herself over and over just to keep Rhayvin safe. The sound of crashing brings my attention back to Rhavyin as she's making her toy cars crash into her blocks and I chuckle. I stand up and kneel down next to her. "Alright, little Rhay. Let's get this all cleaned up and get ready for bed."

Her hair almost smacks me as she whips around and scowls. "No."

Shit.

Okay. This is new for me. *Stern, but not mean.* I take a deep breath. "Rhayvin. It's time to clean up."

She looks at her toys and then back at me, smirking as she smacks her blocks across the floor. Oh, lovely. My daughter has a mix of Lennon-Slater attitude. "You're just making a bigger mess for yourself. The sooner you get it done, the sooner we can read a book."

She stands up, balling her fists and placing them on her hips. "Mama will do it," she says with a snarky tone.

"Rhayvin Grace, that's enough. It is not Mama's job to clean up after you. Enough with the attitude. Clean up. Now."

"You mean Daddy," she replies, her eyes watery and her little lip trembling. *Don't give in, don't give in.*

"Rhayvin. I love you very much, and I'm not trying to be mean but you're not being very nice. You're yelling at Daddy and expecting Mama to clean up after you. That's not okay. So please, clean up your toys."

She sniffles and starts cleaning up her toys, huffing and puffing the whole time. "Thank you, little Rhay."

She crosses her arms and stomps away. I drop to my ass and put my head in my hands. Fuck. I smell Ophelia's familiar shampoo as she wraps her arms around my neck, hugging me.

"Our daughter hates me now."

She pats my chest and kisses my temple. "Welcome to parenthood; where you get to be the superhero and the villain in their story. Just remember, even when she's upset, she still loves you very much."

I grab her hand from my chest and kiss it. "Promise?"

"I promise. Now come on, Bones. Let's go tuck our feisty bird in."

With a heavy sigh, I stand. "You think she'll claw my eyes out with them talons?"

Ophelia laughs and slaps my ass, making me jump. "So dramatic. Move that ass."

I poke my head in her room, seeing that she's laying down with her arms crossed and a pout. She slides a book across her bed towards me without taking her eyes off the ceiling. I look at Ophelia mouthing, "That's *your* daughter."

"If I took a picture right now, you'd see the matching pout you both are sporting," she retorts, rolling her eyes.

I cross my arms. "I do not pout."

As I look towards Rhayvin, I hear the sound of a camera shutter. I whip my head in her direction and see that she's holding her phone up, smiling. I narrow my eyes as she turns the phone around to show me. I attempt to school my features when I see myself standing there, with Rhayvin in the background looking exactly the same. Part of me wants to grumble that it's just a coincidence, but the warmth filling my chest at the sight keeps my mouth shut.

The next day, everyone splits up. The girls are all in the conference room doing recon. Lore gave Rhayvin a tablet so she could play around and pretend she's working with them. All the men are hanging out in the training room bullshitting, sparring or hitting a bag.

I focus on every strike against the punching bag. I spent most of the night tossing and turning, wondering if I've been doing a good enough job with my family. The time that I was Ophelia's boyfriend was really just a blip before I lost her, spent an eternity without her, and now I'm having to figure out how to be a husband and a father. I love my family more than anything, but I don't have a clue what the fuck I'm doing. Am I fucking it all up? Am I everything my wife needs me to be? And my daughter... has the time come where she realizes I'm a monster? That it's my fault her and Ophelia suffered for so long? How do you make up for so much lost time?

Sweat pours from my face and arms with every punch thrown into the bag. I give it my all, my thoughts swirling. I can feel everything building and let out a guttural roar. A touch to my shoulder has me spinning and preparing for a fight, growling like a fucking animal as my chest heaves. Rhys stands before me in a stance, prepared to protect himself.

"Easy, tiger. Hit the showers and then we're gonna have a talk."

Panting for air, I question, "What?" I never grew up with him, but the look he gives brooks no arguments. It encompasses the very meaning of an older brother. It holds a weight I can't explain, like a tether pulling me back to a childhood I never had with him. I nod, tear the velcro straps off my gloves and toss them to the mats. As I'm walking out, I hear Rhys shout for Rhyatt.

Finishing up my shower as fast as possible, I dry off and change into my gray joggers and black t-shirt. I spray myself with my *Azzaro The Most Wanted* cologne and quickly put my socks and boots on. I open the door and find Rhys standing there, getting ready to knock.

"You dirty dog. You didn't have to get yourself all pretty and smelling good for me, baby brother," he smirks.

I roll my eyes and push past him. "Not for you. I want to see my girls before we go."

He roughly smacks my back and I jolt forward with a grunt. "Good call. I need to see my wife."

I snort. "Do you even call her Nova or little star anymore?"

His eyes shine with his smile. "Of course I do. But I *really* love calling her wife now." We walk side-by-side to the conference room, our shoulders occasionally brushing as we go.

Rhys walks in before me and bellows, "WIFE!"

I walk in behind him looking for my girls. I catch the look on Nova's face as she rolls her eyes, smiling and walking over to Rhys. I spot my girls, and stand there watching them. Ophelia is focused on the laptop in front of her while Rhayvin is holding a tablet, sitting beside Lore.

Rhayvin sees me first and practically throws the tablet at Lore. She stands up and runs over. "DADDY!"

I crouch down and catch her mid-jump, standing and spinning her around. "Hello, little Rhay."

She snuggles against me and I hold her a little tighter, whispering, "Does this mean you're not mad at Daddy anymore?"

"Fo now."

I chuckle at her response. "Fair enough. You know Daddy loves you, right?"

She nods against my shoulder, whispering, "I wuv you mo."

Ophelia looks up with a sad smile and I tilt my head in question. Her eyes flick to Rhayvin and I nod. I walk over to Lore and kneel down. "Hey, Lore."

Looking up, she looks at Rhayvin and then me. "What's up, Rhydian?"

"Do you think you could take little Rhay on an adventure?"

I flick my eyes to Ophelia and back to Lore, who meets my eyes with a knowing smile. "Of course. Let's go, Thunderbird."

Rhayvin giggles and pulls away to be put down. "You silly, Auntie Lo." Placing her small hand in Lore's, they leave the conference room.

I walk behind Ophelia and wrap my arms around her, placing my chin on her head. "What's wrong, little raven?"

She melts against me and sighs, pointing to the laptop. I look at the screen and notice a slideshow of different men. I recognize most of them as Cifarelli's men.

"Why are you looking at this?" I ask, gritting my teeth when I see Aldo and Alonzo.

I hate the sad tone in her voice when she says, "Trying to be helpful."

"Helpful how? Cuz it sure as shit ain't helpful to you."

I hold her closer as she grips my arms for comfort. "Seeing if any of them are," she pauses as her breath catches, "the other men that hurt me."

I clench my jaw in anger and slam the laptop shut with a firm voice. "No."

I barely feel her rubbing my arms to soothe me while my chest heaves. "Bones?"

The anger consumes me and I pull away to pace. *Don't yell, don't yell. You're not mad at her. You'll only upset her more.* Rhys grips my shoulder tight to the point of pain and I glare up at him.

He nods towards the door. "Come on, baby brother." He leans forward to whisper, "Kiss your wife so she knows you're not upset with her and then we're leaving."

I scoff, lowering my voice. "Of course I'm not mad at her."

"Trust me. She needs you to tell her. Go."

I take another deep breath and turn towards her. My heart breaks as she stands there with her sleeves over her hands, holding them to her mouth. Her hood is up, but I can still see the tears welling up. I drop my head, ashamed of myself and walk over to hug her. I kiss the top of her head and murmur, "I am not mad at you, pretty girl. I love you."

I feel her nod, and I lean down to look in her eyes. "I have to go talk to Rhys. I love you. I promise. I'm not mad at you. I'm sorry for how I reacted. Can we talk about this tonight?"

I hate how small her voice is when she says, "Okay, Bones. I'm sorry."

I kiss her forehead. "You have nothing to be sorry about. If this becomes too much, you stop helping them with this. Please," I plead.

I follow Rhys as he leads the way. He stops at the armory first and throws a bag at me. I catch it against my chest and look up at him. "Pick your poison. Target practice, baby brother."

Without a word, I walk over to the wall of guns displayed and pick the *Colt M1911A1*. "Well, well, well. Looks like we love the same gun."

I turn to look at him sporting a huge grin. He points at me and his smile morphs to something more lethal. "Don't fuck up my gun, brother."

I snort, ignoring him and pull out boxes of ammunition from the drawers and putting them in the bag.

"Why don't you check out your knives?"

The tone of his voice makes me do a double take at him. "The fuck you do to my knives, Rhys?"

"Relax, Rambo. Go take a look."

I stomp over to the wall. "What the fuck did you-" I forget how to speak when I zero in on my red *Perfect Point* throwing knives. In the middle of the handle, a raven is stamped on each one. I pull one down and run my finger along the stamp in awe. "You guys did this for me?"

"Nothing motivates a man more than keeping their loved ones close. A reminder of who you have waiting for you to come home."

I bite my tongue until I taste blood. I'm not about to fucking cry right now. Who knew the little orphan would grow up to not only get presents for the first time in his life, but to have a family? A real fucking family. I clear my throat and put the knives in the bag. "Let's go."

We walk to the outdoor shooting range and I place the bag down on the table of my booth. "Listen. Shoot a full clip, and then we're talking. You can use your knives after."

I nod, pulling the gun from the bag. I grab the slide and pull it back just enough to find the chamber empty. I push the clip in until it clicks and pull back the slide. I hear the tell-tale sign of a round being chambered, I aim at the target. I pop off round after round, the recoil barely registering. I empty the clip, check the chamber and drop the clip in my hand. I put it all down and wait for the sound of Rhys' ceasefire. Once he's finished, I walk to his side and watch him pull two beers out of a cooler. He uses the table to pop off the caps and hands one to me. With his beer tilted, he points to one of the picnic tables.

We walk over and I sit on top of the table, propping my boots on the bench below. "I can tell you're not ready for this talk, but it needs to happen. You have until I'm done telling you some news to get your shit together and talk. Deal?"

I turn and look at him. "News?"

He nods. "Lore found information on some murders that are taking place in Damascus. A bunch of murders they originally thought were suicides. Ended in a fucking massacre. Rhyatt is gonna go see if it's just a violent outburst from someone having an episode, or if something shady is happening."

I rub the ache in my chest at the thought of him being there alone. "Does he have to go alone?"

"You and I both know that little shit can take care of himself.

Plus, he's mainly supposed to be doing recon on that shit. No reason for him to provoke anyone."

We both look at each other and chuckle. "Good luck with that," I say.

I take a sip of my beer, bracing myself as he asks, "So how are you handling being a dad now? How's Rhayvin doing with it?"

I narrow my eyes. "Did Ophelia say something?"

"No. But I'm guessing there's a story there. What happened?" he chuckles.

I sigh, taking a long pull from the beer. "Man, I don't know what the fuck I'm doing. I'm just fucking winging it and hoping I don't fuck up any worse. I yelled at her last night. I feel like shit, but she's a little spitfire with both mine and Ophelia's attitudes morphed into one. She wasn't listening and got all sassy."

"Listen, I know far less than you do, but I bet you're not fucking up half as bad as you think you are, if at all. You're a better father than ours ever was, that's got to count for something."

I scoff. "It's not hard to be a better father than that piece of shit."

"True, but you have to remember... You never had any type of father figure in your life. And I'm sorry for that. I wish more than anything that things could have worked out differently. Maybe if I found out about you guys sooner. I don't know, man. But for someone who grew up in the environment you did, I think you're doing a damn good job. I'm proud of you for stepping up, no matter how challenging it is."

I look down, running my fingers through my hair. I can't help but feel ten feet tall having my big brother say he's proud of me. They're words I always hoped to hear from him when we finally met. My thoughts go back to Ophelia and the struggles she's been having. I know that Rhys has been there for Nova through all her trauma, maybe he'll have the answers I need.

"Rhys?"

"Yeah?"

I scratch the back of my neck and shyly look at him. "Umm. I need your help man." He sits up straight at my words, the beast in him ready to come out. "Not like that, chill. I just... I know Nova has trauma, and you've had to be there for her through it on the bad days."

I pause and he steps in. "Yeah. Some days are harder than others. What do you need help with?"

"What if I'm fucking this all up too? I don't know how to be there for her. I mean, I try my hardest, obviously, but I don't want to make things worse. Like today when I yelled."

"Listen, Rhyd. There's no handbook on this shit. It's all trial and error. At the end of the day, all that matters is you try. Be there for her. Communicate. Hell, like The Beatles said, all you need is love."

"And if I fuck up?"

"Inevitable, baby brother. We all fuck up. All that matters is you keep trying. Apologize when necessary. Fuck, apologize if you're unsure."

"Thanks."

He slaps my shoulder and stands holding his arms wide open. "Bring it in, baby brother."

I shake my head. "No. Absolutely not." I jump from the table as Rhys starts moving towards me.

"Come on, get back here, you little shit."

"Absolutely not!" I walk faster, but one moment I'm walking and the next, I'm down on the ground. "Oomph! What the fuck?!"

"Give me my hug!"

I grab his arms and roll so he's underneath me. The sky opens up as rain pours down, drenching us. "No!" We roll back and forth as he tries to get the upper hand. My brother is strong as fuck, but I'm stronger. I grip his rain-slicked arms the best I can, get to my knees and stand with him on my back.

"Whoa! Whoa! PUT ME DOWN, ROID DROID!"

I laugh as he panics. "This is hard work, asshole, not roids."

"Well, whatever it is, put me down. I am your big brother and you will listen to me this instant!"

We both start laughing at what he said and I let go. "I'm so telling your wife. Like *Kirishima* says in *My Hero Academia*, not very manly, *Bakubro*."

When you love a girl who's battled trauma, you're really saying, "Love, let me help you heal because I believe you can."
-Kendra Syrdal

CHAPTER FOURTEEN
PANIC ROOM

August 2024

Ophelia

Goosebumps cover my naked body, the cold concrete biting into my knees as I kneel for the man in the ski mask. His muddy brown eyes stare down at me, his mouth curled in a wolfish smile. The sharp points on his incisors match perfectly with the monster that he is. My face burns from shedding useless tears. It's not like they'll pool beneath me and drift me away from this nightmare. I cradle my hands over my bump, protecting my innocent baby. I hope they have no idea of the horrors that exist beyond my womb.

"Unbuckle my belt, whore."

I learned quickly that fighting back means harm to my unborn child, so I do as he says without a biting reply. With shaky hands, I reach up and slowly unbuckle his belt.

"Such a good whore. Undo my pants and pull them down." I pull the button free and unzip his pants. "Slower," he spits down.

I slow my movements down as I curl my fingers in the waistband of his pants and slowly pull them down. He slides the mask off his head, and I watch as his brown hair sticks up like a porcupine in various directions.

"I know I'm supposed to hide my face, but I just can't bear the thought of my view being obscured. You're going to pull my cock out and put it in that well used cocksleeve of yours. Keep your teeth to yourself or I'll break your fucking jaw."

A scream tears from my throat as I jolt upright, clutching the sheets to my chest. Sweat slicks my skin, and I gasp for air. "No!" I cry again, scrambling back as hands reach for me. Strong arms wrap around me and I try to fight, "No, no, please no. Not again!" I cry. I freeze and instantly melt at the sound of Rhydian's soothing voice in my ear, cutting through my terrified haze.

"Come back to me, little raven. I'm here. I have you. I love you. Shh, shh."

My heart races as I try to slow down my breathing, mumbling, "I'm sorry, I'm sorry, I'm sorry."

"Shh. Don't be sorry. It's okay. Shh. I love you so much, Ophelia."

I hear how broken my voice is when I tell him, "I love you, too, Rhydian." I turn in his hold and lay my thigh on his hips, hugging him tight. He immediately hugs me in return, rubbing his hands along my back. "I hope I didn't wake Rhayvin."

I whine at the loss of one of his arms as he moves it and then see the baby monitor brought between us. "She's fine. Still asleep."

"Oh, thank God. I don't want to scare her."

I close my eyes as he kisses my temple. "Do you want to talk about it?"

I grab the back of his shirt and twist it in my hold. "I know I need to."

I hear his intake of breath as he smells my hair and kisses my temple again. "Take your time."

"It was about the guy you're going after today. Rocco-" I begin, taking a deep breath.

"I knew having you look through those pictures was a bad idea."

His grip tightens around me and I can hear his teeth grinding. I nuzzle his neck, hoping to soothe both of us. "Please let me finish."

"Okay, okay. I'm sorry."

"I knew it would be difficult seeing their faces again. At least more than I already do. My nightmares are more like haunted memories. I remember in vivid detail everything I endured. This one was about Rocco and our first encounter. Well, the first time I saw him. I recognized his voice, but he took his mask off this time. Listen, I know this is really difficult for me to do, to revisit it all by going through these pictures, but I already see their faces all the time anyway. At least this way, I can be useful. I can tell you guys who certain ones are, and any information they slipped up with when I saw them. I have to do this. If I can stop this from happening to any other girl, then I'll do it. Whatever it takes."

"Okay. I understand. Fuck, I hate it, but I understand. You're so fucking strong. You know that, right?" I shrug in his hold and he pulls back, looking into my eyes. "You. Ophelia Aria Slater. Are the strongest woman I've ever known. You were strong when we were kids, and you're even stronger now. I am so sorry for everything you went through. I will spend the rest of my life regretting the night I left, and trying to make it up to you and Rhayvin. I wish I could go back and do things differently."

His eyes water and his lip trembles as he looks at me. "I am so fucking sorry, little raven," his voice cracks.

I caress his face and he leans into the touch. "You have nothing to be sorry for, Bones. I told you guys to leave. We were just kids trying to figure things out. We did what we thought was best at the time. We had no way of knowing what was to come. Please don't blame yourself. This isn't on you. This all falls back on Thatcher and the whole fucking Cifarelli crew. We are not responsible for any of their actions."

I place a gentle kiss on his lips and pull away, unable to deepen it. My mind is still flooded with memories of Rocco. I can't muddy the beautiful moments between us with the images running rampant in my head. He grabs the back of my head and gently pulls me forward to kiss my forehead. "I love you, Ophelia."

Unable to look at him, I whisper, "I love you, too, Rhydian."

Lore is hanging out with Rhayvin right now while we all sit in the conference room. She can't be here for this. Who would have thought that the girl who had no one would have so many people to call family? The word family - the idea of it seemed so foreign my whole life. The one thing I wanted most, and now it's here. People who give a shit about me and accept me with open arms. As happy as I am to finally have it, I'm more happy that they're here for Rhayvin. I never wanted her to grow up like me and not know what it meant to have people who love and care about you. People who choose to with no obligations. I melt against Rhydian's chest and rub my clammy hands on my thighs.

Various photos of Rocco fill the screens. I don't realize I've continued rubbing my thighs until he places his hands over mine, intertwining our fingers.

"Sorry."

"Don't be sorry. I'm right here. You're safe," he whispers and squeezes my hands. I nod and continue to stare at the screen. Everyone discusses the plan of action to pick him up.

Their voices all seem to fade to quiet murmurs. All I see is Rocco's face. I'm stuck in a staring contest with him and I feel as if he's smirking down at me again. *I'm not there, I'm not there, I'm not there. Rhayvin is safe.* I'm allowed to fight back now. I glare at him as if my stare alone will stop his blackened heart. Fuck you, fuck you- "FUCK YOU! FUCK YOU! FUCK YOU! I'LL FUCKING KILL YOU! I'LL CUT YOUR TINY FUCKING PECKER OFF, BITCH BOY!" I let out a piercing scream, my heartbeat thundering in my ears. Fuck, I'm flying. No. Not flying. I'm wrapped around Rhydian as he holds me in his arms, rocking me side to side.

"Come back to me. Come on, come on. Look at me, little bird."

I snuggle closer, weakly protesting, "I'm your raven."

He chuckles in my ear as he runs his fingers through my hair. "That's right. You're my raven. My strong, beautiful raven. You're okay."

"I didn't keep my thoughts inside, did I?" I sniffle.

"No, not this time. It's okay. You let it out whenever you need to."

"Did I scare anyone? Fuck." I snap my head up looking around, notice everyone sitting around the table with kind, knowing looks. "I didn't hurt anyone, right?"

Everyone shakes their head, and Nova speaks up while pouting down at the table. "I mean, my Monster was party fouled in an epic fashion. Rhys won't let me lick it off the table. So that hurts."

I can't help but laugh at the absurdity of her statement but I quickly sober. "I really am sorry. I-I didn't mean to."

She stands up and points at me with my shoe. Wait, my shoe. I look down and see my right foot without a shoe. Oops. "You owe me a new one, bitch, let's go. You too, Theia." She roughly kisses Rhys and pulls away while he tries to chase her lips, pouting when she continues to pull away. "You get the honor of cleaning that up, *husband*. Should've let me slurp that off the table."

"I have something you can slurp, *wife*," he grumbles, crossing his arms.

Theia stands, ruffling Dorian's hair and kissing him before walking over to the door to wait. "Put her down, Rhydian. Girl time. You boys go get the fuck who hurt her. Make it count," Nova demands.

He growls, causing me to shiver. "Of course I'll make it count." He kisses my temple, whispering, "I love you," before putting me down.

"I love you, too. I'm sorry."

He opens his mouth and I put my hand up to stop him. "Yes. I know. I have nothing to be sorry about. Please stop correcting it. I'm trying, okay." He nods, and I hobble over to Nova, grabbing my shoe from her and slide it on.

CHAPTER FOURTEEN

Rhydian

It was no surprise to find out that Rocco is a crematorium technician at the only funeral home in town. Rhyatt, Atlas and I never saw him at the Cifarelli estate. Lore dug around and discovered that he was never one of Cifarelli's men, but a friend of Aldo's. From the looks of it, the two of them enjoyed the same dark proclivities and struck a deal. Rocco was allowed to play with whoever Aldo bought or kidnapped, as long as Rocco would cremate them when they were deemed broken beyond repair. At least that's what some of their encrypted text messages said. Fucking scum.

We decided our best course of action was for Lore to intercept their next inventory order, and for Muggzy and I to pose as delivery drivers, with our delivery van bearing the logo of the supply company. We do a quick comms check and get started.

Jade and Sable hide out in the van in case they're needed for back up. Rader and Fish start discussing plans with the funeral director for one of their great-whatever the fuck's. Viking and Mrs. Valour bicker over caskets or urns for their pre-need planning funeral arrangements. Everyone is accounted for and Lore is keeping an eye on everything at the warehouse.

My knuckles turn white with how tight I'm holding the steering wheel. Ophelia's nightmare and her reaction in the conference room swims in my head. "I want him to suffer," falls from my lips when I'm no longer able to stay quiet. Someone starts speaking, not sure who, but I talk over them. "I want him to sweat it out. He'll know his days are numbered, but we're not finishing it tonight. I just want to capture him and make him wait. I need to be with Ophelia tonight."

Fuck, it's weird doing this without Rhyatt. I grab a clipboard with a fake work order, as Muggzy pockets a syringe. We jump out and walk to the giant metal back door. There's faded lettering in all caps that read **CAUTION: CREMATORIUM.**

I knock twice, the metal bellowing and vibrating from the hits. An intercom buzzes next to the door. "Who is it?"

"Delivery!"

The door buzzes and there's a loud click as the door pushes open a crack. I pull open the door and my jaw clenches when I see Rocco. To everyone else, he easily flies beneath the radar. With a pair of oversized glasses and disheveled hair, he looks like an innocent little nerd. The creep's eyes give him away, though.

I see you, fucker. I nod at him and wave the clipboard. "Listen, our boss has become a real stickler about inventory protocols. He wants us to double check you have proper space for the inventory you requested. He said if you ordered too much, we can just give you what will fit and refund the remaining cost."

His nostrils flare and sighs, backing away. "Yes, of course."

We walk in and pretend we're checking out the inventory when we hear V's arrival over comms. I bite back a smile, knowing the shit she's about to pull. I make random checks on the order form and move so I'm just behind Rocco. Muggzy starts distracting him, discussing various items that might be more cost efficient in the long run.

"Do you happen to have darker caskets? I'm thinking, black as night, dark as my so-," V clears her throat, "my super delicious coffee."

I hear one of the funeral directors talking with her, as she cuts him off. "How roomy are these? I know I'll be quite... stiff, and no longer rolling around like I once did, but I definitely don't want my poor body squeezed in there. Of course, I understand bodies are so easy to manipulate any which way to make them fit. But, I'd definitely prefer if I wasn't cracked like a glowstick to fit in here. Actually... you know what... please hold my cane."

I bite my lip to keep from laughing as the sound of laughter fills comms and frantic pleading from the funeral director. "Ma'am! Ma'am, please. You cannot get into the caskets. I'm going to have to ask you to leave the premises, this is quite uncouth."

"My ass will be in one of these anyway. Just think of it as a test drive. Calm down."

Alright. Showtime.

I stealthily sneak up behind Rocco and put him in a chokehold. He claws at my arm, his nails digging into my skin. His feet kick out wildly, searching for leverage. With a sharp kick, I sweep his legs from underneath him but keep my squeeze firm. I lift my elbow high enough so Muggzy can jab the needle in his neck. She quickly pushes the plunger down, and I wait for him to show signs of passing out.

"Every life has a measure of sorrow, and some-times this is what awakens us."
-Steven Tyler

CHAPTER FIFTEEN
BROKEN

Ophelia

Theia and I sit at the table while Nova grabs a *Monster* from the fridge. "Pick your fuel," she demands as she opens it wider. Theia walks over, grabs a strawberry lemonade and they both stare at me. I feel drained from my outburst and walk on shaky legs to the fridge to look. I've been free to make my own choices for a while now and I still struggle with it.

"Whatever the least favorite is here. I don't want to take someone else's drink."

"Yeahhh, we're not playing that game. If you're not sure what your favorite is, pick the one that sounds the best."

I look in the fridge and notice this must be just for the beverages. "Wow. A lot of choices. Umm... can I just have a *Coke*, please?"

Nova gets a big smile and makes herself laugh like a mad scientist. "Oh, this is too good. Yes, Ophelia, you can absolutely have one of those."

Theia holds back a laugh and I look between the two of them. "What's so funny?"

I take the drink from Nova as Theia says, "Those are Rhys'. Apparently she's on a mission to give him a hard time."

"Oh, I couldn't."

I attempt to hand it back, but Nova closes the fridge and opens the drink for me, tilting it towards me. "Yes, you can. You're free now. As long as you aren't hurting anyone, take what you want. Believe me. I know it's difficult, but you have to try, or you're always going to be stuck. Have you heard the saying, *'hurt people, hurt people?'*"

I look down and nod, realizing what she's saying. I know I need to work on that, I just don't know where to begin.

"Trauma affects everyone, including those who care for the one dealing with it. Rhydian loves you. Nothing will change that. Yeah, you're battling some demons. You're a fucking badass warrior, so stand up and fight, but remember you have people behind you. You're not alone."

My nose burns as I fight the tears and whisper, "Thank you. I want to try. I just," I pause with a heavy sigh, "I don't know where to start."

Theia steps forward and hugs me. "One day at a time. If you can't do that, one hour, one minute, one second. Whatever you need. Sometimes we know what sets us off, other times it hits us out of nowhere. It's not easy, but you're safe now. You can do it."

I walk to the table and take a seat, an idea forming in my head. "I think... is it okay if I talk to you guys about sex with Rhydian? Wait, that's weird, right?"

I cringe, waiting for their answer. I don't know how to do this. What are you allowed to talk about with friends... family? Nova breaks out in an obnoxious rendition of *Let's Talk About Sex by Salt-N-Pepa.* Theia and I laugh and join in. We wrap it up and laugh harder, wiping tears from our eyes and clutching our stomachs.

"Okay, okay. What did you want to talk about?" Theia says in between fits of giggles.

I pick at the sleeves of my hoodie, nervous and my face warm. "So. Rhydian has been incredibly patient with me. If I just can't have sex, he's fine with it. Other times, he does things that have to do with what happened to me, but makes me do them to him, giving me all the power. I… I think I want to try and ask him this time. This whole thing with," I swallow down the bile that threatens to come up, "Rocco. I want to try something with Rhydian that he made me do. But I don't know how to bring it up. I also really don't want to freak the fuck out, ya know?"

They both look at me with knowing and understanding looks, nodding. "The great thing about being with your soulmate is you can communicate anything with them. And even if they don't know exactly what the issue is, they can feel it," Nova says.

Theia looks at both of us. "Yeah. It's difficult to approach, especially when you're in the thick of it, but communication is key. And you said Rhydian already does things that empower you, so I really think it's something you can approach and he'll be fine with it, even if you need to take your time."

"I hate to ask. You guys all do so much for us, but is there any way someone can watch Rhayvin for the night? Just in case it becomes too much. I try really hard to keep this side of me from her. Even when we were still with Aldo, I never let her see me upset."

Theia's eyes light up as she elbows Nova. "We can do a sleepover! We'll invite Lore and she'll have a sleepover with all three of us."

Nova grimaces, "How slumber party is this thing gonna get?"

I sit forward, waving my hand. "Oh, nevermind. If it's too much to ask then that's okay. I'll figure something else out."

Nova rubs her face, taking a deep breath. "Listen, featherduster. I'm fucking around. I would love to have a sleepover with Rhayv. I just don't want to do the whole makeup and nails thing. I mean, I'll put makeup and polish on her... just not me. Blech." She shakes her shoulders and arms making a yuck face.

I put my hand up. "Don't even get me started. Nobody prepared me for the life of being a girl mom. I don't know if it's because I was a foster kid or what, but that shit never interested me. Do you know how many fucking *YouTube* tutorials I've had to watch? Hair, makeup, nails, outfits." I put a finger gun to my head and dramatically make the bang noise, pretending to be dead. "Seriously. I'll always let that girl find her own way, but damn. What happened to Chucks, band tees, and torn up jeans?"

They both shout, "YES!"

"This. So much this. Ugh," Nova adds on. I can't help but laugh along with them. This feels nice being able to laugh and talk to people.

Rhydian

I cross my arms and grit my teeth, watching Rhys as he pushes Rocco on a gurney to his playroom. I follow behind as he throws him into a chair, strapping him in with leather cuffs, duct tape and chains. Rhys turns on his music and picks up a pair of pliers, grinning. I stand beside him and smack his arm. He looks at me, still smiling big.

"He's mine to kill, Rhys."

He sobers at my words. "Of course, baby brother. I'm just gonna play with him a little bit."

Rocco's eyes slowly flutter open, looking around in a daze. His shit-brown eyes meet mine, widening, and I'm unable to stop myself. I punch him in the nose and watch as blood pours from his nose. His mouth opens as he howls in pain and I watch as the blood stains his teeth. Rhys pulls his phone from his pocket with a smile that's only meant for Nova.

"My wife says your wife has plans for you. Meet her in the kitchen."

Without a word, I turn to leave the playroom. I can't let the darkness consume me, Ophelia needs me. Rhys shouts behind me, "DON'T BE A PRICK, WRAP YOUR STICK!"

I flip him off as I walk out, shutting the door behind me. Getting closer to the kitchen, I can already smell dinner and smile. Mac and cheese. We lived off that shit. Thatcher always said if we made it to the dinner table in time we could eat, but none of us trusted him or Blake enough to risk eating there. We'd all go to the small store and shove as much as we could in our bags to get us through. Luckily, the only fast food drive-thru in town allowed us to get hot water for free to cook the noodles.

I walk through the door and just about trip and fall on my face. Hot fucking damn. A growl rumbles through me as I watch my little raven bend over and pull dinner out of the oven. She's wearing a tiny black jean skirt that has random tears in it, thigh high socks with *Converse* shoes and a torn up t-shirt. She yelps at my growl and puts the food down. Her curled hair bounces around her face as she smiles and holds her hand to her chest.

"You scared the shit out of me, Bones."

I stroll towards her with determined steps, wrapping my arms around her and pushing my face in her hair. "One of our favorite foods and you looking like this? I thought I already had my birthday, pretty girl."

"I have a surprise for you, but," she takes a deep breath, whispering, "I'm really nervous."

I hold her tighter, rubbing her back. "Why are you nervous?" I pull back to look at her but she refuses to meet my eye.

"I-I want to try something."

I gently lift her chin. "You know I'd do anything for you. What do you want to try?"

She twists the front of my shirt and takes a deep breath. "Remember how you like to give me my power back and rewrite moments from the people that hurt me?" Afraid any words will throw her off track, I nod.

"I want to try something that Rocco used to make me do. Maybe it will help with the nightmares that are happening now that you guys have him." Her eyes widen, her breathing picking up as she grips my shirt tighter. "He's here. Oh my god, I can't believe I forgot he would be here."

"Hey. You're safe. Rhys is with him now. Nobody can leave Rhys' playroom, I promise you. Let's sit down and eat our dinner. Take a breather."

"Okay. Okay. Yeah, good idea." She pulls away and starts dishing up the food. I take the plates and forks from her and bring them to the table. She takes a seat and I look at the distance between our chairs, not liking it.

I grab it and slide her next to me, making her squeal. I can't help but smile at her reaction and grumble, "Too far away." She kisses my cheek and I feel my face heat. I quickly shovel food in my face while she takes slow bites.

We finish up and I help her dry the dishes she washes.

"Ready?"

She grabs my hand, squeezing it. "Yeah. I think I am."

We get to our room and she wipes her hands on her shorts, shaking them out. "Okay, where do you want me? This is your show."

"You can just stand there. I'll be kneeling for you and... sucking your cock."

I choke on my spit at her words and my cock twitches. She needs control here, and I need to give it to her. I drag in a slow, deliberate breath, forcing myself to stay calm. She has to feel safe first. She has to know she's the one in charge. The memory surfaces— her hands tying me up, her hesitant smirk as she tested my limits. I cross the room and take my bag down. I kneel down and unzip it, searching through the contents. I take out one of my long chains, feeling the cool weight of metal against my fingers. I pick it up along with a carabiner and walk over to her. She stammers as she sees what I'm carrying. "Wh-what are you going to do with that?"

I wrap the chain around until it's pressed up against my neck, connect the carabiner to one part of the chain and then attach it to the long part which pools down at my feet. "This is yours to control me. If you get scared, I go too fast, or you just want to feel like you have all the power, you yank on the end of the chain and choke me with it." I watch as she shakily pulls her clothes off. My gaze is glued to her hardened nipples as she kneels before me and looks up. I groan at the sight and squeeze my eyes shut. I hold the length of the chain towards her. "Break free of your chains, little raven."

Ophelia

It isn't until I feel the pinch of the chain in my hand that I realize I'm gripping it tightly. I close my eyes, focusing on the feel of it and the carpet tickling my knees. My eyes open as I take a deep breath and briefly drop the chain. I curl my fingers in the waist-band of his joggers and underwear, making him hiss as the backs of my fingers caress his skin. I pull them down and my breath hitches as his cock slaps against his shirt, bobbing in the air. I squeeze my thighs together for relief, but realize it only makes the throbbing of my clit worsen.

I force myself to look away from his cock and into his darkened eyes. They soften while I look at him and he gives me a small, reassuring smile. "I need you to fuck my face."

He clenches his fists at his sides and I watch as his veins pulsate in his arms. His voice is strained as he says, "Take the chain."

I grab the chain and wrap it around my hand once. I tug on it to test how much I need to pull to make his plan work. Our eyes meet as I open my mouth wide, giving the chain a quick tug of encouragement. I hear the clink of the metal and his choked groan as he grips his cock, slowly stroking. He brushes the tip along the end of my tongue. I feel drool already dripping down my chin, waiting for him to thrust in.

I can hear his heavy breaths as he presses his cock against my tongue and slides it further in. I tug the chain again and with a strained chuckle, he says, "Alright, alright. Barely holding it together here." I can't help but giggle, the sound muffled by his cock filling my mouth and he groans. "Dammit, Ophelia. Killing me, here."

I tug the chain towards me and he lifts his head, gurgling as he starts thrusting in and out of my mouth. He moves faster, grunting with every thrust. The quicker he moves, the harder I feel the tip of his cock against my throat which makes me gag a little.

One moment, I'm fine and the next, images of Rocco flash in my mind. I squeeze my eyes shut and whimper. *No. No. No.* My breathing picks up and I tug on the chain harder. Rhydian immediately pulls out of my mouth, breathing heavily with his head tilted.

"Hey. Can you hear me? It's just you and me here. Nobody else. Tug that chain if you can hear me."

I weakly pull on the chain and he nods. "Good girl. Take a breath for me. In through the nose, out through the mouth."

I follow his directions and feel the clutches of anxiety letting go. "Okay. I'm okay. I'm ready."

"You're sure?" I nod and open my mouth again. I bring the chain towards me, guiding him towards my mouth again. I feel him slide against my tongue as he thrusts in and out slowly, gradually picking up his pace. I keep my eyes open this time, staring up at him. As long as I focus on him, I think I'll be okay. I watch every flicker in his eyes, twitch of his mouth and panted breath he grunts out. He's fucking beautiful. My eyes strain as I watch him, afraid he'll disappear if I blink. Realizing I'm with him gives me the strength I need to enjoy this. I feel myself getting wetter with every sound that falls past his lips. I moan around his cock and suck as hard as he goes.

"Fuck, shit, goddamn. Oh, your fucking mouth, little raven. You're such a good fucking girl. Just like that," he shouts, his thrusts becoming erratic.

Am I supposed to feel so empowered with a cock down my throat? Maybe not. But I fucking do. My grip on the chain loosens and I close my eyes. I listen to every sound he makes and the sloppy sounds of my spit covering his throbbing cock.

"You're taking it so well. Tug twice if I can make you choke on it, pretty girl. I'm so fucking close." I moan loudly in anticipation and tug twice. He groans and grunts from the force of my tugs and he thrusts back to my throat. I hum to force my gag reflex to calm the fuck down and push forward, inviting more of him into my throat. I swallow around him and he shouts, "FUCK!"

His cock is so far back I can't even taste his cum, but I can feel the warmth of it pumping into my throat. He slowly pulls out and I open my eyes, noticing a string of my spit connected from my mouth to his cock snap as he pulls further back. I feel the ache in my throat and jaw, welcoming it. My lips tingle and I brush my fingers against them. He reaches down, picking me up instead of pulling me to stand. I wrap my arms and legs around him, pushing my face into his neck, breathing his scent in. He rubs my back, rocking me back and forth. I fumble with the chain around his neck until I feel the carabiner and unhook it, the coolness of the metal against my hardened nipples making me shiver. I bring the chain down from around his neck, letting it pool between us.

"I'm proud of you for breaking free," Rhydian whispers. I pull back and caress his face with both hands, his eyes flutter shut and he hums in contentment.

"Thank you for being patient with me and helping me heal." His eyes open and I'm sucked into every green, brown and gold fleck.

"You need me in front of you to protect you when you can't stand the thought of standing up and fighting again? I'm there. You want me by your side to fight the problem head on? I'm fucking there. You want to stand up on your own and be the fucking badass that you are, I'll be right behind you to catch you if you fall. Whatever you need, I'm there. I love you, Ophelia. *Nothing* will change that. You ever feel like you're lost and alone, just know, I'll be the motherfucker taking everyone and every-thing down, demons included, to find you. Got it?" He holds up his pinky and I smile, latching my pinky around his.

"Got it."

"The chains that break you, are the chains that make you. The chains that make you, are the chains that break you. And the chains that make you, are the chains you break."
-Anthony Liccione

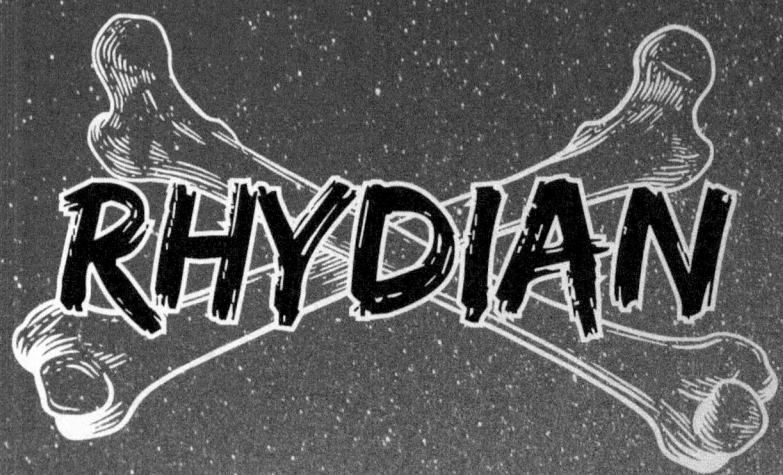

CHAPTER SIXTEEN

I CHOSE VIOLENCE

Rhydian

I spent the night holding Ophelia as she cried and told me every-thing that she endured with Rocco. I felt myself trembling with rage, but needed her to know she could talk about it without dealing with my anger. That changes now because now, I'm on my way to the playroom ready to make this motherfucker pay for what he did and said to her. Give him a... taste of his own medicine. I walk in and find Viking taking a turn. One of his handmade mini cutting boards, glistening with dripping blood, is in his raised hands. He slams it down on Rocco's fingers and I can hear the crunch of his bones echoing around the room. "I didn't realize this is what you made cutting boards for."

He looks over and smirks, blowing loose strands of hair from his face. "*Knotty Viking* boards are *very* versatile."

"Clearly. I'm going to grab a few things I'll need and then it's my turn. I have a treat for this little bitch boy."

Rocco pants and glares up at me. "Fuck. You."

"I hope you enjoy eating those words." I turn away and dismiss him as I go through the various items on the table. I have a plan in place, but something else just clicked. With a dark chuckle, I pull my phone out and text Rhyatt. I'm so glad he's back from that recon mission in Damascus. He's the only one I could send this crazy ass text to.

> Listen. I have kind of a strange favor to ask.

> You know me, I love strange. What's up?

> I'm in the playroom. Can you cum in a cup and bring it here?

> Cum again? Wow, brother, I didn't realize you were so fucking kinky.

> Shut the fuck up. Can you do it or not?

> I gotchu. I'll be... coming soon hehe.

I shake my head and pocket my phone. Idiot. I put aside pliers, one of my knives and the mini blowtorch. The door is opened and Rhyatt runs in with a cup in his hand. "I'M COMING! Well, I came. But you know what I mean."

"Quit running with that shit before you make a mess." I gag at the image of his cum splattering around the room. Fucking gross. "Viking, do we have anything to use to keep his mouth open?"

"I think that can be arranged." He smashes the cutting board against Rocco's mouth. "Oops." Rocco screams in pain and Viking takes advantage of his open mouth. He places the cutting board in a standing position between his bottom and top teeth.

"Too bad you can't use this as advertising, Viking."

"That's why I just tell people... once it's theirs, they can do whatever they want with the item," he laughs.

Rhyatt pushes the cup towards me and I cringe away. "No. You can serve it up yourself."

I look at Viking. "Be ready to yank that thing back so we can shut his mouth." Rocco's tongue lashes against the cutting board as he attempts to push the intrusion out of his mouth.

"It sucks when there's unwanted shit in your mouth, huh? Let's see how you like being forced to drink down someone's cum, you pathetic parasite."

He attempts to shout and shake his head as Rhyatt moves closer with the cup. He tilts the cup and cum drizzles down into Rocco's mouth. He screams and whines, trying to fight it. Viking quickly pulls the cutting board back and Rhyatt and I immediately grip Rocco's jaw, shoving it shut. He continues to struggle, and a snort causes cum and snot to shoot from his nose.

"Oh, fucking foul, dude." I angrily chop his index finger off and wipe the snot and cum from his nose and mouth with it, shoving the finger into his mouth. "Suck." Unable to stop, he sucks the mix from his chopped finger, gagging and crying. I pull the finger from his mouth and throw it behind me, looking at Viking.

"Hey, do you have one of your bigger cutting boards here?"

He shakes his head. "No, but I can go get one."

"Thanks, man. Make it the heaviest one you have." He nods and walks out while I grab a pair of scissors. I slice Rocco's pants and underwear away, leaving the shreds lying on either side of him.

"What the fuck do you think you're doing?"

I look at him and find myself smiling at the drops of cum on his lips. "I really can't take you seriously when you have baby batter for lip gloss."

"Fuck you!"

"Is that the only thing you know how to say? Sorry to disappoint, but I'm not on the menu tonight. It's all about self-love tonight."

He scrunches his face in confusion. "What?"

"I hear it's your favorite dish to serve. Figured it's time for you to try it yourself."

Viking walks back in with one of his large cutting boards. I take it from his hands and immediately feel the weight of it. "Damn. Is this the big boy special?"

"Big boys like to cook, too."

I press my lips together and shrug. "Fair." I turn towards Rocco and fidget with the cutting board. "Remember when you used to tell my wife you'd break her fucking jaw if she used her teeth on your millimeter peter?"

His eyes widen as I grip the cutting board tight and swing it at his jaw like a bat. I watch as his jaw is pushed too far to the right, and the distinct sound of a cork being popped from a champagne bottle announces the break. Blood drips down his chin. "We got all the information from him we needed, right?" I direct my question at Viking.

"Pussy has a set of pipes. Sang like a fucking tweety bird just to get us to stop," he smirks.

I snort. "Of course he did."

I drop the cutting board on the table and grab the blow torch, handing it to Rhyatt. His eyes light up and he smiles with a goofy laugh, lighting it. I pick up the pliers and knife, walking over to Rocco. I look down at his shriveled cock in disgust. He attempts to talk but everything comes out in a drooling slur. I clamp the pliers onto his cock and give it a tug. He squeals like a pig, morphing into guttural screams as I slice through it like butter. Blood spurts out like a fountain.

"Rhyatt, cauterize that shit."

"Gladly," he laughs. Rocco's screams grow louder as Rhyatt burns him. His screams fade away as he passes out and his head drops forward. A mix of drool and blood slowly drip off his chin. Rhyatt turns the torch off, inspecting his handiwork. "Dude! Look!" He quickly grabs a screwdriver and points towards the inside of the mangled mess. "It's like a face! Those top two squishy circles are like eyeballs and the little one has a baby mouth."

He pushes the tip of the screwdriver in the small opening he calls a mouth and wiggles it. "Hi, everybody, I'm mini Rocco," he says in a high-pitched voice.

I elbow Rhyatt away. "Back up. Stick to playing with your own cock, bitch."

He grabs his junk and jostles it. "Gladly, jerk."

I roll my eyes and jab my knife inside of the cock a few times, loosening everything up. I hear Viking and Rhyatt behind me.

"Ouch."

"Yikes."

I carefully dig the knife around inside, pulling free bits and pieces of the spongy insides. I drop it all in his lap, and then throw the knife on the table. I snatch the screwdriver from Rhyatt's hands and he pouts.

"Hey!"

I grip the metal of it and shove the handle inside. Making sure it's snug, I remove the pliers and drop them on the table. The beauty of pain is it can make a person pass out and shut the fuck up, but if reapplied it can also wake them the fuck up. I slap his broken jaw and watch it wiggle as his eyes shoot up and he screams in agony. I wave his severed cock in his face and Rhyatt steps up, giggling.

"Say hello to your little friend."

I snort and shake my head while Rocco gurgles loud nonsense. "Remember when you shoved this nasty thing in my wife's mouth? It's your turn. Eat up, cocksucker."

I shove his mangled cock into his mouth, thrusting it in and out. His top lip quivers and his tongue wiggles as if he's trying to close his mouth to get it away.

"That's it, suck your own cock. How's it taste?"

Vomit erupts from his mouth and down his chest. I grimace as a bit hits my boots. "I figured as much. Keep going, cockslut." I shove it further back into his throat and he gags, vomiting more. "Attached, this little thing could never do that, but look at it now. Choke on it."

I shove it down as far as I can until my knuckles graze his teeth. He gags and whines the best he can with his cock blocking his throat. His chest rises and falls slower and slower and his eyes start to roll back. "Give me a hammer, Rhy."

He pushes the hammer into my hand and I tap it against the end of the screwdriver, pushing his cock further down his throat. His gurgled gasps slowly quiet to a hiss, like air being let out of a tire. I watch the light fade from his eyes as he stares blankly up at the ceiling. "Good riddance."

I close my eyes and remember every tear Ophelia shed while telling me what she went through with him. With a guttural roar,

I slam the hammer into his face over and over. Blood spray hits my face, but I'm too lost in the anger to give a shit. The hammer is yanked from my grip and I'm gripped from behind. My chest heaves from the exertion. Viking slaps my chest over and over.

"Clean up. Take a walk. We got it from here."

I stare at Rocco's mangled face, torn between continuing and getting the fuck out of here and checking on Ophelia. Rhyatt tilts his head so I can see him. "It's okay, Rhyd. Go."

I nod and walk over to the sink, turning on the water and washing the blood from my face. How do I tell my wife I'm my own brand of monster? The one I became without her, and the one I've morphed into in order to protect her and Rhayvin, and get revenge against the fucks who hurt her. Can she really love the real me?

"Heroes and villains both thrive on violence, but we're still categorized. 'You're good' 'You're evil'. That's how it is! Symbol of peace? Hah! In the end you're just a tool for violence, made to keep us down. And violence only breeds more violence."
- Tomura Shigaraki (My Hero Academia)

CHAPTER SEVENTEEN

FEEL THE LIGHT

September 2024

Ophelia

I wake up to the feeling of the bed jostling and the sounds of Rhayvin's sweet giggles. I open my eyes and smile, this moment reminding me of the time her Uncle Rhy-Rhy did this to wake me up.

"Good morning, my bouncing bird."

"Good mohnin', Mama. Guess what, guess what, guess what?!" She squeals. I tickle her legs and she giggles, falling on top of me. I hug her tight to me and kiss her head.

"Tell me, tell me, tell me!" I respond, matching her enthusiasm.

She looks up at me and smiles big. "Watuh pahk, Mama!"

Her excitement for this family trip warms my heart. I never thought this was something I would ever get to do in my life, let alone with a family of my own. "That's right! We get to go to the water park today. Is Daddy packing without us?"

She nods frantically, her hair smacking her face as she bounces. "Mhmm."

"Okay, let's go help Daddy. The faster we pack, the faster we can go."

She screams and jumps off the bed. I laugh and get up, following behind her. She runs in her room and jumps on Rhydian's back as he kneels in front of her dresser. Her light weight barely registers but he gasps and drops the bag, dramatically falling to the side.

"Ahhh, I've been attacked! Help!"

She rolls away from him, giggling more, "Daddy, it's me, Wayvin."

He lays beside her with his hand over his heart and looks at her smiling. "Phew. I'm so glad it's you. I was so scared."

She hugs him tight and he looks over her shoulder, smiling at me. "Good morning, little raven."

"Hi, Bones. Do you want to keep packing for all of us, or start breakfast for our sweet girl?"

"Oh, breakfast is covered. Jade said she was going to get a big breakfast started for everyone before we hit the road. We'll also be making a stop at the store for last minute things."

"Not just for us, right? Everyone needs to pick up something?"

"Yeah. Everyone is going to pick out drinks and snacks, and then a few of us have to pick out swimsuits. I was thinking we could find those cool arm float things for Rhayvin."

I frown, remembering the last time she was in a pool. I don't even know if she's ready for that part of the water park. I look at Rhydian as he pulls his phone out of his pocket. "Hey. Can you come get your niece and take her to breakfast while Ophelia and I pack?"

I hear Rhyatt respond loudly and Rhydian says, "Thanks. Just head to Rhayvin's room when you get here." He hangs up the phone and pockets it. "She's going to have some Uncle Why-Why time."

Rhayvin bounces in his arms, squealing, "Yay! Uncle Why-Why!"

Rhydian looks at me again and I mouth, 'thank you'. He winks and I feel my cheeks heat. He smiles wide at my reaction and I flip him off, sticking my tongue out. Rhyatt barrels into the room, Lore following closely behind. I bite back a laugh at how obvious they are, even if she tries to hide it.

"RHAY-RHAY!" Rhyatt shouts.

She tries to pull away from Rhydian as he holds tighter. "Daddy! Uncle Why-Why needs me. Let go!"

"Yeah, Daddy! Let go!" Rhyatt says in a high-pitched voice.

Rhydian flips him off and kisses Rhayvin's head. "Fine, fine. Go hang out with your Uncle Why-Why. I love you."

She kisses his cheek, "Love you, Daddy." She runs to me and hugs me. "Love you, Mama."

I hug her back and kiss the top of her head, pushing some hair from her face. "I love you, too, baby. Be good for everyone, okay?"

She pulls away and takes hold of both Lore and Rhyatt. "Yes, Mama."

"Hey, why don't you go ahead with Auntie Lore real quick. I'll be right there, promise." Rhyatt says. He puts his hands on his hips as he peeks out the door.

I can hear Lore as she shouts back, "Stop looking there, heathen!"

He giggles and looks at us, schooling his features with a shrug. He clears his throat and scratches the back of his head like he's nervous. "Listen. I haven't had a chance to tell you guys yet. It's not an emergency or a big deal, but it felt weird not sharing. Everything is all clear with that Damascus massacre. The story is honestly wild." He pauses and waves his hand. "That's for another time. Anyway, while I was in there, you will never fucking believe who I ran into!"

Rhydian crosses his arms and I tilt my head as we ask, "Who?"

"That creepy fucker, Blake!"

I look away as I recall a memory from that night. "Holy shit! That's what they meant!"

Rhydian walks over to me. "What who meant?"

I grimace before saying their names. "Aldo and Alonzo. That night Aldo told Alonzo to make a call, get him sent to Damascus and make it known who killed Thatcher. I think they pinned everything on Blake. Made it out that he lost his marbles and killed him."

"Listen. That fucker was already fucked in the head, but that place did a number on him. He spent his time isolated and quiet. He lost his shit once while I was there. This cool dude, Karver, told me how Blake would scream at the tv if we were on the news. He said it was weird, because he's always very with-drawn, practically mute. Of course, I had to go see for myself. So I peeked through the little window of his door and he saw me and woooo! That dude has a set of pipes on him and was bouncing around like a fucking bouncy ball pinging off the walls. Like I said. He's locked up in that place, and he really seems wayyyy far gone. We're safe from that fucker. Ya hear me, Ophie? Safe."

"Okay. Yeah." I shake my head and smile. "Yeah. Thank you for telling me. Is it wrong I... don't feel bad for him at all?"

Rhyatt snorts. "Fuck no. He was a creepy little bastard who wanted to create the ultimate incest-fest and diddle all of us, including Daddy dearest." He shivers and gags. "I'm out of here. Hurry up and pack, you two! We're going to the water park!" He runs out like a kid hopped up on sugar. My head almost spins from how fast he goes from serious to goofy fucker.

Rhydian pulls me to him. "Do you want to talk about that, too?"

I'm already shaking my head at his question. "No. We already have enough we need to talk about and honestly, Rhyatt said we're safe. I don't really want to add that shit to a pile of real worries, ya know?"

Rhydian nods and quickly finishes packing Rhayvin's bag. I take his outstretched hand as he guides me to our room. He lets go of me and goes to the closet to pull down one of our bigger duffle bags. Grabbing his clothes, he starts, "So, what had you frowning in there?"

I sigh while opening my drawers. "I know Rhavyin is really excited for the water park, but I'm worried about her." I walk to the bag and drop in some of my clothes as Rhydian puts his in on one side of the bag.

"Worried about what?"

"I think she'll do great with most of the things there, but I think it would be best to not take her to the pools. I know she hasn't had any nightmares about what happened that night in the pool, but what if getting in one triggers something for her?"

He nods in understanding, looking away in thought. "What if we gave it a try at the hotel pool? We can ask her first and see if she's comfortable. If she is, we take it slow, go at her pace and see how she does."

I sit on the end of the bed, absentmindedly refolding all of my clothes from the bag. "I know. I just... I tried so hard to keep her safe, and hide the darkness of that world from her. But they went and fucked everything up that night. She had to bear witness to things no child should ever have to. I wanted better for her than we did as kids, ya know?" A tear falls and I quickly swipe it away.

Rhydian kneels before me, holding my hands. "Hey. You are an incredible mother. I am so sorry you went through everything you did. You are a fucking force to be reckoned with. I wish our baby didn't have to experience that night, more than anything. But you need to know, you did so fucking amazing with her on your own. Anytime Rhayvin talks to me about life with you, she has so many happy memories. The things that happened there, not many could say they made it through that unscathed. You took control of the situation the best you could, and that night was one that just wasn't possible to take on all on your own."

I nod and sniffle, my voice broken. "Thank you for not hating me."

He squeezes my hands, his brows furrowing. "Hate you? I could never hate you, Ophelia. Why would you think that?"

"Because I didn't go with you guys that night. I didn't fight harder to get away from Aldo. I didn't get Rhayvin and I out of there. So many things."

"I need you to listen to me, okay?" I look up at his stern, broken tone. "We were kids, Ophelia. We both could have done things differently that night. We did the best we could in a fucked up situation. You don't think I have carried that burden with me everyday? Wishing I did things differently? That I found you sooner? This time with you and Rhayvin has really opened my eyes, though. I'm going to ask you the same question I had to ask myself. Would you blame Rhayvin if she made the same choice? Would you hate her?"

A sob falls from my lips and my heart shatters. "Never!"

He scoops me up and sits with me in his lap, rocking me back and forth. "That's right. We would never blame her for that. Because she's a child, and would do the best she could. Just like we did. Okay?" I sniffle and nod against his shoulder, trying to steady my breathing. "Let's get you cleaned up and go join our family on this adventure, pretty girl."

I rub my temples as we wander through the store, the chaos of our entire family buzzing around me. This trip better be worth it. The guys dart off to the men's section, yanking random swimming trunks from the racks with barely a glance. Moments later, they charge back and toss the entire armful into one of the carts we girls are pushing, as if their mission is complete. Viking grabs one from Mrs. Valour.

"We're going to go get car essentials and emergency kits in case of a breakdown. It shouldn't take too long, we can meet up to grab snacks and drinks after you girls are done picking out swimsuits."

Rhayvin pouts at me from the kid seat. "Mama, can I go with Daddy and my uncas?"

I smile. "Not this time, baby. We're going to go pick out a very special swimsuit for you."

Her eyes light up and her mouth drops as she gasps. "FO ME?!" She squeals.

I chuckle at her excitement and nod. "Yup. Let's go."

Most of us pick out our suits fairly quickly, only leaving Rhayvin, Lore and Nova to decide. Rhayvin slides the suits back and forth on the rack, making the hangers squeak and click as they go. "Do you have an idea of what you'd like to wear?"

"Mama. I like dahk, but I also like pwetty."

I look at the suits and eye one that is the perfect mix of both. I tap my chin, pretending to be in thought. "What if I told you that you could have both?"

"Two?!"

I laugh and shake my head. "Not two suits. But one that is dark and has pretty things on it."

"Ooo! Yes! Yes! Yes! Please, Mama!"

I pull the one I found off the rack and show her. It's all black with rainbow sequins on the skirt. Her eyes grow big and she jumps up and down pulling on it. "I WANT IT! I WANT IT! I WANT IT!"

"Yay! Put it in the cart."

I pick Rhayvin up and put her back in the children's seat, pushing the cart towards Nova and Lore. Nova grabs different swimsuits, feeling the material and stretching it out. I notice Lore standing further back with her arms crossed and a scowl on her face. I can practically see the fire in her eyes, as if she could scorch every suit here.

"Hey, Lore." She looks over and I smile. "You could always pick a plain black one and maybe a pair of black shorts to go with it. They also have these cool mesh things you can wear. Some women only wear them out of the water, but you can get them wet. It can either cover your arms and most of your body, or if you wanted you could tie it up to at least show the shorts."

Her demeanor changes with the new information. "Really?!" She clears her throat and looks around, schooling her features. "I mean, that's cool. Thanks, Ophelia."

"Of course."

Nova practically growls, yanking a suit from the rack and tossing it in the cart. "Fuck this."

"Rhayvin, check this out," Rader says.

We both look over and she shakes her suit. "It looks like *R2-D2*."

"Oh, that's a great find."

Rhayvin tilts her head. "What's ah-2-D2?"

Rader puts her hand over her heart and glares at me. "I'm stealing your kid for a *Star Wars* marathon."

I put my hands up in surrender. "Don't shoot me, yeesh. And if you do, I hope you have the aim of a *Stormtrooper*."

"Guys! We should do a Horde movie night with a marathon of the *Star Wars* movies," Jade says.

Lady Sable smiles. "That'll be an easy sales pitch to the guys."

I nod. "Okay, sounds good. Maybe we can schedule it for some time after this trip, though. I think after all the excitement of the water park, Rhayvin will be too tired to watch that many movies."

"Nuh uh!" She gasps.

"If you say so, baby bird. We'll see."

Vanessa looks at our carts as Lore brings her items over. "I think that's everything. Someone wanna call the children and tell them to meet us to pick out food and drinks?"

Theia pulls out her phone. "Guys, we might all have to call. Who knows what the hell they're getting into over there."

"Who wants to bet they ended up in the toy section?" Nova laughs.

Before the rest of us can pull our phones out, Lore lets out an evil laugh while tapping on her phone. She looks up and grins. "Wait for it."

The sound of multiple emergency alerts ring out loudly throughout the store. We look around and back at her as she throws her head back laughing. "I sent out a mass text to them, and made it to where their phones all go off with emergency alarms until they open it."

One by one, the sound quiets until it's silent as we all laugh and make our way to the food section. I look around at the group and can't help but smile. I hope this isn't a dream.

"Family is laughter, love, happiness. Everything."
-Unknown

CHAPTER EIGHTEEN

THE BEST OF TIMES

Ophelia

We pull into a parking space at the water park and Rhayvin and Rhyatt immediately cheer excitedly. Rhayvin insisted we get here as early as possible so she didn't miss anything. The poor girl has seen far too many *Disney* parades and thinks they are events that happen at all fun locations. The rest of us moan and groan as we pile out of the vehicles. The adults were up far too late watching movies and bullshitting. I reach for our backpack, ready to sling it over my shoulder, but Rhydian swoops in and takes it first. He presses a quick kiss to my cheek.

"I got it," he says with a grin.

"Thank you, Bones." As we approach the entrance, I notice there's a massive line of people. My palms are slick with sweat and my heart races. My eyes bounce frantically around, searching for Rhayvin and Rhyatt.

I clutch Rhydian's arm, forcing him to stop. He looks down at me, his brow furrowed. "Hey, what's wrong?"

"Rhayvin. Get Rhayvin. Now."

"Hey, hey, breathe."

"GET RHAYVIN!" I whisper-shout, my voice edged with panic.

"Okay, okay. RHY!"

Rhyatt runs over with a shaking Rhayvin, clutching him tight.

"Look, Rhay-Rhay, here's Mama, it's okay," Rhyatt says gently.

Her head shoots up and she practically jumps in my arms. I hold her tight to my chest and rock her back and forth. I feel slightly better with her close, but the unease still lingers within me. There's so many people. How do I keep her safe with so many people around?

Rhydian wraps his arms protectively around us. "What's wrong?" he murmurs against my ear.

"It's usually just us with family. Our biggest trips have been to the store or *Swan & Scribe*. There's so many people. How do we keep her safe?"

Rhayvin hugs me tighter. "Mama, I okay."

"Are you sure? This isn't too much?"

"No, Mama. I wanna have fun. Can you and Daddy stay wiff me?"

"Of course, baby."

She looks over at Rhyatt with a pout. "Will you be okay, Unca Why-Why?"

He rubs his chin in thought. "Hmm. I will miss my sidekick. But I'll be okay. I'll spend time with your Auntie Lore."

Rhayvin giggles. "Okay, Unca Why-Why."

"We're going to have so much fun. Daddy and his girls on a wild adventure. Hop on Daddy's back."

He turns to give her his back and she leaps on top of him. "Oomph. Ugh. Easy. Loosen that grip, anaconda."

We all pay and make our way to the bathrooms so everyone can get changed. Rhydian kisses my forehead as I pull Rhayvin into my arms. "Everything will be okay. Look how big our group is. Nobody wants to fu-" he stumbles on his words, looking at Rhayvin in my arms, "fudge, nobody wants to fudge around with us."

Rhayvin squeals, "FUDGE?! I want some!"

He ruffles her hair, chuckling. "Maybe later. Go with Mama and get your super cool swimsuit on." I spin around so he can pull his swimming trunks and slides out. "I love you, girls."

Rhayvin and I both smile. "I love you," we reply in unison.

We all shuffle outside to the lockers. The sound of flip-flops and slides slapping against feet and asphalt surrounds us. The guys meet us there, a few of them already have lockers open for us to put our bags and shoes in. I notice Nova hesitantly hold her backpack against her. She looks at the bag and up at Rhys. She looks around at the group, and I busy myself messing with my bag in my locker as if I'm searching for something. I sneak a peek at her and everything clicks as soon as she puts the backpack in her locker. The unmistakable glow that has nothing to do with the sweat on her brow, mint in her mouth, and the subtle bump she can't help but cradle.

My eyes water with the realization. I'm so happy she won't be alone in this. I walk over and before reaching her, call out, "Please don't be mad."

She drops her hand and looks at me, confused. "Wha-" I cut her off by wrapping my arms around her tightly. Her arms flail wildly, and she lets out a screech.

"Noooo touchy. Why?! Why?! What's happening!?"

I whisper in her ear, "Congratulations." Her breath hitches and I feel her whole body tense. "Please stay away from the water slides. I don't think they'd be very safe for you right now."

"Don't make me cry, asshole. Let go, let go, let go."

I pull back and give her space. Her eyes water and she looks up, trying to keep the tears from falling.

Rhys swoops in and hugs her from behind. "What's wrong, little star?"

"I don't know how, but Ophelia knows," she whispers.

Rhys smiles wide at me. "Yeah, I did that."

I can't help but laugh at his response, as Nova reaches back and slaps his thigh. "Ooo, feisty mama."

"Cut it out, we said we were keeping it quiet," she hisses.

I put my hand up. "I won't tell anyone. Not until you're ready. I just… I'm so happy that you'll have people around for this experience. And I really couldn't keep quiet about the slides. I would've felt like shit if I didn't say anything."

She looks at me and takes a deep breath. "Thank you. We're just trying to decide the best time to tell everyone."

I nod. "I understand. Let me know if you have any questions. I know it can be different for everyone, but I did a lot of research with Rhayvin."

She puts a fist out and I bump mine against hers. "Thank you, Ophelia."

Rhydian walks over with Rhayvin on his shoulders. "Everything okay here?"

He looks between all of us and I smile up at him. "Yeah. Let's go take our baby on that adventure."

We make it back to the hotel and everyone finds a place to collapse. Rhayvin is fighting how tired she is, and she's on one final burst of go-go juice before her inevitable collapse. She jumps up and down tugging on my shirt. "Mama, Mama, Mama."

I rub the top of her head, looking at her with a tired smile. "Rhayvin, Rhayvin, Rhayvin."

"Can I make bwacelets?" She looks around and whispers, "I not weddy fo da pool."

I kneel down in front of her. "That's alright, baby. We won't try until you're ready. We just thought you would like the stuff you did at the water park, and then try the hotel pool when there weren't so many people. I promise we'll only do it when you're ready. Go ahead and grab your beads and string and you can start making bracelets."

Viking plays another *Star Wars* movie for us to work our way through them. Rhayvin lays on the floor and starts setting out different colors. She crawls over to me and shakes my knee. "Mama, I need help."

"What do you need help with?"

"I want to make bwacelets fo evweeone," she says, brimming with excitement. "Wiff names."

"Okay, baby. I can help with that." I get down on the floor next to her. She giggles softly as she shares her ideas, pointing out beads for each person's bracelet.

"The fuck. You read?" Rhyatt asks in shock.

I look up and see him hovering over Viking. He pulls the book from his grasp and looks at the book like it's a foreign object. "Dude. This is Shakespeare."

Viking laughs and yanks the book back. "Of course I read. Who do you think taught Dorian about the cookbook?"

"Cookbook? Like recipes or something?"

Dorian laughs nervously. "Yeah, or something."

Once finished, Rhayvin looks at me and holds up a bracelet with black and rainbow colors that says **MAMA**. I slide it onto my wrist and gasp, clutching it like a treasure.

"Rhayvin, it's beautiful! Best bracelet I've ever had! Thank you!"

She beams, her little voice chirping, "Yo welcome, Mama."

She shows me everyone else's, before excitedly running over to them and sliding it on each of their wrists. I walk over to Rhydian and sit in his lap. He wraps his arms around me, pulling me closer.

"I love our family," I whisper as I nuzzle against his neck, my voice soft and full. "We made it, Bones."

"And suddenly you know: It's time to start something new and trust the magic of beginnings."
- Meister Eckhart

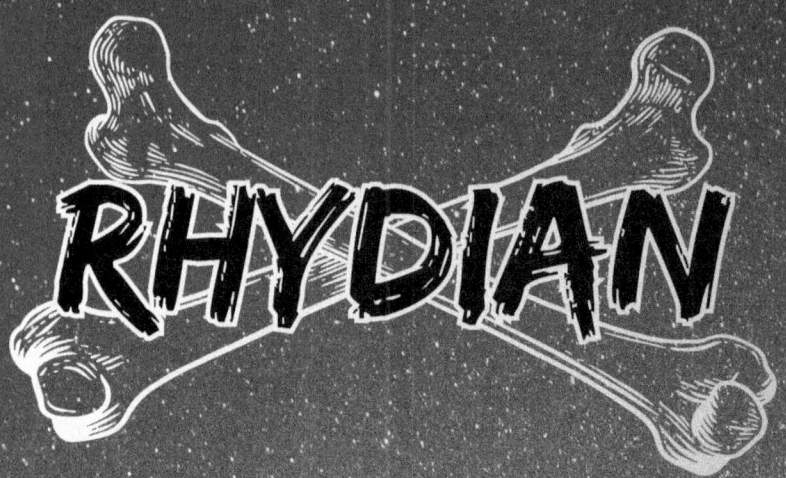

CHAPTER NINETEEN

KNOW YOUR ENEMY

October 2024

Rhydian

I look at the screens as Lore pulls up the surveillance of our new target, Deacon Foster. I feel Ophelia's hand over mine after I squeeze her thigh. At this point, we're comforting each other. She's torn between looking at the pictures of yet another man who fucking touched her, and staring at the laptop, pulling up another man's picture over and over. Me, on the other hand, I'm ready to fucking tear this guy's head off.

It's bad enough he's one of the men who dared hurt my little raven, but this fuck is a vice-principal at the local high school. Not only does he play with the trafficked victims, but he fucking helps recruit. He pretends to give a shit about the kids who fall through the cracks, while simultaneously serving them up like pigs for slaughter. He gets a taste as long as he keeps pointing them in the right direction. Fucking disgusting.

"Everyone needs to be on their best behavior tonight," Lore pauses and stares at everyone before continuing. "I know we'll all want a piece of this fucker once we see him at the carnival, but we have to wait. Timing is everything."

Dorian gets up and grabs the clicker from her. "Thanks, Lore." He points the remote at the screen and clicks. The surveillance all disappears and is replaced with a map of the carnival grounds.

"Alright, first job– scare workers. It'll be Rhys, the twins and myself. We'll keep an ear out for anything important, but we'll also be scaring the kids away if they hang around Deacon for too long. We haven't found any surveillance of him physically helping with kidnapping these kids, but anything is possible. There are distractions everywhere, and it's far too easy to run off with someone unnoticed."

Rhyatt laughs and drums on the table. "I am so ready for this. I can't wait for you guys to see what I picked out to wear. Totally got inspo from that wild *Tik Tok* app."

"Of course you did," Lore scoffs, rolling her eyes.

He winks over at her. "Just you wait, little succubus."

Dorian laughs at the two of them before straightening up. "Anyways. We're all going to have to work together – split up, keep an eye and ear out on everything. But we also need some people with Rhayvin and Ophelia. Ophelia will be taking our resident princess to do all the fun things you're supposed to be doing at a carnival. We don't want to make it too obvious, so we can't have two of you hulking fuckers with her. Miss Rhayvin will have one auntie and one uncle guarding her at all times."

Ophelia finally looks up from the laptop when Rhayvin is brought up and she smiles. "Thank you. I know we've gotten somewhat better with crowds, but it still brings me some anxiety.

I'll feel better knowing you guys are there to help keep my baby safe."

Nova crosses her arms and sits back, grumbling, "I wanna do fun rides with Rhayv."

Rhys rubs the back of her head. "I'm sorry, little star."

Everyone looks at them and Dorian lifts a brow. "Why can't you go on the rides with her, SuperNova?"

Her eyes widen. "Uhh, I... just..." She pinches the bridge of her nose. "Ghoulie, I don't want to wait anymore. I hate sneaking around like this."

He kisses the top of her head, his voice soft. "Whatever you want."

She drops her hand to her stomach, her fingers absentmindedly rubbing over it. "No rides with Rhayv," with her other hand she points to her stomach, "semen demon on board."

The room erupts in cheers, my eyes widen in surprise. "Holy shit! Congrats!"

V and Ophelia both let out a sigh. "Finally," they both say.

"Wait. You two already knew?"

Nova points at V. "Told her," then points at Ophelia, "a-hole figured it out."

Ophelia smiles awkwardly. "Sorry. I kept quiet, though, so that counts for something, right?"

Dorian and Rhyatt both start climbing over the table at the same time, wrestling each other to go first.

"Get out of my way, Dorki. I need to congratulate Nova," Rhyatt grunts.

"No way, SlayBell. I knew her first!"

"Get off the table, children!" Nova shouts.

They both hold onto each other but stop wrestling, and look up at Nova with a pout, grumbling.

"Sorry, Nova."

"Sorry, SuperNova."

She starts gesturing around the room. "Seriously. All of you stay the fuck back. No hugs. Hug each other or something."

Dorian lays back on the table, smiling. "I can't wait to tell Theia."

"Make sure to tell her while you're getting ready. You know she'll try and hop on a ride with me and Rhayv," Nova says.

He scrambles off the table, shouting, "EVERYONE GET READY NOW!"

The group starts laughing and breaking off to go get ready for tonight. I look at Ophelia, who's biting her lip with a furrowed brow, staring at the guy's picture again.

"Do you recognize him?" I ask.

Without looking at me, her only response is a murmured, "Huh?"

I point at the guy's face on the screen. "Do you recognize him? Is he one of them?"

"It's driving me crazy, Bones."

"What is?"

"He just… I swear I recognize him, but he wasn't one of the guys who touched me. I'm afraid to say yes, I recognize him, and you guys hurt some random, innocent man."

I grab her chin and turn her head to look at me. "You know we always do our surveillance, especially if you're unsure. We never go after an innocent. We'll look into it, okay?"

She pulls from my hold and closes the laptop. "Okay. I'm sorry," she nods. I growl at her apology and her breath hitches as she slowly turns to look at me.

"Did you just growl at me?"

I smirk and lean in close. "I did, but it looks like you enjoyed it, little raven."

She scoffs, shaking her head. "N-no."

I pick her up from the chair and throw her over my shoulder, smacking her ass. She yelps and moans, slapping my back. "What the hell, Rhydian?! Put me down!"

"Don't think I didn't hear that moan. Don't hide what you love. I'm your husband, Ophelia, not some random schmuck you can't be yourself around."

She rubs my back and a shiver runs up my spine. "Don't distract me, woman. We have things to do."

A sharp sting on my ass makes me stumble "Oww, what the fuck? Did you just bite my ass?"

"You asked for it. Now put me down. We have to get ready."

"Ugh, fine. I have to go get something from Rhyatt's freaky ass, anyway."

"... all around me are familiar faces..."
-Gary Jules (from the song: Mad World)

CHAPTER TWENTY

TAG, YOU'RE IT

Ophelia

"Alright, baby. Time to get you ready for the carnival."

Rhayvin squeals and runs to her room. I smile and follow behind her as she opens her closet, jumping excitedly. "Mama! Mama! Pwease!"

She points in the closet to show me what she wants to wear. I had a feeling this would be her pick, so I already texted the group and asked if they would join in on the fun. I pull everything out of the closet that she needs for the outfit and throw it on the bed. Rhydian comes running into the room and picks Rhayvin up, spinning her around. She wraps her arms and legs around him, throwing her head back and giggling.

He kisses the top of her head. "I love you. Daddy has to go. I can't wait to see your super cool costume. You be good for everyone tonight, deal?"

He puts his fist up and she punches it as hard as she can. "Deal!"

She winces and he pretends to howl in pain. "Ouchie, you're so strong."

He puts her down and slowly prowls towards me with a smirk. I shake my head, pointing a warning finger at him. "Don't you dare, Bones." He lunges for me. "BONES!" I yelp, laughter bubbling out of me as he grabs me by the thighs, lifting me off the ground. My legs wrap around his waist instinctively, and my hands grip his shoulders for balance. "You don't listen for shit."

He nuzzles my neck, leaving small kisses. "Always pretending you don't love it."

My stomach is in knots and I hug him tight, whispering, "Please be careful."

He holds my face and leans in to give me a kiss. He lingers for a moment before Rhayvin pipes up, "Yuck!"

We pull away laughing and look at her. She has her hands on her hips making a sour face. Rhydian pulls away, putting his hands up. "Fine, fine. I'm out of here. I love you both."

"I love you," Rhayvin and I say back. I watch him leave until I feel fabric pushing against my hand. I look down and see Rhayvin trying to shove her outfit in my hand.

"Mama! Let's go!"

The twins, Rhys and Dorian left first for the carnival. I was tempted to ask for a comms device to listen in as well, but I don't think I'd be able to focus on that and Rhayvin properly. I unbuckle her booster seat and help her out. She jumps out of the van next to me and copies my movement of brushing off my black jeans. Her eyes light up when she sees that a lot of the girls dressed up as rockers like her.

She spins around, looking at everyone and gasps, "Wow! So pwetty!"

Rader walks over and smiles. "Wow, Rhayvin, your costume is amazing!"

She looks up at Rader and checks out her costume. "You da lady in da movie!" She gasps.

Rader chuckles, twisting the buns in her hair. "Princess Leia," she says.

"Oh no, I don't match. Is this costume okay, Rhayvin?" V asks.

"Oh shit, cool costume, V."

She taps her staff twice. "Thank you."

Rhayvin squeals, jumping up and down and tugging on V's outfit. "YOU MEFUHSENT!"

"Yesss, I am Maleficent."

"So cool," Rhayvin sighs. I follow behind her as she checks out the rest of the costumes, asking questions about each one.

I grab her hand as we walk to the entrance and pay for our tickets. They hand each of us a map of the carnival and where each ride, game, food booth and bathroom is located. I breathe in the smell of all the delicious food and groan. "At some point, we need to get some of that food."

Nova steps up beside me and rubs her belly. "Bitch. I'm gonna need one of everything. Somebody get me a towel. Drool, on aisle me."

I look over and the sight before me is like a scene from a movie. Holy shit. I gently elbow Nova. "You're really gonna need that towel now. Look."

"Wha- oh fuck, I'm about to get pregnant again."

I can only guess the elbows continue down the line as Theia says, "Oww, what? Oh, hello, D'oro," she practically purrs.

The boys walk side by side in all black clothes and face paint. Aren't these supposed to be scary costumes? The only thing scary is the throb between my soaked thighs. I tilt my head and before I have a chance to question the knee pads they're wearing, they all start slip-skating towards us in a synchronized motion.

Rhayvin tugs on my hand as she jumps up and down screaming, "Mama, look!" Rhys slides in first, stopping just before Nova. Rhyatt is next, moving towards Lore, and then my Bones and Dorian slide at the same time. I smile down at Rhydian, my hand stopping before touching his face. It's covered in face paint that morphs his face into a skull. My eyes fall on a choker around his neck. *Well, that's fucking hotter than expected.* I practically pant at the sight. "Hi, Bones," my voice comes out huskier than I intended.

Rhayvin gasps. "Daddy! You look so cool!"

"I do?! Do you think it's scary enough for other people?"

Her hair flies around her face as she nods. "Yes!"

Rhyatt's silly laugh has me looking over as he kneels before Lore. "Hi, little succubus. Like what you see?"

"Mmm, you make my girlhood tremble."

I slap my hand over my mouth, laughing. His eyes light up. "REALLY?! That's fucking hot."

She rolls her eyes and snorts. "No."

The fake blood dripping down his face gets in his mouth with his dramatic pout. "You wound me, baby girl."

"Not yet. But keep it up, I'll add some real blood to that pretty face of yours."

He clutches his chest and falls back with a sigh. "YOU HEAR THAT?! MY SUCCUBUS THINKS I'M PRETTY! I CAN DIE A HAPPY MAN NOW!"

She kicks his foot and hisses. "Get up, heathen! Knock it off!"

"I'm gonna need mouth to mouth, baby girl. Save me."

I feel Rhydian's hold on my chin as he turns my face to look at him. "Hi," he smiles.

"Hi," I whisper in return.

"Close your eyes and put your hand out."

I lift my brow in confusion. "Why?"

"Please?"

I sigh, "Fine." I close my eyes and hold my hand out. I feel hard plastic placed in my hand. "What is that?"

"Open your eyes." I open them and look down at the tiny, round remote in my hand.

"What's this for?"

"If you get scared, press the button."

He winks and walks backwards. "Let's go, boys."

"Mama, can we go now?" Rhayvin questions, tugging on my hand.

"Yeah, baby. Let's go." I look at our group. "So, who is walking with us?"

The group stares at each other, nobody stepping up to volunteer. V stands in the middle of the group and strikes her staff on the ground twice. "Hey! Focus! Who is going with who?"

Muggzy steps up. "Always making shit complicated. Listen– Viking, Sable and Fish, you three stay with the precious cargo. The rest of us can fan out. We're all on comms and armed. Frequent check-ins."

I kneel down next to Rhayvin and show her the map. "Alright, baby bird. Where to first?"

She looks at the map, squinting, and over at Nova's belly. She taps her chin in thought. "Auntie Nova?"

Nova holds her hand over her belly and kneels. "What's up, Rhayv?"

"Can you and da baby go on any wides wiff me?"

Nova smiles at Rhayvin, her eyes watering. "Dammit." She swipes away the tears. "Not a word, any of you." She looks back at Rhayvin. "That's so sweet of you to ask. Let's take a look here."

They look at the map together and Nova points out the slower kid rides that she can get on. "Is that okay, Rhayv?"

"Mhmm."

Nova stands and Rhayvin hugs her, kissing her belly. "Hey, you. We gonna have so much fun!"

"Oph, tell your kid to stop making me emotional," Nova whines.

"Sorry, Nova. Unavoidable. Gotta love those hormones pumping through ya," I laugh. She grumbles and walks away. We follow behind and make our way to the carousel first.

After a few rides, Viking taps my arm and points to his ear piece. "Rhayvin is gonna stay with the group. Rhydian asked that we head to the haunted house."

I look down at Rhayvin and the rest of the group. "But? What about Rhayvin?"

"Rhayvin will be safe. Everyone heard the plan on comms and is moving in. Rhayvin will be surrounded by the rest of us. She's safe. No harm will come to her."

I feel the remote in my pocket and I'm tempted to push the button. I shove my hands in my jacket, squeezing them tight. This is not the kind of fear Rhydian was talking about, I have to leave it alone. Viking nods in reassurance and I kneel next to Rhayvin, hugging her tight. "Mama, you hug me too tight."

I reluctantly loosen my grip. "I'm sorry, baby bird. Mama is gonna go check out the haunted house with Uncle Viking. You're gonna hang out with the rest of your aunties and uncles, okay?"

Rhayvin taps my arms. "Okay, Mama."

She pulls away, effectively dismissing me. That hurt more than expected. "I love you, Rhayvin."

"Love you, Mama," she says without looking.

I stand up and follow Viking, turning to look over my shoulder in her direction until she's out of sight. I pull the remote out of my pants pocket and put it in my jacket pocket, keeping my hand around it. These kind of things don't usually scare me, but I find myself more on edge without Rhayvin or Rhydian close. I notice Dorian walking over to us, his face paint cracked slightly by his grin.

"Follow me."

He guides us to the front of line, the people behind us bitching and groaning that we cut the line. The door behind us closes and darkness surrounds us. The only light guiding us are glowing arrows on the floor and walls. A gust of wind hits us in the face and blows my hair back. "Jesus, thanks for the glaucoma exam," I retort.

There's spooky music blaring, which is occasionally overshadowed by the sound of screams. We make our way through the maze when I see a glowing sign that says **STOP**. I follow the instructions, bracing myself for the inevitable jump scare. A wall crashes down in front of me with a deafening boom, red lights flashing in slow pulses. "What the fuck?!"

There's a crescendo of slamming noises and I turn to look, realizing there's now a wall behind me, separating me from Dorian and Viking.

"Hey! What the fuck?!" I bang on the walls surrounding me, panic rising in my chest. "Ha ha, very funny. Now move these fucking walls!" The flashing red lights stop, leaving me in a dark abyss.

I feel a whoosh of air behind me and goosebumps prickle my skin. I hear breathing behind me and squeeze my eyes shut. A hand slaps over my mouth, while an arm snakes around my waist. I scream behind the hand and kick my feet out. Remote. I need the remote. I press the button over and over. A familiar growl in my ear makes me stop.

"Bones?!"

"Mmm, hi, little raven," he whispers before gently biting the shell of my ear.

"What the fuck are you doing?!"

"Just giving you your power back."

"What? How?" He spins me around and puts my hand against the choker on his throat.

"Push the button again." With a shaky hand, I push the button again. The collar lights up and Rhydian grunts. I gasp and let go of the button.

"Oh my god, Bones! What the fuck?!"

"Listen, if you need me to completely stop, press that button over and over. If you need me to slow down, press it three times. And if you just want to boss me around, hit the button once. It'll be like a shocking whip to get me to do what you want."

He grabs my hand and pulls me through a narrow walkway, lit up with the little arrows. "Watch your head," he whispers. I duck and move slower behind him. I look up, squinting when I feel dust fall on my hair and face.

"What the- pfft pfft," I spit dirt out of my mouth. The music dies down, the sound of footsteps and creaking boards right above us.

"Bones?"

He puts his finger over my mouth, shushing me. "Shh. You don't want them to hear you, do you?"

My eyes widen. "Bones! Don't you dare." I murmured sharply.

"If it's a no, press that button over and over. But if it's a yes, then be a good girl and pull your pants down."

My thighs clench instinctively. "Dammit, Bones."

I pocket the remote and do as he says. He grabs me, shoving me against the wall, my back to his chest. I shiver when the cold air hits my exposed ass and thighs as he yanks my pants and under-wear all the way down.

"Oh fuck."

I shake in anticipation, my hands clawing at the wall before me. The music starts up again, the sound vibrating through the walls and my body. An uneasy feeling creeps in when I realize I can't actually see or hear that it's him behind me. My heart pounds and my stomach rolls. *Fuck, fuck, fuck.*

I scramble for the remote in my pocket and try to remember how many times I'm supposed to hit the button. Shit. Once? No, no, maybe again and again or? It's getting harder to breathe as I try and figure out the remote and how to get his attention. His grip on my hips gets tighter and tighter with every push of the button. I feel his breath against me and then his voice. "Ophelia?"

I let go of the remote and sigh. "One for more. Three for slow. Over and over for stop. Okay? Are you good?"

I nod, remembering he can't see me and press the button once.

"Good girl." I feel my pussy clench at his praise, wishing it was filled. "We have to be quick, okay?"

I push the button again and he groans, "Good fucking girl. Goddamn."

I feel his cock against me and no time to prepare as he thrusts forward, filling me completely. I shout, pressing the button again. His punishing grip on my hips gets tighter as he thrusts harder and faster. My hands slip against the wall as I try to hold on for dear life. I slide them down in front of my face as a barrier to keep my face from getting smashed in. With the remote between my hands, every thrust makes me hit the button. We create our own rhythm that brings me closer and closer to the edge, without even touching my clit or nipples.

With every press of the button, he moves deeper, his thrusts precise and unrelenting, hitting the perfect angle. My mouth falls open, a breathless gasp escaping as pure ecstasy ripples through me. My pussy clenches around him as the tension coils tighter, hotter. The orgasm tears through me, stealing my breath and every coherent thought. I slump back against the wall, my thighs trembling as aftershocks ripple through me. My chest rises and falls with shallow, uneven breaths as I ride the waves of pleasure that refuse to subside. Just as everything comes into focus, I feel the warmth of his cum spurting inside me. I moan at the feeling.

Fuck, why does that feel so good?

I almost become one with the wall as he pulls my underwear and pants back up, fastening them for me. He spins me towards him and holds me close, his own breathing heavy. "You did so good, pretty girl. I'm so fucking proud of you."

I caress his face until I find his lips and lean in, kissing him hard. My lips vibrate with his groan and he swipes his tongue along my bottom lip. I open my mouth, letting him slide his tongue in, flicking against mine slowly. He pulls back and gives me a quick peck. "You keep that up and we'll be caught for sure. Let's go."

He guides me out of the haunted house and slaps my ass startling me into a yelp. "Bones!"

He points to his mouth and then me, smirking. "You got a little something there." I narrow my eyes and notice his face paint is smeared. I touch my lips and feel the greasy paint there. *Dammit.*

I flip him off and listen to his laughter as I walk over to Viking. "Gods, I hate that I know what you two were up to." He shudders and continues walking. We find the group quickly and Rhayvin runs over, jumping in my arms.

"Well, hello to you, too."

"I hungwee, Mama."

"Oh, of course. That's why I got such a wonderful greeting from you. Okay, baby, let's find out what everyone wants."

As we walk up, I notice Lore staring in the direction of the haunted house and spinning some of the beads of the bracelet Rhayvin made her. Sometimes she seems so fucking distant and lonely. I blame myself sometimes. It's not that I didn't notice her in high school. I mean, I obviously noticed her a lot more when I met the twins, but I never did anything about it. I should've befriended her. She needed someone as much as we did. I need to fix this. I sit next to her, putting Rhayvin in my lap. "Hey, Lore?"

"Hmm?" She asks without looking.

"I was just wondering if you would come with me to get the food for everyone." She looks up at me confused, pushing her glasses up. "Me?"

I smile and nod. "Yeah. Please?"

"Okay," she shrugs.

"Hey, Nova, I'll make you a trade."

"What kinda trade we talkin' here?"

I stand and lift Rhayvin in the air and she giggles, kicking her feet. "You watch my bird and I'll get you and your semen demon food."

She snaps her finger, giving me the finger gun. "You got yourself a goddamn deal! Get on over here, Rhayv."

I put her down and she runs over to Nova, hugging her leg. We start to turn away as Nova shouts, "I swear to fuck, y'all better get *all* of the food. You're gonna have to ask those fuckers for a food cart. Wheel the food on over, and then you'll have to use that thing to roll me outta this joint. Got it?"

"What Mama wants, Mama gets. On it."

I take a deep breath before starting. "Can I ask you something, Lore?"

"Uhh, I guess."

"If you are, it's totally fine, and I'll understand. But are you mad at me for high school?"

Lore stops and stares at me. "Huh? Why would I be mad at you?"

"Honestly? I feel bad that I didn't try to be your friend. I knew you existed. Especially after meeting Rhyatt. But I just never made the effort. And it really had nothing to do with you or not wanting to. I just... I went from being all on my own to having the twins, and even that's a lot for someone who used to have nobody. But the more I think about it, I think you were in the same boat. I think that maybe you needed someone, too. And I'm really sorry that I wasn't that person for you if you needed it."

"It's okay. I'm not mad. I never was."

She walks past me and starts ordering food. "I really don't think Nova was kidding about the food."

Lore laughs. "True. Excuse me, do you guys have a food cart? Our friend is growing an alien and wants everything you have."

The kid working chuckles and then coughs, staring at us. "Wait. You really want everything on the menu?"

"Sure do, kid. Can we get our cups for drinks while we wait?"

"Umm, okay, yeah."

He hands us a stack of cups. "This will take awhile, you know that right?"

"That's fine. We'll just wait right over here out of the way."

The kid's voice squeaks as he looks around the space. "Oh man."

I grab the cups and follow Lore to the soda machine. Lore grabs one cup and starts adding a little bit of everything to it. I curl my lip. "What the fuck is that?"

"You've never had this?! It's called a graveyard, or a suicide. Whatever tickles your pickle. It's delicious. Great hacker fuel, honestly."

"Hmm. Interesting." I start filling a cup like she did, stopping when I hear the sound of ice and liquid splashing against the ground. I turn and find Lore standing there frozen, gasping for air.

"Lore? Hey, Lore? What's wrong?"

I step up next to her and notice the man standing on the side of the food booth. He smirks, blowing smoke through his decayed teeth. I grab Lore's arm and glare at the man. "Who the fuck are you?"

He shakes his head, strands of his greasy black hair tumbling forward. "Lore, where are your manners? Tell your pretty friend who I am."

I grimace at him calling me pretty. I pivot my legs so I can see her and the creep. "Lore? Who is this?"

Fear is etched across her face as she stammers, "M-my... father."

I look back at him. "Okay, well this doesn't look like the kind of family reunion she wanted. So we're just gonna get going now."

A dark chuckle falls from his mouth as he throws his smoke down, stomping on it. He reaches into his pocket and in the blink of an eye, we have a gun pointing at us. "Yeah, that's not how this is going to go."

I open my mouth to scream and he points the gun towards Lore.

"Don't," he seethes. Anger pours off him in waves. He pulls a phone out of his pocket with his other hand. "Why don't you take a look at your family over there."

Fear courses through me as I slowly turn and look towards the group. I see Rhayvin getting tossed in everyone's arms, giggling away. I notice a man standing off to the side, glaring as he answers the phone. The man behind me starts talking. "Wave at us, friend."

The man looks over and smirks while waving. He stays on the phone and continues watching the group. I grit my teeth. "Stay the fuck away from them."

"Hmm. That depends on if you play nicely."

I glare at him, a bit confused. "What do you mean?"

"You two are coming with me. You little bitches ruined every-thing four years ago. It's time for you to pay for ruining my life."

"Wait. What?"

"You little sluts were sold off to Aldo and Alonzo. You," he points at me with the gun, "got away and weren't supposed to."

He points the gun at Lore, his hand shaking as he sneers. "And you. You fucking ran and ruined the whole fucking deal. You know your mother is dead cuz of you. If you would've just stayed, they wouldn't have made me kill her."

Lore gasps, trembling. "Y-you. You killed her?"

"That's on you, Lore the whore." A tear falls down her face. "You two are going to come with me. There will be no fighting or screaming. You will come with me willingly and not cause a fucking scene. That guy I called isn't the only one here. I have enough to take on your whole group. They'll bring *all* the girls in, including that little girl of yours. There will be no mercy this time, either. No exchanging yourself for her. That deal is off the table. So what's it gonna be?"

I swallow the bile creeping up, tears sliding down my cheeks. "Not her. Don't you touch her."

Lore is already stepping forward to follow him. I grab her wrist as I walk beside her and the guy turns to lead the way. I look around trying to come up with a plan. I make sure he's not looking and yank on Lore's bracelet, the string snaps and the beads all fall to the ground. I clamp my hand over her mouth to muffle her gasp. She cries, watching the beads bounce on the ground. I put my finger to my mouth to shush her.

I hold onto my bracelet as we walk and carefully snap it, holding all the beads in my hand. As we walk I drop a bead here and there as we go, leading all the way to the man's parked truck. Instead of breadcrumbs, I've left beadcrumbs for them. *Please find us.* I drop the final bead as he shoves us into the truck, slamming the door behind us. The sound makes me think of a final nail placed in our coffin. I put my hand on the window and stare at the carnival grounds. My heart shatters at the realization that this is it, our days are numbered.

Lore and I jump when the truck backfires and I close my eyes, whispering, "Until we meet again."

"The story of life is quicker than the blink of an eye. The story of love is hello and goodbye, until we meet again."
-Jimi Hendrix

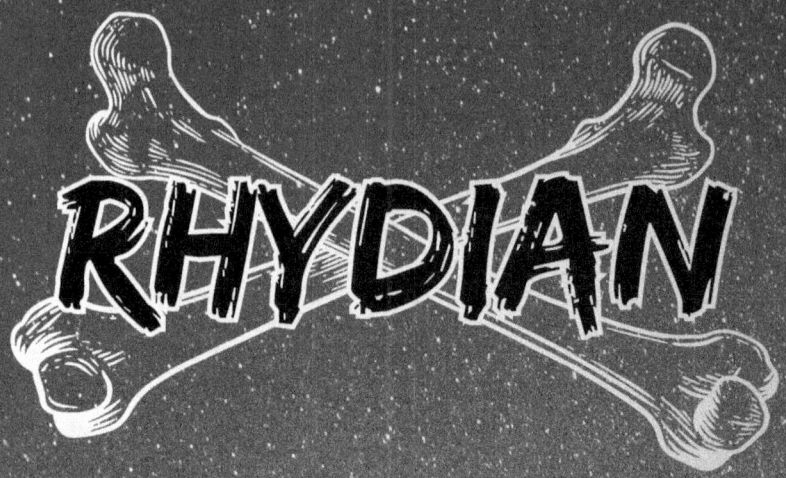

CHAPTER TWENTY-ONE

CAN YOU FEEL MY HEART

Rhydian

I spot a group of kids hanging too close to Deacon and narrow my eyes, a low growl rumbling in my throat. I break into a run, dropping into a slide across the pavement on my knee pads. The kids jump in surprise, their giggles echoing as they scatter like startled birds. Deacon jolts a bit with a laugh as I make sure to slam into his leg. I grunt and get up. I stare at him and tilt my head, like a predator sizing up his prey. He chuckles nervously as I continue to stare. I ball my fists at my side, my chest heaving. I take a menacing step towards him and he instinctively takes one back.

"Umm," he stammers out, looking around as if searching for an escape. I'm ready to advance towards him again when the sound of a truck backfiring catches my attention. *Don't engage, only recon.* I shake my head and walk away as I hear Nova on comms, groaning about how long Ophelia and Lore are taking with the food.

I turn and walk away. "Where are you guys at?"

"Food benches by the Ferris wheel," Fish says.

"Copy. I'm heading over."

I make my way through the crowds effortlessly as everyone quickly moves out of my way. I cross my arms and look around at everyone in the group.

"Rhydian, there you are! Your wife and Lore are taking forever," Nova whines.

"Where's Rhayvin?"

I look around the group and find her with Theia. "DADDY!" I pick her up and hold her tight, walking back to Nova.

"How long have they been gone for?"

Dorian and Rhyatt walk up as Dorian looks between me and Nova. "Why do you look consternated, Rhydian?"

Rhyatt guffaws. "How do you know he's constipated? That's weird, Dorki."

Dorian pinches his nose with a sigh. "Consternated. Not consti-pated. There's a difference."

"If you say so," Rhyatt snorts.

I ignore them and look at Nova again, anxiety welling up inside me. "Nova. Please. How long have they been gone for?"

She sits up straight, noticing my unease. "Shit. Umm. I don't know. I just know it's been awhile. I mean, I did give them a big order though, so that's probably the hold up."

"Wait, who's gone?" Rhyatt asks.

I ignore his question and ask Nova, "What booth did they go to?"

"I think they were maybe going to start on one end and work their way down."

"Daddy, what's wrong?"

I kiss her head. "Nothing, baby. Here, go back to Auntie Theia." Theia looks at me with concern and quickly grabs Rhayvin. I kiss Rhayvin's head again, "I love you."

Without a word, I head towards the food booths, Rhyatt following beside me. I look in every direction as I move, my heart feels like it's beating out of my chest. I put my hands on my head, looking everywhere. Something's wrong. *This isn't right. Fuck, fuck, fuck.* "OPHELIA?!" I feel the veins in my neck bulging out as I scream.

I can hear everyone talking over comms, but I can't make out anything they're saying. As soon as I say *bird* she'll shout back, I know it. She has to. "LITTLE BIRD?!"

Come on, come on, come on. Give me that attitude about you being my raven.

Rhyatt starts frantically shouting as well. "LORE?!"

We both start rubbing the ache in our chests, feeling each other's pain and worry. "LITTLE SUCCUBUS?!"

I cringe when an obnoxious ringing hits the ear piece. Viking is now shouting over the line. "GUYS?! WHAT'S GOING ON?! DO YOU COPY?!"

I grit my teeth. "COPY! We have a situation! Ophelia and Lore are missing. Everyone fan out."

I reach the food booth at the end and notice a busted cup on the ground. I kneel down and look around the area. The light from above shines down and I notice the light glinting off something. I crawl across the ground and find scattered black beads, some of them lettered beads. I stare at them, immediately recognizing, **L**

O R E.

"RHY!" Rhyatt rushes over and drops to his knees. He looks at the beads in my head and shakes his head.

"No. No fucking way. No." He rips the beads from my palm and starts picking up the rest, "No. Not possible." He shoves the beads in his pocket and pulls out his phone. "Come on, come on, come on. God dammit, Lore! PICK UP THE PHONE!"

Not again. This can't be happening again. I whip my head back where Rhayvin is with everyone else and shout over comms. "GET MY LITTLE GIRL OUT OF HERE NOW!"

I spot a red bead a little ways away from Lore's beads and pick it up, turning it over in my fingers. A ringing fills my ears, sharp and unrelenting, and the world narrows to a tunnel. Another bead— a green one this time — catches my eye. Behind me, Rhyatt's voice cuts through the haze, sharp and frantic.

"LORE! OPHIE!"

The beads lead me further as I go and stand and stare at the letters I just picked up.

M A M A.

Everything spins as I stare at the letters. I squeeze my eyes shut, feeling out of control, hoping when I open them I won't find those letters staring back at me. I slowly open my eyes, seeing them still in front of me. The beads blur as my vision swims, and my chest tightens until it feels like I can't breathe. I shake my head, no, this isn't happening. I follow the beads and stop at the last one, spinning in a circle.

"OPHELIA! LORE!"

I scream their names, over and over, until my throat feels like sandpaper.. Reality kicks me in the fucking gut. I double over, retching onto the pavement, my stomach twisting itself into knots. The sour taste fills my mouth, but I barely register it. I stand up and wipe my mouth, walking around the parking lot, looking for any other sign. I feel a grip on my shoulder and I yank away. "DON'T FUCKING TOUCH ME!" I snarl.

Rhys is standing there with his hands up. "Hey, easy, baby brother. I know this is tough, but you need to keep your head in the game."

"YOU DON'T KNOW SHIT!"

He holds one hand up and the other out towards me, walking with slow, measured steps. "Yes, I do. I know what you're feeling right now. Nova's been taken from me before, too. We have to breathe. We have to focus. Ophelia needs you to do that. Do you hear me?"

I spit, my mouth bitter with vomit. "I can't do this again, man. Not again. What the fuck am I supposed to tell my daughter? She's gonna ask where her mama is. Her aunt. What the fuck do I say?" My voice cracks. I take a deep breath, trying and failing to get my emotions in check.

"I'M NOT FUCKING LEAVING! GET THE FUCK AWAY FROM ME! LORE! COME ON, BABY GIRL, WHERE ARE YOU?!"

I look where Rhyatt is, pulling away from Dorian and screaming throughout the parking lot. I bring my fist to my chest, hitting it over and over.

Focus, focus, focus.

My family needs me. I crack my neck and walk towards Rhyatt.

I grip his shoulder tight as he shouts, "NO!"

"Rhy. We have to go."

He looks at me like I've lost my mind. I have. "What the fuck do you mean we have to go? Our girls are gone, Rhydian!"

My voice cracks, feeling his pain and my own. "I… I know. But we have to," I hunch over, holding my knees and breathing deep. "We have to… we're gonna…"

Rhyatt grabs me, pulling me into a rough hug, gripping me tight. "We have to find them, Rhyd. We have to. This… We gotta find them, Rhydi."

I hold him back just as tight, repeating myself as I nod against his shoulder. "I know, I know, I know."

I close my eyes and I remember the night I lost her the first time. This feels worse than that. Much worse. Lightning strikes in the sky as rain pours down upon us. *Why is there always a storm when I lose my little raven?*

"And once the storm is over, you won't remember how you made it through, how you managed to survive. You won't even be sure, whether the storm is really over. But one thing is certain. When you come out of the storm, you won't be the same person who walked in. That's what this storm's all about."

-Haruki Murakami, Kafka on the Shore

CHAPTER TWENTY-TWO

HEARTBEAT

Ophelia

The gravel crunches underneath the truck tires as we leave the carnival grounds. My heart sinks as the truck turns out of the parking lot. I turn my head to check in with Lore. She's sitting stiff as a board, trembling, her wide eyes darting around like a cornered animal. When I lean in to check on her, she looks at me blankly, her breathing shallow.

I lean in to check on her and we both freeze at the sight of a gun being placed between us.

A man with a deep, raspy voice says, "There you are, sweetheart. I was looking everywhere for you."

I tremble in fear and slowly turn my head, looking at the man holding the gun. The cab light illuminates the truck and my eyes widen when I recognize the man sitting there. Tousled brown hair, dark eyes, and dimples that form with his smirk as he chews on a toothpick. It's the man whose picture I kept staring at, trying to place him. I tilt my head, my voice wobbly but low.

"I know you, don't I?"

"Normally," he drawls, "it'd hurt my feelings real bad that a pretty girl like you doesn't remember my name. But for you…" He pauses, the grin sharpening into something colder. "I'll make an exception." I grit my teeth, forcing myself not to recoil as he leans forward, the gun still trained on me. If this is my final moment, I refuse to cower.

"Our previous encounters were… fleeting."

As if to finalize his statement, a crack of lightning illuminates the sky, followed by pouring rain. The wipers squeal as they fly back and forth across the windshield, barely keeping up with the downpour. I watch as we turn onto a side road bordered by trees and the truck stops. The headlights cut through the darkness just enough to reveal a vehicle in front of us. The man in back leans forward again, the seat beneath him squeaking.

"Alright, ladies. My name is Howl, and I'll be your guide this evening. I know Silas told you if you fought back at the carnival, we would hurt your family. The threat still stands. I'm going to let you out of the truck and you're going to walk to that vehicle without a fight. Understood?"

Lore and I both nod like bobbleheads. Every jostle of the truck has me on edge. We both jump when he slams his door shut and tremble when he opens ours. He points the gun at us and gestures wildly, "Out."

I push myself out of the truck and try to remain standing on shaky legs. I step aside for Lore, catching her arm as she stumbles. "I got you."

The ground has turned to mud from the rain, squelching beneath us with every step. Howl pats me down and pulls my phone out, then does the same to Lore. He throws both of them in the direction of the main road and turns to us, his gun raised. He flicks his wrist with a sharp motion. "Walk."

We obey, arm in arm, clinging to each other like a lifeline. We're soaked from the rain, shivering both from the cold and the fear that chokes us. I open the sliding door of the utility van and step in. I start to slip and grab hold of the driver's seat to keep from falling. I turn and reach out for Lore, helping her in. The man that goes by Howl steps in after us and waves his gun towards the bench seats. Lore stands frozen as she watches her dad jump in the driver's seat.

"Lore," I hiss, yanking on her arm, my voice sharp with urgency. She just stares at him, rainwater dripping from her hair onto the van floor. Once we're sitting down, Howl ducks as he walks through the van and pulls out two sets of handcuffs.

"Wrists."

Lore just stares at her dad, as if she's in a trance. I pick her wrists up first and Howl puts them on her. The metal clicks a few times and I watch as he puts his finger between the cuffs and her wrist.

"Make sure they're tight, Howl. My daughter is a slippery little bitch," Silas seethes. Howl tightens Lore's cuffs, shaking his head with a heavy sigh. Why is he so reluctant to harm her when they live off doing that very thing? He steps in front of me and I put my wrists out. He loops my arm under hers and then slaps the handcuffs on me. My wrists pinch as he tightens them. He mumbles and I swear it's an apology.

"Lore?" She stares blankly at her dad, her gaze unwavering. It's hit or miss if pain will pull someone from dissociating, but I have to try. I grab one of her cuffed wrists and tighten it more. She sucks in air and glares down at her wrist and at me,

"Oww, Ophelia."

"I'm sorry, I'm sorry. I had to. Listen. I know you're having a hard time right now with whatever memories plague you, but we're going to need to help each other out, okay? I'll be here for you with whatever you're remembering, but I'm really going·to need your help, too. They're taking me back to that place," my heart pounds and my stomach rolls as I suck in air, "that place where," I shake my head, focus, Ophelia. "That place where I remember all of the bad things that happened. I was free. I'm supposed to be free. Please help me, Lore. I'll help you, too, okay?"

"Of course, of course," she nods. She shakes her head, a grimace marring her features. "I'm sorry. This has to be incredibly difficult for you, too. Yes, I'll help you."

After driving around for what felt like hours, I finally feel the van lurch as we stop. Howl slides a black pillowcase over Lore's head and then covers mine. The fabric is breathable, but I still feel like I'm suffocating with the fabric flapping inside my mouth every time I breathe in. The van rumbles as it's shut off and I hear the door slide open. Lore yelps and then I'm tumbling over, I can only guess she's being dragged, which in turn drags me with her. I feel like I'm free-falling and then I'm yanked back by my shirt. I grit my teeth, forcing myself to shut the fuck up. The scent of animal shit wafts through the pillowcase and my eyes water as I gag.

I really hope this isn't pig shit, because if it is, that only means one thing. This is our final destination. My shoes dig into the gravel as we walk, and there's a loud creak coming from somewhere in front of us. The harsh crunch of the gravel below us becomes softer, almost muted. I hear scraping metal and whip my head behind me when the sound is now behind me. There's grunting and shuffling noises ahead of us. I feel a whoosh of air and then the only sound that can be heard is our breathing.

I close my eyes, trying to focus on what else I can hear and smell, when the pillowcase is ripped off my head. I squint at the harsh light surrounding us. We're surrounded by metal walls and flooring, a square country-style throw rug covering most of it. Silas pulls back the rug, revealing a floor hatch connected to it. He tosses it open, the door slamming down next to us. Lore and I stumble over each other trying to jump away. He looks up at us, laughing at our expense, until his laugh turns into a wet cough. Spittle flies from his mouth as his face turns red. He jabs his finger down, gasping for air. "Get. Down. There. Now."

I take a step forward but am jolted back when Lore doesn't move. There's a gleam in her eye as she watches Silas practically hack up a lung. I pull her closer to me.

"Lore, let's go."

She briefly closes her eyes and opens them, finally looking at me. "Yeah, sorry."

I look down and see a dimly lit, metal staircase. "You hold one rail, I'll hold the other, okay?"

"Okay," her voice shakes. A rattle of clacking noises echo in the tiny space as we all walk down the stairs. The space narrows further as we reach a metal door with a keypad next to it. The air grows colder with every step, seeping into our skin. Lore and I shiver, our teeth chattering.

"Move." Silas snarls and shoves Lore, making her slam into me. We grab each other, trying to stay steady. He rubs his forearm across his forehead trying to wipe away the sweat dripping down. With his back to us, he looks over his shoulder while punching in the code. The keypad beeps, followed by a click of the door. Silas pushes the door open all the way and stands in front of it, crossed arms and panting like he ran a marathon.

God, I hope he has the most drawn out heart attack ever.

We jerk forward when Howl nudges our backs with the gun. We walk in and my heart shatters. My breath catches, and Lore lets out a shaky gasp as we're forced forward into the room beyond. There were never this many girls before. In the center of the room are at least ten naked girls, teenagers and young adults, one even looks like she could be a fucking preteen. My eyes water at the realization that this could have been Rhayvin if we didn't get her out. They all huddle together and tremble in fear. Tear-stained cheeks and eyes wide in fear, waiting for what's to come.

"Uncuff them, Howl."

The cuffs click as he frees us from them and we both rub the burning, tingly sensation in our wrists.

"Get naked," Silas barks.

Lore murmurs over and over, "Not again, not again, not again."

I tilt my head to catch her eye and grip her arm tight to get her attention. "Lore."

She looks up at me, her eyes brimming with tears and her bottom lip trembling.

"I know this fucking sucks. I'm so sorry, but it's so much worse if we don't comply."

My movements are jerky, reluctant, but I manage to yank the hoodie off and throw it to the floor. She follows suit and starts removing her clothes as well.

"FASTER!" Silas' shout slices through the room like a whip. Everyone jumps and the girls huddled on the floor gasp and whimper, trying to shrink into themselves. Quickly removing the rest of our clothes, Howl picks them up and opens a metal cabinet, where a fire roars inside. He throws the clothes in, they singe and sizzle before my eyes until he slams the cabinet shut.

"Howl, go prepare their meals. I'm going to mix the old with the new for a little bit."

Silas pulls out a chair and sits down, unzipping his pants. Lore sniffles behind me as he says, "Just like old times huh, Lore the whore?"

My nostrils flare as I breathe heavily, adding him to my mental list of people I kill in my head everyday. My eyes flick to the metal cabinet with a fire inside, and my first thought is shoving his head inside. In order to survive, will I in turn become my own brand of monster?

"I feel terrible, like there's a weight on my chest." -Howl, Howl's Moving Castle

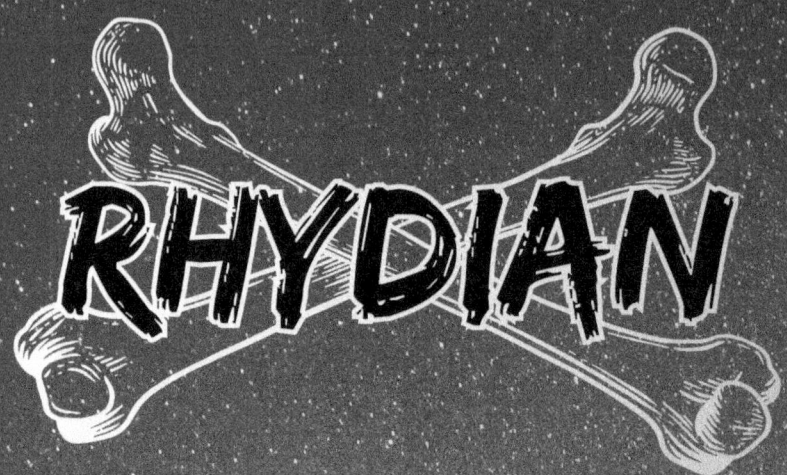

CHAPTER TWENTY-THREE

HAVE YOU EVER SEEN THE RAIN

November 2024

Rhydian

I cradle Rhayvin in my arms while she sleeps. With every stir and whimper, my grip around her tightens, reminding her that she is still safe. How do you convince your child they're safe when you couldn't even protect her mom and aunt?

As soon as the rest of us got back to the warehouse, she ran to me and looked around, asking where her mom and Auntie Lo were. I choked on the words, trying to find a way to tell her the devastating news. She flailed against my chest, sobbing that we needed to save them from the bad, bad men. I thought my heart was aching before, but witnessing my child crumble in my arms completely shattered it. I failed my family. Again. I vowed to protect them, and in one night I broke it. I have to find them.

I carefully stand with her in my arms. I look around the room while everyone quietly discusses plans. Dorian sent different angles of footage to a few, and everyone is combing through it. My heart races and I can't seem to get my feet to move in a proper direction. I take a few steps to the right, freeze, and then move to the left. The room around me fades and all I hear is my racing heart and harsh breaths.

Rhayvin is pulled from my arms and I shout, "NO!" Not her, too.

Everything comes into focus and Nova is cradling Rhayvin in her arms, covering her ears, while Rhys is standing in front of them. I look at Rhayvin, making sure I didn't wake her up or scare her and put my hands up. "I'm sorry. I'm sorry," I pant. I run my hands down my face and take a deep breath.

"We need to get Deacon. I can break him. He'll talk."

Rhyatt stomps over, jaw clenched. "Me too. I want them all."

I nod and we both look at Dorian. "I want to look at every bit of footage of Deacon, and every angle of the girls at the food booth."

Dorian looks at us remorsefully. "About that."

"What?!" I snap.

"The carnival grounds themselves don't have any surveillance, other than the food booths, and they're pointed at the registers. I can pull audio, but there won't be a view of them. Our best footage is the parking lot. A few of the street lights have cameras."

I shake with rage and bite my tongue, trying not to shout and wake Rhayvin. "Please tell me that footage will give us something, *anything*," I seethe.

He nods. "We'll get answers. The good news is, there are houses along the roads around there. Maybe some of those people have cameras we can hack into. We're going to do everything we can."

I look at Nova. "Can you guys stay with Rhayvin while I do what I have to?"

"Don't ask stupid questions, Rhydian. Of course we'll watch her. I'll protect her like she's my own. Go get them back."

Breathing in, I sigh and step around Rhys, dropping a kiss to Rhayvin's head. "Thank you, Nova."

I look at the clock on the wall and see we have about thirty minutes until school is out for the day. "Dorian, will you guys keep looking and let us know what you find when we get back?" He starts to respond when Rhys steps forward.

"Back from where?"

"We're getting Deacon."

"Fine, but you're not going alone."

"We're not alone, Rhyatt and I have each other."

Rhys glares and crosses his arms. "Excuse me? No," he shakes his head with an unamused chuckle. "No. There is no more you and Rhyatt against the world. You have us and we have you. I will not lose you two. Both of you are angry and on edge. How many times now have you zoned out? You cannot afford distractions like that. It's not safe and you'll fuck up. Do I make myself clear?"

I feel like a small child every goddamn time he goes all big brother on us. I cross my arms, my jaw clenched. "Fine."

"It's cheating to go all big brother on us like that when we're upset, ya know," Rhyatt pouts.

Rhys' lip twitches, suppressing a smile, and points towards the door. "Armory. Now."

Walking back to the conference room, I nudge Rhyatt. "Do you think they'll even agree to this?"

He shrugs. "It's worth a shot, and if not, we'll figure out a way to pull it off."

"Good luck convincing Dor," Rhys chuckles from behind us.

Rhyatt scoffs, "Oh, come on. We're the Slater bros, it should be totally fine. He trusts us." The three of us just stand there once we reach the conference room.

I elbow Rhyatt again. "Ask."

He returns the gesture with his own quiet outburst. "You ask."

"It was your idea, bitch." The group all stares at us while we go back and forth.

"Fine, jerk!" Rhyatt takes a deep breath and looks at Dorian and Theia. He scratches the back of his neck with a nervous chuckle. "Hey, umm, question."

Dorian and Theia both look at each other puzzled and back at us.

"Yeah?" Theia asks with some hesitation.

"So we had this idea," Rhyatt begins, his words tumbling over themselves, "to get Deacon to pull over and help us on his way home. I was thinking of using those window marker things and writing like a homecoming proposal on the back window."

He turns and looks at Rhys, "I swear I'll wash Beauty."

Rhys narrows his eyes. "You're not just washing her window, you're washing all of her, and you're going to do a damn good job. Full detailing."

"I said I would," Rhyatt whines. "Anyway, we figured Deacon would be more willing to help if it was a young girl he saw that needed help, rather than us. So, heh, what do ya say, Theia? Wanna pretend to be a high school girl?"

Theia opens her mouth to respond as Dorian shakes his head. "Yeah, no, that's not happening."

She glares at him. "Excuse you?"

He shrinks like a kicked puppy. "I just... oh come on, sunshine. It's dangerous."

"We'll keep her safe. You know this," I step in.

She lifts a brow and waves her hand towards us. "See. I'll be safe."

"I don't like it."

"You have surveillance to look at. You can stay here and not like it, while I go help," Theia snaps. Her voice softens slightly. "It would be nice to do something useful to help get the girls back, so I'm doing it."

For a moment, Dorian stares at her, clearly torn. I see it then—the subtle flicker in his eyes. When he speaks again, it's Atlas, not Dorian, facing us. "You will keep her safe. No harm comes to her. Not even a fucking scratch."

I nod in agreement as Rhyatt interjects. "Okay, but what if she accidentally scratches herself? We can't be held accountable for that."

I pinch the bridge of my nose. "Let's go."

"How much time do I have to get ready?" Theia asks.

"The amount of time it takes for me to write the homecoming message on the back window." Rhyatt responds.

She slaps her thighs and stands. "Okay, then." She puts her hair up in a messy bun, pulling down a couple strands by her face. She pulls on her shirt, showing her cleavage and I look away.

Rhyatt is more dramatic about it, throwing his hands up. "Ayo! Come on! Oh my god, is this what it's like to have a sister who does stuff that creeps you out?"

"Oh my god, calm down," she snorts. She ties the hem of her shirt and tucks it in the back. She then rolls her skirt a few times to shorten it and even I feel grossed out.

"Seriously, you too, Rhydian?"

I put my hands up, shaking them. "I'm sorry, I'm sorry. It's just weird."

Dorian watches her with a mix of resignation and desire. She quickly kisses Dorian and pulls away as he tries to reach for her. "I love you, I'll be safe."

In a daze, he responds, "Luh-yoo."

"Alright, let's head out. We need to beat him out there."

We walk out to Beauty, where Rhys and Theia take the front seat. Rhyatt pulls out the window chalk and writes, **HOCO OR NAH, BABY GIRL?** I curl my lip and look at him. "Really? That's the best you could come up with?"

"What? I'm hip with the way these kids talk. Watch. He'll believe it."

I shake my head and we jump in the back of Rhys' truck as he starts it. Rhyatt crawls up to the seat and leans over it to talk to Theia. "Okay, so all you have to do is stare under the hood like you're really confused. He'll pull over and try to pretend he's some white fucking knight and help you. Just act really confused, like *'oh no it stopped working and won't start again.'* He'll most likely ask if you have jumper cables or tools. Tell him you have them in the back of the truck."

She nods and takes a deep breath. "Okay. I can do that."

I kneel next to Rhyatt and tap Theia's shoulder. "Listen. We'll be right here the whole time. Nothing will happen to you. Plus, this guy just points them in the right direction. He doesn't do the kidnapping, okay? When you go to open the back, just act like it's stuck and you need his help. When he steps in to help, you move to the passenger side of the truck, out of the way. We'll take it from there."

Rhys pulls over to the side of the road and puts his emergency lights on, shutting the truck off and pocketing the keys. He pops the hood of the truck and unbuckles, turning to look at all of us. "Alright. Plan is in place. Theia, are you sure you're good with this? We can find another way."

She quickly shakes her head, unbuckling, "No. I can do this. I want to help. Please, let me help."

He opens his window a crack. "Alright. Just remember, it's okay if he sees you nervous. If you think you're showing too much nervousness, pull the shy, naive act. Okay?"

She nods, hopping out of the truck and opening the hood. She hops, trying to push it all the way up. The hood squeaks and Rhys sits there flinching, dying to jump out and help. "God. She's hurting my Beauty. I can't watch this."

We move out of the way as he crawls in the back with us, plugging his ears. She finally gets the hood propped up and I slap his leg, nodding towards the front.

"She's got it."

"Finally. And everyone wonders why I don't want anyone messing with Beauty. That was painful."

Our phones all buzz in unison and we pull them out.

DORIAN: Is she okay?

DORIAN: Is everything okay?

DORIAN: She's safe, right?

DORIAN: Hello?

"Rhys, call your bestie and tell him to chill," Rhyatt says with a chuckle.

The line barely connects before Dorian's voice explodes through the speaker. "IS EVERYTHING OKAY? WHY AREN'T YOU GUYS ANSWERING?"

Rhys pulls the phone away from his ear, grimacing. "Dude. Chill. She's fine. Quit distracting us so we can focus on her safety, Dori."

"Don't you call me that right now, Reese's Pieces! I'm worried!"

"Okay, I get it, you're worried, but you distracting us isn't helpful, now is it?"

Rhyatt crawls closer. "Hey, hey! Request." He snatches the phone from Rhys. "Hey, Dorian. Tell someone to make a quick run to the store. Tell them to grab a random doll. Any doll, totally doesn't matter." There's a pause in the conversation and I see the gleam in Rhyatt's eyes. "Please. It's important. Just get someone to do it. Probably best if it's one of the girls. Might look weird if one of the dudes do it. Okay. Okay. OKAY! Sorry, krrrr, sorry, bad, krrrr, reception."

CHAPTER TWENTY-THREE

He hangs up the phone and tosses it to Rhys, laughing.

"What the fuck is the doll for?" I ask.

Rhyatt's smile grows. "Necessary evil."

"Incoming," Rhys warns. I look out the back window and recognize Deacon's car. We all lay down and keep an ear out.

"Wait! Wait! Pull over! Please help!" Theia shouts in a high-pitched tone. "OH THANK GOD!" She shouts louder.

"Hey there, everything okay?"

"Oh my god, Mr. Foster! Thank you so much for stopping! My daddy is going to be so mad at me. I don't know what happened. It just stopped working. And then every time I tried to start it, it made creepy noises."

"You one of my students?"

She giggles obnoxiously. "Duh, Mr. Foster. GO TIGERS!"

"Mhmm, go Tigers is right. So, uh, were there any warning lights that popped up beforehand?"

"Ohhhh. There were a lot of them. Is that wrong?"

The guy chuckles. "Yeah, sweetie, that's not good. It could be a bad creepy sound, or something as little as the battery. Do you have any cables?"

"Cables? I'm not allowed to have a tv in the car."

I bite my lip to stop from laughing, while Rhys and Rhyatt slap their hands over their mouths. Theia is way too good at this. "I'm sure there's something in the back I can use to help you."

Theia gasps. "You think so?"

His voice deepens, making my skin crawl. "I know if I was your daddy, I'd have just the tool for you to use."

"R-really?" she stammers.

"Mhmm. Let's go take a look, sweetie."

"Okay. Thank you again, Mr. Foster."

I hear the handle on the back of the truck move and we all slowly kneel, ready to pounce. I crack my neck, pushing back images of bashing his face in over and over.

"Ugh, it's stuck!" She whines.

"Here, sweetie. Let me give it a try."

"Oh, thank you. Darn thing won't move." There's a slight tap on the passenger's side, letting us know she's out of the way. The back easily opens and I watch his smile morph into surprise.

"What the-" I leap towards him and tackle him to the ground.

"Ahhh! What is happening?!" He tries to push and pull at me, wriggling beneath me.

"Shut the fuck up, Deacon!" I scream and punch him in the face. His head flies to the right, blood flying from his mouth. Images of a terrified Ophelia flash in my mind and I see red. I barely register that I haven't stopped punching him until I'm pulled back and I roar, "NO!"

"Easy, little brother. He'll get what's coming to him, but not here in the open." My chest heaves while I try to calm down. "I'm fine, I'm fine. Let go."

Rhys slaps me over the chest. "Good. Then let's get this fucker in the back."

I feel a drop on my cheek and look up as the rain falls harder. I look down and watch as it washes away the blood I spilled.

CHAPTER TWENTY-THREE

"I will destroy you in the most beautiful way possible. And when I leave, you will finally understand why storms are named after people." - Caitlyn Siehl

CHAPTER TWENTY-FOUR
FIRE IN THE WATER

Ophelia

Silas throws a baking sheet full of food between us all. It looks like bread and some sort of veggie and meat slop that's already soaking the bread. Some of the girls divide the meal up for everyone. Each girl huddles closer and gives a majority of their small portion to the little girl. One of the oldest girls waves Lore and Lover.

"We just got here. Split my portion."

"Mine too," Lore whispers.

Without hesitating, all the girls slide our portions to the little girl's pile of food as well. The little girl trembles and whispers, "You guys need it, too."

"You keep your strength, honey. We're okay," I smile halfheartedly, shaking my head. Missing my family more than ever, I extend my pinky to her. "Promise."

Trembling, she reaches forward and hooks our pinkies.

"Eat up."

She pulls away to eat her portion. The other girls take their bites in silence, then, without looking, slide the next one closer to her.

"Is this all you guys get for the day?"

One younger girl finishes her bite and mutters, "Depends on their mood."

I spin my wedding ring round and round, grateful they haven't taken it from me. The door clicks open and I freeze at the sound of the voice that follows.

"You've come back to me. I knew you would."

I squeeze my eyes shut. *No, no, no. I'm not ready*. I look down at the grip on my left hand. Lore holds me close and my breath hitches as she slowly pulls my wedding ring off.

"I'll keep it safe," she whispers.

My eyes brim with tears as I look at her and mouth, '*thank you*'.

I can feel him behind me before he says another word and my whole body tenses. My hair flutters as he breathes against my ear, practically panting. "Aren't you happy to see me, piccolo prigioniero?" I bite my tongue until I taste the sharp tang of blood in my mouth. I desperately want to fight back. Part of me thinks for just a moment that I'm free to do so because Rhayvin isn't here, she's safe. Until I hear a small whimper and look over, catching the look on the youngest girl's face. All I see is Rhayvin when I look at her. I can't let them hurt her. My eyes flick around every girl huddled together and they all morph into Rhayvin.

"Hello, Aldo," my voice cracks. He nuzzles my neck, inhaling my scent.

"I'm very upset with you," he growls. The only warning I have is the subtle brush of his fingers through my hair, before he grips it tight and yanks me up. I yelp, quickly scrambling to my feet. My scalp stings with how tight he's gripping my hair. He starts walking, using my hair as a leash. I fist my hands at my sides until I feel the pinch of my nails against my palms. I look at the terrified girls and mouth, 'it's okay'.

He drags me into one of the rooms and kicks the door shut, shoving me to the ground. As I land on my hands and knees, sharp pain shoots through my wrists and my knees. "Stand."

The ache in my wrists and knees slows me down. He kicks me in the center of my back, sending me sprawling down. The soles of his shoes scrape my back and I bite back a scream.

"I said stand."

I stand up, gritting my teeth. *I am standing you fucking piece of shit.*

"Turn."

I slowly turn to face him and he smirks. "Mad, are we? Your anger is nothing compared to mine." I keep my head up, holding his stare. "Arms up."

I bring my arms above my head, and my body shakes harder the closer he gets. The cold metal bites into my wrists as he cuffs them both to a chain. The jingle of the chain as he picks it up is my only warning before it's yanked, pulling my arms up higher. I grit my teeth, my shoulders screaming in pain due to the unnatural angle.

He connects the chain to a hook to hold me in place and slowly circles me like a vulture. So much for breaking free of my chains. He runs his fingers down my ribs and stops at my stomach, pinching it. "You've really let yourself go. We'll have to work on that." He draws a lazy circle on my stomach and pats it. "Is this weight gain due to another pregnancy? Hmm?"

Even with all my years with him, I'm honestly still not sure what the best answer is here, so I remain silent.

"We won't be making love tonight, piccolo prigioniero. I'm too angry with you."

He pulls his phone out of his pocket and the familiar tune that haunts my nightmares begins playing. I barely have time to brace myself as he rears back. Pain blooms across my cheek with the first hit. Heat radiates from the sting, my jaw hurting and my tongue sore from biting it. I take a deep breath and brace for the next hit.

"You earned this for leaving me."

The next hit is directed at my ribs. Pain bursts through me and my shoulders throb as I sag against the chains. I look up and attempt to stand up tall to get some relief. The sight of the chain reminds me of Rhydian and all the work he did to help me heal. *My Bones. I need my Bones.* My thumb twitches towards my ring finger, as if to twirl the ring that's no longer there.

"Mama, Mama, I want this one!" I glance over at Rhayvin, who is holding a pretty white dress up with a purple ribbon around the middle. She jumps up and down, shaking it towards me. I smile and kneel down in front of her.

"This is beautiful, just like you. This is what you want to wear?"

"Yes, yes, yes. Pwease."

I can't help but laugh at her enthusiasm. "Of course you can get this one. Will you help Mama pick hers out?"

She throws her dress in the cart and grabs hold of my hoodie. "Let's go, Mama." Lore follows behind us as we go to the women's section.

"Lore, feel free to wear whatever you want. I don't want you to be uncomfortable."

She pushes her glasses up her nose and nods her voice soft, "Thank you."

I feel a sharp pinch to my nipple and scream. With labored breaths, I look down and watch as Aldo continues to twist and pinch it.

"There you are. Pay attention to me, Aria. You owe me that much."

My body aches and feels wet, unsure of all the damage my body has endured. Another punch to the face has my eyes rolling back. Everything blurs and then nothing.

I bounce on my toes, waiting in the bathroom for our cue to walk. Rhayvin walks out with her flower petals. I peek out the bathroom door and watch as she drops petals as she goes. Every few steps, she does a twirl while throwing petals up in the air and giggling. She hugs Rhydian's leg and then gives a knuckle bump to Lore. Fire In The Water by Feist plays and Rhyatt loops my arm through his and pats my hand.

"You look beautiful, Ophie. You ready?"

I smile up at him. "Thank you, Rhy." I take a deep breath, preparing myself for what's ahead. "I'm ready."

He walks me out of the bathroom and into our living room. Rhydian looks up, and the moment our eyes meet, my breath hitches. The intensity of his stare freezes me in place, and it feels like nothing else exists. Nothing can break me from this moment as I watch his eyes look at me with desire and life-altering love. My cheeks ache with how big my smile is and I feel the sting of tears the moment I see his eyes water. Rhyatt hands me off and smacks Rhydian's chest.

"Now, listen here, boy. You take good care of my Ophie, ya hear?"

We all laugh and Rhydian pushes him to the side. He reaches for me and his first tear falls. "You're beautiful," his voice cracks.

I wipe his tear away and sniffle, "Aww, Bones." I feel a tug at the back of my dress and turn. Rhayvin is holding my dress and looking up at me smiling.

"Mama, you bootuhful."

I kneel down and smile. "Thank you, baby. I think you're the prettiest princess here."

"Auntie Lo is a pwetty pwincess, too."

I look at Lore and back at Rhayvin, smiling. "That's right. You're both very pretty princesses. Auntie Lore is more of a badass goth baddie though."

Her face scrunches. "Auntie Lo not bad."

I throw my head back and laugh. "You're right. Can I marry your Daddy now?"

She rolls her eyes, "Duh." I stand and turn to face Rhydian again, holding his hands.

"That's your daughter," we both say in unison and laugh.

I feel myself coming back to consciousness. *No, no, not before the best part.* My breathing slows once again and I'm out.

"I have my own vows prepared," Rhydian says before taking a deep breath.

"Ophelia. My beautiful, strong, little raven. Who would've thought two orphans like us would hit the family lottery? It all comes back to

you. You became the sister Rhyatt always needed, and you became the healing balm to my tattered soul. I never knew what home was until you. Every cheesy, sappy love cliché there is all make sense now. You're my lighthouse in the storm, my northern star. The bird that guides me back to its nest. You're the most incredible person I've ever known. You carried, birthed and raised our beautiful Rhayvin. She's the coolest kid ever, but also the kindest, smartest ray of sunshine. And that's cuz of you. I vow to do a better job of cleaning up after myself. I vow to be the husband you deserve and the father Rhayvin needs. I vow to always tell you that you're right when we argue, because let's be serious, you totally are. Without you, I was just a shell, a machine. With you, I'm whole and alive. You breathe life into me, pretty girl. And I vow to fiercely protect you and our daughter with everything I have. And when I feel like I can't give anymore, I'll push through and give more. I love you, Ophelia."

Tears fall down my face and I laugh. My heart is so full. I clear my throat, "I have my own vows as well. I can't believe you're making me follow that up, you show off."

He gently cradles my face, wiping away my fallen tears. With a shuddering breath, I start. "Woo. Okay. I can do this," *I fan my face in an attempt to compose myself.*

"Rhydian. My Bones. Ugh, thanks a lot for stealing the name thing at the beginning there. Make me look like I'm copying you. I knew you were a protector from the start. And I've been blessed to be protected by a man like you. But you are not just a protector. You are a healer. From the very beginning, you started to heal the broken little girl that was left abandoned and abused. You took my broken wings and mended them. You helped me fly again. Not once, but twice. You showed me that I was safe with you, that not all men are the same. I found my home with you. My safe place. My Bones. The foundation of my nest. You have always been so patient with me and understanding. You show me the pieces of myself that I find tarnished in a different light. You allow me to see myself through your eyes, and through them, I am beautiful and deserving of your love. You are an incredible father to our daughter. You're giving her everything we had wished for growing up. She knows what it is to be loved and protected. Cherished. You were the dream I was afraid to hope for, but am so happy I found. I love you, Rhydian."

"Whatever our souls are made of, his and mine are the same."

-Emily Bronte, Wuthering Heights

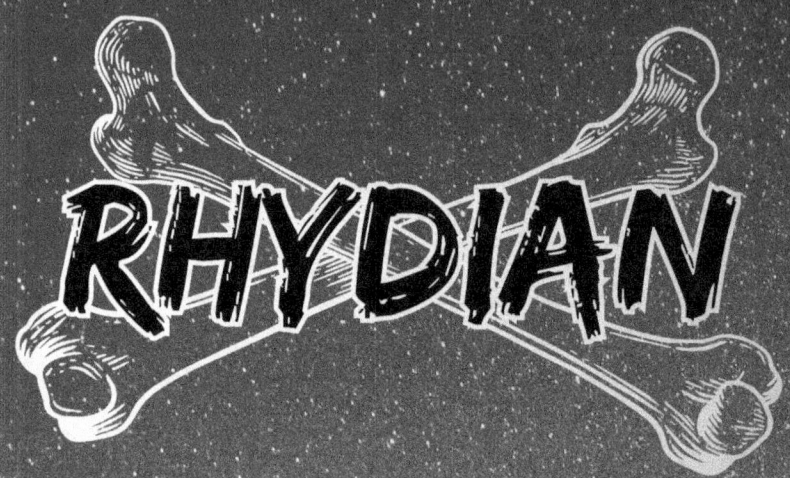

RHYDIAN

CHAPTER TWENTY-FIVE

WHERE'S MY LOVE

Rhydian

I sit on the edge of Rhayvin's bed and watch her sleep. "I'll get Mama back, little Rhay," I whisper, leaning forward and kissing her head. Before leaving her room, I stand by the door and watch her for a moment longer. I lightly tap the door frame and nod to Nova in thanks for keeping an eye on her. As I head to the play-room, I shed my role of father and let the monster within take over.

I walk in the playroom and pull down the hose that Rhys has on a pulley. I spray Deacon in the face with the freezing water and he gasps for air, sputtering on the water flying in his mouth.

"Rise and shine, bitch. It's Monday morning, class is in session."

He sputters and gags, his chest heaving violently as he tries—and fails—to catch his breath.

"Drink up. Don't want you dehydrated."

I release the handle and let the hose fly up into place above me, cold droplets hit my head while I wait for Deacon to shut the fuck up with his choking. He finally gasps for air, his chest heaving and then he starts to whimper.

"P-please. Please. You're making a big mistake. Why are you doing this?"

I walk up to him and raise my arm, swinging hard and back-handing him across the face. His head whips to the side and he yelps, crying harder.

"Shut the fuck up! Those poor women and children you hurt are fucking stronger than you."

He looks up at me with eyes wide with terror. "Wha-. I-I don't know what you're talking about," he sputters but looks away.

"Tch, looking away? That just won't do."

Shaking my head, I walk to the table and grab a pair of needle nose pliers and the surgical staple gun. When I turn, he tries to jump in his seat, unable to move while strapped down.

"No, no, no. What are you doing? Please no," he begs. Pinching his eyelid with the pliers, I peel it back against his forehead. He squeals and tries to shake his head. "You're making it worse for yourself, but please continue. At the rate you're going, the damn thing will tear off and I won't even need the stapler."

Deacon whimpers, his thrashing slows as sweat pours down his forehead. I force his eyelid to his brow with the pliers. Pushing the stapler against the two, I pull the trigger and the first one goes in. It clicks in place and his scream rips through the room. I grit my teeth, annoyed by the sound of him, and staple the rest of his eyelid to his brow. I move on to the next one and watch his eyes roll back as he passes out.

"Pussy."

I toss the pliers and staple gun on the table and sit on the edge of it. Rhyatt marches in with a grin on his face, holding a grocery bag.

"Ooo, perfect timing, he's passed out. Help me get him strapped to the gurney."

He quickly puts the bag on the table and rolls the gurney over. The two of us work in silence, unhooking the chains wrapped around Deacon's body. My knife slices clean through the duct tape binding him, and his limp form slumps forward. Rhyatt walks over and takes one arm while I take the other and we drag him to the gurney. His chest lands on the gurney with a thud and we each take a side as we haul him all the way up. Deacon groans and his body starts to twitch.

"Rhyatt, get the rope!" I demand, as I push my hands against Deacon's back, holding him down.

Deacon's screams are muffled by the gurney until he turns his head, screaming louder. "Let me go! Please!"

Rhyatt yanks on his arms and Deacon's face and chest slams down. Rhyatt tightly ties his arms together underneath the gurney. He kicks wildly, and I slam my elbow in the center of his back.

"Seriously, stop fucking moving. The more you fight, scream, and cry, the slower I will kill you."

He squeaks and nods his head before freezing in place. I pull a piece of rope away from Rhyatt and tie Deacon's knee to the hand rail. Rhyatt gets the other side and then we both work on tying his ankles to the rail as well.

"Get the hose ready, I have a feeling he's gonna make a mess," Rhyatt says with a smirk and an evil gleam in his eyes.

"Not yet."

Rhyatt stops and looks at me confused, "What do you mean not yet?"

"We have to try and get some answers."

Rhyatt rolls his eyes and groans, whining like a child. "Fiiiine."

I walk over to Deacon and grip his hair, pulling his head back. He yelps from the pain, his bloodshot eyes pleading.

"You help Aldo Cifarelli, yes?"

There's a flicker in his eyes and I know he's about to lie. He's more afraid of Aldo than me. Big mistake.

"I-I don't know who that is."

With a heavy sigh, I look down at him. "Sooner or later you're going to realize it's in your best interest not to lie to me." I lean in close to his face, my nostrils flaring.

"You know what's worse than the devil you know?" I spit in his face and he grimaces. "The devil you don't know."

I look at Rhyatt and nod, he pulls out a knife and slices the back of Deacon's pants open. Deacon's tries to move around, thrashing and flailing. "No! Oh god, please, no!"

"Shut up! You don't get to beg for mercy! You won't find it here." My voice cuts through his pathetic whimpering. "Just like those poor, defenseless girls found no mercy from you and those other fucking perverts. Believe me when I say this: You will know desperation. You will know fear. Pain. Embarrassment. Shame. But no matter how much damage we inflict, it will never compare to what you did to those innocent girls. This is for them."

I sneer down at him and then move to the end of the gurney across from Rhyatt. He pulls a *Barbie* from the grocery bag and I lift a brow. "What the fuck is that for? I know Rhys calls this the playroom, but it wasn't meant literally. Play with your dolls another time."

Rhyatt flips his imaginary long hair. "I can play with my dolls wherever I want."

"Seriously, whatever you're about to do, I've decided my daughter doesn't get any fucking dolls ever again."

"No worries there. I tried to give one to Rhay-Rhay and when I tell you the sass that came from her. Whoo! She did one of these," he puts his hands on his hips and pops one hip out. I can't help but chuckle, imagining Rhay standing exactly like that. "She told me 'Unca Why-Why, I don't pway wiff dolls anymoh. I'm a big gohl, duh.'"

"What would your daughter think, if she knew you were doing this to someone?" Deacons says. I freeze at his words, and I feel my body vibrate with anger. The air around me thickens with fury. I stomp over to him and grip his jaw tight, turning his head to the side. "You don't fucking talk about my daughter. Do you understand me?!"

I squeeze his jaw tighter and he whimpers, "I-I'm sorry, I-I just-"

I lean closer and scream, spit hitting his face. "YOU DON'T TALK ABOUT HER! TELL ME WHAT I WANT TO KNOW! WHERE DID THEY TAKE MY WIFE?!"

"I don't know what you're talking about!" He squeals.

"You work for them! You send them girls! You know! TELL ME!"

"I don't know, I don't know, I don't know. Please," he cries.

I look at Rhyatt. "Do it."

"What are you doing? What-what is happening. Don't do this, please!" His pleas turn into screams as Rhyatt starts pushing the feet of the doll into his ass.

"Sucks when someone puts something in you that you don't want, doesn't it?" Rhyatt's lip curls in disgust while he continues to push the doll further in. Sweat, snot and tears all mix together, running down his face. "How many of you were at the carnival that night? There was a plan in place. Break it down for us."

"I swear, I don't know. They don't tell me anything. I just point out the kids nobody will notice are gone. Kids people don't care about. In exchange... in exchange I get to play with who they have. That's it, I swear!"

"Ugh, dude, now get the hose! Fucking gross man!" Rhyatt shouts. I pull the hose down and see the mix of shit and piss pooling beneath him.

"Move, Rhy." He steps back, grimacing and I spray the hose at Deacon. He shouts from the freezing temperature, trembling when I stop spraying. I let go of the hose and step beside him again.

"Ugh, gross. I can't believe you forced yourself to shit to get that thing out." Rhyatt gags and shoves the doll back in, holding it in place. "Don't you fucking dare do that shit again!"

I look down at Deacon. "Who else is there when you go visit? How many?"

"Those of us that just visit never exchange names. I only know of two men there that work for them."

"NAMES!" I shout.

"S-Silas and-and H-Howl," he sputters.

"You done back there, Rhy?"

His jaw is clenched as he looks down at Deacon. "Yeah, I'm done." He pulls back and steps to the side in case Deacon tries to shit the doll out again. I nod and turn back towards Deacon.

"You pretend not to know the evil you have become and which you surround yourself with. You turn a blind eye." I jam my thumbs in his eye sockets and push. He screams as I push harder and his eyeballs burst like a spoon through gelatin. Blood and other liquids squirt over my thumbs as I keep pushing.

"See no evil." I pull my thumbs back and wipe them on my pants.

"My eyes! My eyes! I can't see!" He screams wildly.

"Hand me two sharps, doesn't matter what, Rhyatt."

Looking down at the table, he shakes his head while trying to pick something out. He carefully hands two scalpels over to me. "Hold his head face down."

Rhyatt nods and grips his hair tight, lifting his head up and then slamming it back down to the gurney. I hover above Deacon, pointing the scalpels next to each ear. "You pretend not to hear their screams and cries for help, for all of you to stop." I jam both of the scalpels deep into his ears and his guttural screams don't let up, his body trying to thrash, but unable to move much.

"Hear no evil."

I rip one of the scalpels out and a squirt of blood chases the blade.

"It's a shame you can't hear this or see it coming now. It's your turn to be stopped from shouting what you're desperate for. Just like them."

I slice his tongue down the middle, blood pooling in his mouth. Unable to stop, I yank the scalpel out and shout, "SPEAK NO EVIL, BITCH!"

I press the scalpel just below his ear, pushing deep and then slide it across his neck. His muffled shouts now morph into labored gurgles and chokes as he drowns in his own blood. In almost mirrored movements, Rhyatt and I rub our fist over our hearts and drop to our knees, screaming. All this bloodshed will never fill the void, but it will feed the beast I need to be. They will all suffer just as we have.

"Nothing about me is original. I am the combined effort of everyone I've ever known."
-Chuck Palahniuk

OPHELIA

CHAPTER TWENTY-SIX

MY BLOOD

November 2024

Ophelia

I wake up to the sound of hushed whispers. All of us are huddled together for warmth, and I'm hoping none of them wake up and interrupt the conversation. I steady my breathing and keep my eyes shut, hoping to gain new information from them.

"At the end of the day, this is your operation. But I have to tell you some things I've observed. Is that alright?"

It takes everything in me not to tense up when I hear Aldo respond, "Spit it out, Howl."

"I know your plan was to sell Lettie, the youngest, first. But I don't think that will go over too well. I think she needs to be sold last. The only thing keeping the rest of them in check and not fighting us is that little girl. You get rid of her and they will team up against whoever is here at the time."

"I see your point. Also, don't call her Lettie. They no longer have names. I'll message you about that later today. Anyway, from what you've seen, who would they care less about leaving?"

"Obviously, your girl is off the table."

Aldo growls while I swallow the bile threatening to spill at being called his.

"As much as she'll lash out, I think Lore would be best. The other girls haven't known her as long. They'd be upset, but they're not close enough yet for them to care. I can take care of transport and everything."

Aldo clicks his tongue. "As tempting as that is, no. I bought her from Silas years ago. She needs to pay her dues just as he has. Take a day. Keep an eye out and let me know the next best option. I have to find another person to help us find girls. Deacon Foster has disappeared. You know what that means."

"It's those fucks from before, isn't it?"

"Yes," he seethes. "Keep me posted."

I hear the beeps of the code being put into the keypad and then the click of the door before it opens.

As the door shuts, I slowly release the breath I was holding. My breath hitches when Howl whispers behind me, "You can stop pretending to be asleep now."

I wait until his footsteps fade away to crack my eyes open. My eyes adjust to the dim lighting of the room, and watch as he walks down the hall that leads to the small kitchen.

"Girls. Time to get up."

I whisper and shake each one of them awake. "Hurry. Wake up. Howl is in the kitchen and Aldo just left."

A few of the girls quietly whimper. "Shh, shh. It's okay, you're okay. Remember. We need to be alert to everything. They're trying to decide who to sell next. They want it to be whoever they think we won't fight for. I know Lore and I are the newest here, but if we want to survive we need to show that we're all united. This doesn't mean fight and rebel right now. We need to bide our time. We have to be smart about this."

I hear Howl's footsteps grow louder and immediately stop talking about it. I quickly change the subject and look at all the girls. "How is everyone feeling? I think it's almost breakfast time."

Everyone's eyes flicker around our group and each murmurs.

"Good."

"Hungry."

"Tired."

"Lettie, honey, why don't you curl up a bit, okay? Hug your knees." She nods and quickly hugs her knees, the rest of us scooting in as close as we can.

Howl walks in whistling and carrying a tray of breakfast for all of us. I try to hide the way I watch his every move and my confusion with him. Whenever Silas feeds us, it's like pigs eating slop from a trough. When Howl does, he makes sure to provide all of us with our own bowls or plates and plasticware. The only thing he makes us share is a pitcher of water, milk or juice.

"Alright, eat up girls. You'll need the fuel to get you through today."

He sets the tray down behind me and Lore and then walks over to his chair. He sits down and starts scrolling through his phone, not even paying attention to us. He looks up and narrows his eyes. He pulls his toothpick from his mouth and barks, "Eat!"

Some of the girls yelp in fear and curl in on themselves, as Lore and I start handing everyone their own bowl of oatmeal. I grab my bowl last and stir the peanut butter and sliced banana around. That's another difference when he feeds us. We don't have to share with Lettie when he cooks. He provides a healthy amount of food to fill us all up. Howl's phone pings and I can't help but glance over. He hasn't noticed me staring yet, and I watch as his jaw clenches at whatever message he received. My eyes fall to his chest, noticing he's wearing two necklaces with matching pendants. The only difference is one has a blue jewel and the other has a red one. He shoves his phone back in his pocket and I quickly look down at my bowl, taking a bite.

Hours have passed and the door sounds, alerting us to someone coming in. We all brace ourselves for whoever it is, and I feel Lore tense up beside me as the open door reveals her father. He's carrying a duffel bag in his hand and smirks. He zeroes in on Lore.

"Hello, Lore. Did you miss Daddy?"

My stomach rolls and apparently Lore's does as well, as a bit of her oatmeal is puked up and falls past her lips. I grab her hand and squeeze it, letting her know she's not alone. He winks and walks over to the metal cabinet and opens the door.

The fire roars inside, and he unzips his bag. He pulls out a handful of metal rods and puts them directly in the fire, only leaving the ends sticking out. Reaching into the bag, he grabs a pair of heavy duty working gloves and tosses them at Howl. He catches them against his chest and takes a deep breath, cracking his neck.

Silas drops the bag and stomps over to us, kicking a few of us out of the way, "Move!" He grabs Lettie and yanks her up in the air.

She screams and fights in his grasp. "No, no, no!"

We all stand, moving towards him, shouting, "Leave her alone!"

"No, not her!"

"Please!"

He reaches back and pulls out a gun, first pointing it towards us and then bringing it to her temple. We all freeze and put our hands up, stepping back. "That's what I thought," he sneers.

Howl's gaze flickers between them and then back at us, he seems almost defeated when he shouts, "Line up! Those that have been here longer go first, newbies, go last."

He pulls off his hoodie, revealing his cut-off shirt. A cherry blossom branch runs down his left arm, and ends with a giant cherry blossom on his hand with blood splatter. His other arm is covered with various forms of Japanese art. He slides the gloves on while we line up, each one of us bracing our hands on the back of whoever is in front of us. He pulls out one of the metal rods and slowly steps up to Silas and Lettie. Silas looks at all of us with his smarmy smile.

"From this moment on, you no longer have names. You will now be the number branded on your skin, like animals ready for slaughter."

"Hold her tight," Howl demands. She whimpers when Silas squeezes his arms around her, keeping her arms pinned to her sides. He holds the rod up and presses it against her tiny forearm, the room immediately reeking of burned flesh. Her skin sizzles and she attempts to thrash around and pull away from the pain, screaming and crying.

"Please! No! It hurts, it hurts. MOMMY! I WANT MY MOMMY!"

My heart shatters at her screams for her mom. "It's okay, Lettie. It's okay. Listen to my voice. You're okay, honey. Deep breaths."

The other girls pitch in, trying to soothe her.

"Shh, shh."

"It's okay, Lettie."

"You're okay, Lettie."

"You're so strong."

Howl pulls away and an angry, red and white brand is in her arm, **1**. She stops screaming, but continues to cry softly. Her body sags as the fight leaves her. I look at Howl's hand holding the rod. His knuckles are white, flexing over and over, and a slight tremor can be seen. He throws it against the wall and it clatters to the floor.

"Next! Get over here, now!"

Each girl goes and braces one hand on the wall, stretching out their arm for Howl to brand. They all stare at Lettie, as if to remind themselves why they're not fighting back. It's my turn, and the more I watch his reactions to this and everything since we've come here, I've realized there's a chink in his armor. I intend to crack at it every chance I get, until it shatters completely.

Instead of looking at Lettie or looking away, I make sure he meets my eyes before branding me. There's a flicker of something in his expression and he quickly looks down at my arm as he brands me. I tremble and bite my tongue, holding my scream as I stare defiantly at the side of his face. He pulls away, tossing that metal rod down as well. When he refuses to return my stare, I look down at my arm instead. Blood bubbles to the surface throughout the brand. This is the second time Aldo has taken my name from me. Only this time, I've been reduced to a number.

Goodbye, Ophelia.

Hello, **12**.

"I have nothing to offer but blood, toil, tears, and sweat." - Winston Churchill

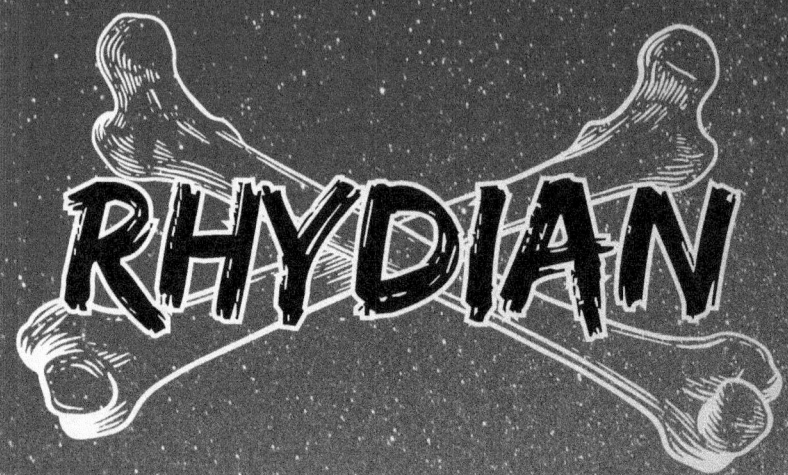

CHAPTER TWENTY-SEVEN
ANOTHER ONE BITES THE DUST

Rhydian

With my headphones on, I listen to the carnival food booth audio on a loop. I cross my arms and sit back, observing everyone in the private book-nook work on different things. I don't care how often we've listened to this or looked at the parking lot footage, I refuse to miss a single thing. I will pick every last detail apart. Anything could be a fucking clue, and I refuse to fucking miss it.

The door opens and a disheveled, blushing V walks in, adjusting her hair and clothes. I hit pause and pull my headphones off as everyone starts to hoot and holler. She holds up an envelope, waving it.

"I had to go grab a delivery from Cal. He said it was hand delivered."

"He hand delivered that dick to you," Nova says while laughing.

"It was a big delivery. Huge," V retorts.

"Get you some, V. That man is too hot not to mount," Nova says.

Rhys' eyes darken and he turns and looks at her. "Excuse me?"

"Oh, calm down, Ghoulie. The man is hot. Doesn't mean I want him. My best friend should have someone hot to fulfill all her package needs." Nova laughs and brings Rhys' hand to her belly. His eyes soften and he smiles.

"You're fighting dirty, wife."

"Okay, enough about my sex life. Did you guys not hear me? Cal says this was hand delivered to him this morning. Why would someone hand deliver an envelope to my barista? That doesn't make sense."

Everyone sits up straight, more serious with the realization that this is strange.

"I'll pull up the surveillance here. Did Cal say what the guy looked like?" Dorian asks.

"He said the guy had hair like fire and soulless eyes."

"So, a ginger?" Rhyatt asks. He can barely contain his laughter through each word, "V, does your boy believe the myth of soul-less gingers?"

V glares at Rhyatt. "Nene, cállate."

"I know there's a shut up somewhere in there, but my name is Rhy-Rhy not Nay-Nay, thank you very much." He dances around and singing, "Watch me whip, mm, yeah, watch me nay-nay. Whipped cream and banay-nays."

V lifts her brow and sighs, shaking her head. "Pendejo," she mutters with a smile.

Great, now the lyrics to the actual song are floating in my head. I roll my eyes and snap at Rhyatt. "Rhyatt. Shut up and sit down. Lore needs you."

Rhyatt immediately freezes, and I watch as my goofy ass brother morphs into a broken boy again. He sits down looking broken, and I rub the ache in my chest. I feel like a dick for the low blow, but I need him to focus.

"What the fuck," Dorian says. He's furiously typing away, but shaking his head.

"What's up?" Rhys asks.

"Everything is gone. There is no footage here from midnight to an hour ago. Not even static or a loop. Just. Gone. All gone. What the fuck is going on?"

He tugs at his hair, looking at it as if it's a puzzle to be solved.

"Okay, time to open the envelope. Maybe we'll find answers in there," I say, pointing at the envelope in V's hands. She tears it open and slowly dumps the contents out on the table. A stack of papers, surveillance photos and a plastic case with an SD card falls out with a note attached. A few of us stand, spreading the papers and photos out.

"What the fuck?" I whisper. I pull the note from the case and open it.

I will save them all. I swear I will. I just need some help. Help me, help you.

Rhys slaps his thighs and stands, helping Nova up. "That's our cue. Nova grab Rhayvin. All of you who work your asses off behind the lines, you're coming with us."

He turns and points at V. "You better hope Cal isn't in on this. I'm sorry. I'm happy for you, but if he fucks with our family, he's fucking dead."

V shakes her head, sighing. "I'll kill the country boy myself if he's out to hurt our family. I really don't think he's involved in this, though."

Muggzy picks up a surveillance photo of a man unbuckling his belt. "Someone needs to talk to Cal. Get as much information as possible on whoever handed this to him. Just don't bring him in here. He doesn't need to see any of this if he really is clueless."

"Daddy?"

I look down at Rhayvin, her eyes pleading. I pick her up and hold her in my lap. "Hi, little Rhay."

"Are you coming home, Daddy?"

"Yeah, baby. I'll be right behind you."

She holds her tiny pinky towards me. "Pwomise?"

I wrap my pinky around hers. "I promise."

Everything inside the envelope was split up. Everyone is analyzing every pixel of the photos and every line of intel. In between Dorian's clicks on his laptop, I look up and ask, "Dorian, what's on that SD card?"

"So far, it's looking like all of that information in digital format. There's an audio file as well, I'm getting ready to pull it up. One says original and the other says enhanced background."

I wait for the audio to begin when there's a scuffle to my right. I look over and Rhyatt is trying to snatch pictures from Fish.

"Give me them, you fucking guppy!"

Fish holds the stack of pictures behind him, shouting over his shoulder, "Someone take the fucking pictures! They don't need to see these!"

They? I quickly stand up. "What pictures? Who doesn't need to see them?" I watch as the pictures make their way down the table to each person. "What the fuck are in those pictures, Fish?!"

The pictures reach Rhys and he looks down at them. His jaw clenches and his eyes darken with every picture he flips through. He looks at us and back down at the pictures. My heart races and I'm terrified to know what they're seeing. I feel like I'm being torn in two different directions. The fear of the known and the fear of the unknown.

"We can't hide it from them. They have to see."

The group bickers about it and I stand on the table, shouting, "SHUT THE FUCK UP! SHUT UP!" I'm breathing heavy and staring at the group as they stop and stare up at me.

"Just stop. Let us see the pictures. Until you're in our shoes, you don't get a fucking say! You all know damn well you'd want to see. So give us the fucking pictures!"

Rhys walks over and places the pictures between Rhyatt and I, face down. We both reach for them, our fingertips just barely grazing the edges before he slides them away.

"Look at me, little brothers."

Looking up at him, he looks down at us with a sad smile. "Use it as fuel, but don't let it cloud your judgment. We need you both to keep your head in the game. Okay?"

Rhyatt and I look at each other and then back up at Rhys, nodding. He pushes the pictures towards us and stands behind us. He puts a hand on each of our shoulders and squeezes, reminding us he's there for whatever we find. Together, we flip the pictures over. The first one shows a man smirking, and the girls just behind him, crying in the carnival parking lot. Rhyatt snatches the photo from my hand. "Wait. Is that?"

He brings the picture closer to his face, his eyes flicking back and forth. He tosses the picture to the table and stands. Grabbing his chair, he lifts it over his head and slams it against the floor, one of the legs cracking. He smashes the chair against the floor repeatedly, screaming, "FUCK! FUCK! FUCK!"

He tosses the last remaining piece of the chair down, his fists clenched at his sides. Rhys and I walk towards him as he continues to scream. Spit flies from his mouth as he continues to growl and scream. He spins away from us and walks up to the wall, punching it. The sight of blood on the wall makes us both step in and grab an arm each. He fights our hold and we kick his legs out from under him, pinning him to the floor.

"Breathe, Rhy, breathe. Shh."

He opens his mouth to speak—then shuts it again, lips trembling. It's as though he's searching for words, but all that comes out is a dry, guttural croak. I can feel his pain and I look at the group, who are standing and staring.

"Clear the room!"

Without a word, everyone heads to the door, with one last look from each as they go. The door shuts and Rhyatt lets out a choked sob.

"I should've killed him when I had the chance."

"Who? Who should you have killed?" Rhys asks.

"Rhy! Who?!" I beg.

Rhyatt grits his teeth, spit flying through as he screams, "Lore's father."

"Learn how to see. Realize that everything connects to everything else." -Leonardo da Vinci

CHAPTER TWENTY-EIGHT

I HOPE YOU DANCE

December 2024

Ophelia

Time no longer exists. There's no way to count the days that we've been down here. We started with twelve girls, and we're now down to three: **1, 11, 12.** The number dwindled down over time, and it always happened the same way. Howl would snatch one of the girls as they screamed for help and he dragged them behind a closed door. Her muffled screams would turn to silence and we would all hold on to each other, holding our breath. Waiting. He'd open the door and they'd lie limp in his arms, blood trickling from their head. We've waited for more girls to arrive, and so far none others have joined us. I'm thankful no other girls have been taken, but it leaves me on edge. There are no answers as to why there aren't more, and it almost feels ominous. As twisted as that sounds.

I watch as Howl paces back and forth, looking at his phone. Silas is sitting in a chair against the wall, passed out with a hand down his pants. Lettie's back is against mine, while Lore sits in front of her. A notification sound goes off on Howl's phone and he mutters, "Shit."

He looks over at us, chewing on his toothpick harder. It snaps, one end falling to the floor and he spits out the other end. He shoves his phone in his pocket and walks over to Silas, kicking his shin. Silas wakes up with a grunt.

"What the fuck?"

"Get up. Boss is on his way down, look alive. I'm gonna go play for a bit."

Silas smirks and looks over at us. "Which one?"

My body tenses and I feel Lettie trembling behind me. Howl prowls over, looking at me first and then past me. I look over my shoulder as his hand shoots past me. For a moment, I think he's going for Lore but instead, he snatches Lettie up.

"No!" I shout, as Lettie screams, her tiny body flailing in his arms.

"Not her, take me, not her!" Lore begs. Lettie kicks and struggles around in his arms as he grunts and carries her to one of the rooms. He kicks the door shut, and I can still hear her muffled cries for help.

I start to get up when I hear the telltale click of a gun. My breath catches in my throat when I see Silas with his gun pointed in Lore's direction. He keeps the gun towards her but looks at me.

"Sit. Down. Now," he demands.

I immediately drop to the floor, wincing at the pain in my knees. The only sound in the room is mine and Lore's shaky breathing. *Why can't I hear Lettie anymore?* I look over my shoulder towards the door, my eyes brimming with tears. *Please don't be dead.* I look back at Silas as his gun remains steady and aimed at Lore.

"Please, please. I did what you asked. Please!" I beg.

"I like hearing you beg. Do it again." With his other hand, he reaches down and rubs the front of his pants.

"Please!"

He moans and rubs himself. "Again."

"Pl-"

The door clicks and he immediately jumps, putting his gun away. I stare at the door as it slowly opens and blindly reach for Lore. My fingertips brush against her skin and she tightly grabs my hand, quickly scrambling to sit right beside me. The door bursts open and Aldo walks in with a cigar hanging from his teeth with a smile. He has a Santa hat covering his head and a tiny tree over his shoulder.

"Merry Christmas, my hoe, hoe, hoes."

Christmas? It's already Christmas? Tears prick my eyes at the thought that I'm missing Christmas with Rhayvin, and shortly after, her birthday. Aldo tosses the tree and kneels before me, blowing his smoke in my face. My eyes sting from the burn of the smoke. He wipes a tear away from my cheek and licks it from his thumb.

He mocks me, cooing, "Aww, what's the matter, 12? Did you just realize you won't be spending Christmas with little Rhayvin?"

My nostrils flare in anger, yet more tears fall down my face. He pats my cheek gently at first, each pat getting harder and harder. He rears back and smacks me hard enough that the sound echoes throughout the room, and I fall to the floor holding my cheek. "I really did want to have a beautiful Christmas with you. Decorate the tree. Eat a meal. Make love. Unfortunately, your family has really fucked with my business. Someone has to pay for that. And until I get my hands on them, it'll just have to be the three of you." He looks past me and shouts, "Howl!"

I roll my head to the side and watch as the door opens and Howl peeks his head out smiling. "Yeah, boss?"

"Call the buyers. Tell them there's a slight delay in transport. Depending on how these two behave, I will decide whether 1 leaves breathing or not."

Lore and I both sob, "No."

The door clicks shut behind me and Aldo looks at Silas. "Go hook 11 up in the room. 12 and I will be right there."

Lore whimpers the closer Silas gets. He chuckles and walks behind her, quickly bringing his arms around and holding her over her breasts. Lore sobs and shrieks at the vile touch from her father. He drags her to the room, laughing the whole way.

"Aldo, please, please don't hurt them." I yelp as his hand strikes like a snake, latching around my neck and squeezing tight. I gasp for air as he squeezes tighter and tighter. I can hear my heart pounding and my body feels like it's tingling. I try to slap at his hand but his grip remains.

"You would think after all this time, you would know not to tell me what to do, 12." Drool spills from my mouth as I cough and gasp for air when he lets go. I bring my hand to my throat, rubbing it and wheezing. "Get to the room."

I put my hands on the floor and push myself up, stumbling to the room. Lore is dangling from the chains, sobbing and with puke dripping down the front of her body while Silas continues to caress her.

"Get out Silas," Aldo barks. He immediately steps back, scurrying out of the room head down like the fucking rat that he is.

"We're going to do things a little differently tonight. What better way to celebrate Christmas than creating new memories and starting new traditions?"

The opening notes to his favorite song fill the space and I fight to focus. I desperately want to disappear, think of happier times, but I can't leave Lore alone. I have to stay for her. For Lettie. *They need me.*

"Clean her up."

I flinch, my body jerking, realizing how close he is, breathing in my ear. Swallowing hard, I force myself to move. I walk up to her and try to wipe the vomit off of her body. My stomach rolls at the feeling of her vomit in my hands. I gag as I shake the excess vomit off of my hands, pieces of it slapping against the floor.

"So close. Now lick the rest off."

My eyes widen and I stare at him. "Wh-what?"

With a bored expression, he pulls his gun out, cocks it and aims it in our direction. "Lick. It. Off."

I turn to Lore. "I'm sorry. I'm so sorry."

She squeezes her eyes shut, crying. "Just do it," she mumbles in resignation.

I lean towards her belly button and stick my tongue out. The bitter, acidic taste hits my tongue and I try to hold back my gag. I lap at her stomach and chest like a dog, trying to get it done as quickly as possible. My eyes water with every barely restrained gag. I lick the last of it from her nipple and quickly spin away, vomiting on the floor.

I spit and my tears rush down my face. "I'm sorry, I'm sorry. I'm so sorry, Lore."

With a shaky, tearful voice, she tries to soothe my conscience. "It's okay, I promise, it's okay. I'm okay, we're okay."

"Stand next to her and close your eyes. Arms to your sides." I do as I'm told and squeeze my eyes shut, my body trembling in trepidation. I ball my hands into fists, forcing myself to keep my eyes shut while I hear Lore sniffle and gasp.

"Bellissimi Gemelli." Beautiful Gemini. *No. Oh, please no.* "Open your eyes, 12." Tears spill from my eyes as I open them and I can't help but look at Lore's stomach. Uneven dots adorn her torso, matching the scars on mine.

My voice cracks as I beg, "Aldo."

He looks at me and smiles, tilting his head. "Why so sad?"

"I don't want you to hurt her."

His smile grows and his eyes darken as he points a knife towards me. My breath hitches and my stomach tenses, waiting for the first stab. "I'm not going to hurt her."

"Y-you're not?"

"No." He spins the knife around, the handle pointed in my direction now. "You are."

I'm already shaking my head and taking a step back. He clicks his tongue and points his gun at her head with his other hand. "I'll shoot her and then have Howl bring 1 in. You'll watch us take turns with her until she takes her final breath. All the while, you'll be picturing Rhayvin's face. Do you want that?"

I sob at the thought. "No, please, no."

"You have to do it, Oph. Do it for those little girls, please! You have to!" Lore pleads.

My eyes flicker back and forth between Aldo and Lore. Her eyes plead with me and she nods. My hand shakes as I take the knife from Aldo. "Don't do anything stupid. Give her the marks."

Tears blur my vision and I quickly swipe them away with my knuckles. I stand in front of Lore and look up at her. "I'm so sorry." She starts humming a tune that seems almost familiar. Her hums turn into broken singing and I realize she's singing *I Hope You Dance* by *Lee Ann Womack,* the song Rhayvin and I danced to at my wedding. I sob harder at the memory, remembering such a beautiful moment.

I look up at her and she nods again with a sad smile, then sings the rest of the song with a wavering voice as I begin puncturing each dot on her stomach. Every push of the knife into her skin is punctuated by a keening cry. Her breathing is heavy as she forces the song out. Blood drips warm and slick from every mark I make. I finish the last one and hear the faint clink of Aldo's belt behind me.

"Rub your hand through her blood."

I look at him as he reaches inside his pants. "You're gonna need it."

"Is it really a choice when we have no other option?" - Hobson's Choice

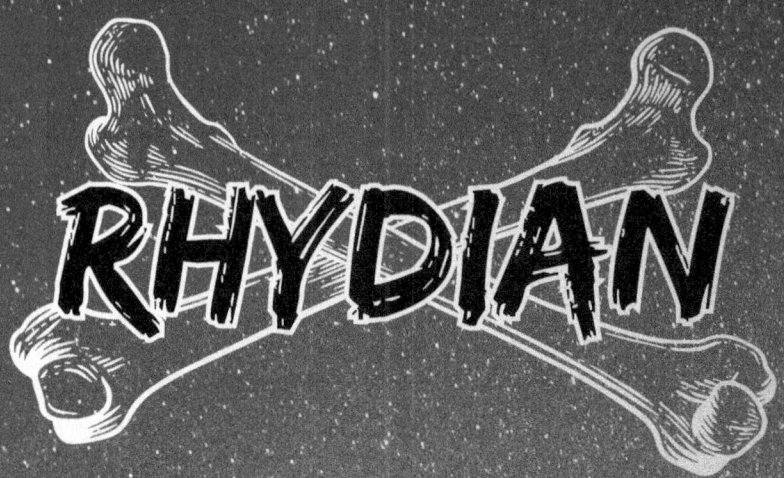

CHAPTER TWENTY-NINE

RISE

January 2025

Rhydian

The table practically shakes as all our phones go off at the same time.

> UNKNOWN: 911. Meet at Swan & Scribe.
> DON'T SHOOT THE MESSENGER. They will
> have vital information to save the girls. Trust is
> hard, I know. But we've been helping the best
> we can. Please remember that.

All at once, we pocket our phones and our chairs squeak against the floor as we get up.

"Someone call V. Tell her there's some sort of emergency and the store needs to close early. Get everyone out of there," Rhys says.

"On it," Dorian responds, already pulling his phone out again.

"I'll be right out, don't leave without me. I'm gonna go say bye to Rhayvin."

"We're right behind you," Rhys says as Dorian and him fall in line behind me. Our boots clomp against the floor as we rush to my little apartment.

I open the door and Rhayvin runs over. "Hi, Daddy!" I kneel down and open my arms for her.

"Hi, little Rhay. Daddy has to go for a little bit, so you're gonna stay here with Auntie Nova and Auntie Theia, okay?"

She pulls away from my hug and pouts. "Do you have tuh go, Daddy? You always leavin'."

I push some of her hair back and try to muster a smile. "I know, baby. Daddy's just working real hard to get Mommy back."

Her eyes water and her little lip trembles. "Bwing Mama back, Daddy. Pwease."

I hug her tight, "I'm working on it, baby, I promise. You be good for your aunties, okay?"

"Mhmm." She kisses my cheek and walks away to play with her toys.

The drive is silent the whole way there. Walking towards the entrance, V is already pushing the door open for us. "Go to the usual book nook."

Rhyatt whistles and looks back at her. "Damn, V, did you threaten to chancla everyone in here to get them out so quick?"

"Move along before you find one lodged in your ass."

Rhyatt puts his hand over his ass. "You keep that thing on your foot and out of my ass, spicy lady."

I shove him forward. "Keep moving, bitch."

"Paws off, jerk."

One by one, we make our way into the book nook and stand around. I cross my arms and watch the door, ready for whoever walks through. Viking taps one of the tables and captures our attention.

"Remember. We can't attack first. We need to see what this person knows. We all know how to defend ourselves and each other. We'll see the signs if they're lying. Plus, there's more of us than one fucking messenger." He briefly pauses and sighs, "I vote the twins hang back."

"WHAT?!" Rhyatt and I shout.

"Listen! Just go to the back of the fucking room. You're still going to be a part of this, but that way you have more of us to go through in a fit of rage. Emotions get high and you two lose your fucking minds, every time."

Rhys nods at us. Great, the big bros have spoken. "Fine," we both grumble and push our way to the back of the book nook. We both cross our arms and kick a leg behind us, our boots propped against the wall.

Dorian gasps and points. "See! It's fucking creepy when they do that shit!"

Annoyed by being pushed to the back, I snap at Dorian, "What?"

"Oh settle down, grumpy. I always say how creepy it is when you guys do the same thing at the same time, or say the same thing at the same time. And you guys are doing it right now."

"You realize that you and Rhys do the same thing, right?" Rhyatt asks.

In unison, Rhys and Dorian say, "No we don't."

Rhyatt points and shouts. "AHH! Right there! Caught ya, jerks!" They both make faces mocking Rhyatt and turn to look at each other. A look of realization crosses their faces and they quickly turn away, grumbling.

The moment is interrupted by the door opening.

"You're going to get me killed with this plan, man!"

Everyone stares and our jaws collectively drop. "They're all looking at me. I will seriously haunt your ass if they kill me. No. Don't you, don't you dare hang up on me!" He glares down at his phone. "I disown you," he seethes. When he finally looks up, he scratches the back of his head, his expression a mix of guilt and nerves. "Uh, hey guys. Umm. Surprise?"

V steps forward, her voice cracks in betrayal. "Cowboy?"

He sighs, shifting his weight while barely meeting her eyes "Hi, darlin'."

"Don't you darlin' me, Cal! What the fuck is going on?"

"Please. Please, hear me out. I know this looks bad, but I swear we've been doing all we can to help."

I push off the wall and crack my neck, making my way towards him. The group immediately turns and puts their hands up.

"Wait! We listen first, then decide from there," Rader says.

I growl in frustration and glare at him. "Sit the fuck down and start talking. Your fucking life depends on it, motherfucker."

He puts his hands up. "Okay, okay." Rhys kicks a chair towards him, Cal barely catches it before it collides against him. "Yeesh."

He takes a seat and looks around, his eyes falling on V once again. She crosses her arms and glares at him with barely restrained fury. He puts his head down, sighing in defeat.

"If we could have got them out of there sooner, we would have. When they were first taken, there were eight other girls already there. One... one of which is just a little girl. We wanted her out of there first more than anything, but we knew it would turn into a bloodbath if we did. She was the only thing keeping the other girls from fighting back. My cousin Sage, or Howl as they know him, is in charge of watching the girls and transporting those that die or get sold. He's developed a system to try and help the best he can. To give some of the girls a break from the men who show up, he'll pretend to stake a claim on them for the evening and drag them to a room. He'll drug them with the Dimenticare and just sit in there while they sleep it off. He'll ruffle their hair a bit and try to make it look believable and then bring them back out. He does the same thing for the girls that are to be sold."

I stop my pacing and glare at him. "We're just supposed to let you live after telling us he's still helping sell these girls?!"

His eyes widen and he shakes his head. "No, no, no. He's not really selling them. He creates the illusion that they're being sold. He tells that Aldo fucker that he found a buyer. I'm his DorLorean of sorts, heh," he clears his throat and cuts off his laugh. "Sorry, no time for jokes. Anyway, I siphon money from Aldo and every other piece of shit we come across. When the buy takes place, that's where Sage gets the money from to pay for the girls. He then takes them to the hospital in our home-town, Ingary.

With an astronomical donation, the hospital there was able to build a wing specifically for sex trafficking victims; *Jenkins Moving Castle*. Go ahead. Look it up. It's real. I know you can confirm all of this, Dorian. You have the skills. I've seen it. You're a damn good hacker, definitely been making me jump through hoops like crazy."

"So wait, no soulless ginger delivered that envelope? It was you?" Rhyatt asks.

Cal laughs softly and nods. "Just me. Sage wanted you to have as much information as possible to work on taking out those involved in the ring. If he could've cloned himself to do it all, he would've. He needed help on the outside so he could focus on what needed to be done on the inside. I think this is the most difficult job he's ever been on. Don't get me wrong, they're all rough, but this one… it's the longest job he's been on." He looks off into the distance, his eyes glazed over. "I don't even know if he'll ever fully recover from it this time."

It feels weird being so angry with a person, but at the same time being grateful for the amazing things they've been doing for victims. I scratch my head thinking and turn towards him. "So is there a plan in place here or what?" I put my hands on my hips, waiting for his reply.

Rhyatt's obnoxious giggle rings in my ears before he slaps my back. "I'm about to start calling you Rhay-dian. Holy shit, you're in her sassy pants stance."

I drop my fists, shaking them out. "I am not! Shut up." He opens his mouth to talk and I put my palm over his face, pushing him back. "Anyways. Is there a plan in place or not, Cal?"

He sits up straight and smiles brightly. "Yeah, we have a plan." His smile falters for a second. "We don't have much time to put it all in motion, though. You guys were able to wipe out all the key players. Sage has all the girls out except for Ophelia and Lore. This is the perfect chance to get it done."

"Okay, great. When?"

CHAPTER TWENTY-NINE

"Tomorrow."

"You cannot alter your fate. However, you can rise to meet it if you choose."
-The Wise Woman, Princess Mononoke

CHAPTER THIRTY

SKYFALL

January 24, 2025

Ophelia

Lore and I are all that's left of twelve girls. Lettie was taken on Christmas while Aldo forced me to mutilate Lore. The thought of fighting our way out of here seemed so much easier when there were more of us, but we refrained to keep Lettie safe. They made sure she was the last one taken before us. I'm sure it was to fuck with us. As if to say, *there you go, try and fight back now*.

Problem is, we're weak and tired. With every girl they took, our food portions dwindled. The only thing keeping us going is the glimmer of hope that our family will find us. Some days that glimmer fades to nothing, and we lie side by side staring at the ceiling in defeat.

Howl walks out and hands the both of us big cups of smoothies. I look inside at the green goop, and my stomach swoops at the memory of how much it fucked me up last time. I grimace and shake my head, refusing the drink.

"Come on, it's good for you," he says, pushing the cup closer to me.

I roll my eyes. "What? A customer coming today that's into shit play?"

He scrunches his nose at my question and shakes his head, pulling his toothpick out of his mouth and pointing it at me. "That's nasty, girl."

"What's nasty is your smoothies and what it does to my stomach."

Silas stomps over and picks up the cup, seething. "Drink it, you ungrateful bitch!" He grabs my hair and yanks my head back, dumping the contents over my face.

Howl groans, "Now I have to throw them in the shower room, Silas." Silas smirks at Howl and chucks the cup at the wall, turning to Lore.

"You want some, too?" She whimpers and quickly picks up her cup, downing it as quickly as she can. Reflexes dulled, she's unable to dodge the rageful backhand to her face. She cries out in pain, holding her face as he kneels down. "Stupid bitch. Always ruining my plans. How are you still so goddamn useless?"

"Why don't you clean up the mess you just made, so I can get them in the shower room."

He jabs his finger in Howl's face. "You can't tell me what to do, boy!"

Howl stands taller, looming over Silas, forcing him to shrink back. Fucking coward. "I can't? How do you think the boss would feel if he knew what you just did to 12 with the drink? You know the rules and you broke them."

I can't help but smile at the fear in Silas' eyes. *Good. Feel the fear that we do.*

Howl looks down at us. "Let's go, girls."

Lore and I grab onto each other and stand on shaking legs. We follow Howl to the shower room and step in. With our hands on the wall, we hear the click of the door shutting and brace ourselves for the freezing water. We both jolt when the water hits us then sigh, realizing he's using warm water. At the same time we look at each other with confused expressions.

Howl steps between us, his movements quiet and deliberate. He reaches up, looping the hose around a pipe overhead, his expression unreadable. From his pocket, he pulls a roll of electrical tape and wraps it tightly around the trigger and handle of the hose. "There. Stand under that and keep warm," he says in a hushed tone.

We huddle together under the spray and stare at him.

"I need you both to just stay quiet and listen, okay?"

Hunched under the warm water, we wait for what he has to say. What? Does he expect us to just say, *'yeah, sorry, not listening to you'*?

"I'll show you proof when I'm done explaining. I know you feel like you can't trust me, but you can. I'm not one of them. I know you've noticed things here and there that separates me from them. My real name is Sage. Sage Jenkins. I'm in a similar line of work as your family. My main focus is sexual assaults and human trafficking," he pauses. "Stumbling on this ring was pure coincidence. I happened to overhear the brothers talking about the operation they had. It was supposed to be hush hush, even from their daddy Cif. I paid my dues, I played my part. I've saved as many as I could along the way."

He lifts his shirt sleeve and shows his cherry blossom branch down his arm. Numbers 1 through 12 are on different blossoms and the rest have letters. He points them out to us.

"The ones that aren't tainted are the ones I've been able to save. The ones with blood are the ones I wasn't able to. I carry all of you with me every single day."

"Lettie?" I ask tearfully.

He nods and points to the blossom with a 1. "I took her to my hometown. There's a hospital there with a wing specifically for trafficking and sexual assault victims. She's safe. I swear. I can show you proof of that later as well. My cousin has been helping me on the outside. I'm sure you both know him. Cal? Works at *Swan & Scribe*."

My eyes widen when I realize I do remember Cal, the barista.

"He's basically my Dorian and Lore all wrapped into one. I give him as much information as I can. I've sent him updates on you guys and information that your family needed on the other key players of this operation. He's working with them now on a rescue mission for you guys. I'm waiting for word from them to get you out of here. I promise."

Standing up straighter, I narrow my eyes at him. "How do we know we can trust you? Have you forgotten we've watched you drag girls into the rooms to have your way with them? And every single one has come out of there bleeding, unconscious or dead in your arms."

"All an act. An illusion. I would never fucking touch women or girls like that. When I take them to the room, I drug them with Dimenticare. I know you guys have heard of that. I let them get some real rest. When they start to come to, I ruffle their hair a bit. Make it look like I had my way with them, and due to the drug, they don't remember what happened so they can't ever slip up about me taking care of them. The blood you've seen? Fake. Again. Used to make it look like I've harmed them."

He pulls his phone out and starts tapping. "One sec. I'm going to show proof from Cal that he's working with your family."

A soft click from the door stops us all cold.

"Wasn't that already closed?" Lore whispers.

Howl, Sage, what the fuck ever, clenches his jaw. "Yes. Yes, it was." He grabs a new toothpick and places it between his teeth before pocketing his phone. "Stay here."

He walks towards the door and tilts his neck side to side before opening the door a crack. He peeks out through the crack, leaning in to listen.

"Motherfucker," he hisses under his breath. He looks over at us, eyes sharp. "Stay. Put."

He yanks the door open and stomps out, his voice booming, "WHAT THE FUCK IS UP, SILAS?!"

Lore and I sneak towards the door and listen.

"You're a fucking traitor! And now you're gonna fucking pay!" Silas' voice is wild. "Boss is coming for you, boy. He's coming for all of you!"

Fuck. I reach for Lore as she reaches for me, our slick hands sliding against each other's arms as we try to latch on to one another. My heart hammers in my chest as I gently push on the door and cringe, squeezing my eyes shut as it creaks. I slowly open my eyes and see them both staring at us.

Sage looks panicked, his jaw tight and Silas has an evil gleam in his eye. He nods towards us. "Yeah, you bitches are done for."

Sage balls his fist and throws his fist up against Silas' chin. His shout of pain dies off in his throat as he passes out before he even hits the floor. "Girls! Time to go!"

We scurry out of the shower room as Sage runs back towards the kitchen. I jump at the sound of cupboards and drawers being slammed. The sound of scraping captures my attention and I look to the left. Lore is picking up one of the branding rods and lays it over her shoulder. She walks over to Silas, tremors wracking her body as she hovers above him.

"Lore?"

"Never again," she shakes her head. She lifts the rod above her head and with a guttural scream, swings down against Silas' face over and over. Bones crunch and blood splatters the tiles with every hit.

"NEVER AGAIN! NEVER AGAIN! FUCK YOU! YOU'RE THE WHORE! YOU'RE WORTHLESS! PATHETIC! DISGUSTING! I HATE YOU!" She lets out a blood-curdling scream and slams the rod against his face one last time.

"Holy shit," Sage murmurs beside me. He hands an unzipped backpack to me. "There's clothes in there for both of you. We have to go, so you're going to need to help her." I'm frozen in place looking at the bag, then at Lore and down at what's left of Silas.

"Ophelia."

I turn to him, my voice trembling. "Proof?"

He sighs in frustration and pulls his phone out, unlocking it. "I'm your only hope, Ophelia," he says as he turns the phone towards me. The screen glows with a message thread marked with a flame emoji. The text exchange shows everything he said: information he gave Cal so the group could take out key players, updates on both Lore and I, pictures and videos of all the girls he saved. He pulls the phone back and scrolls a bit, showing me the phone again.

"I had him send this one for you." I grab his phone and my eyes brim with tears. Rhydian sits holding Rhayvin as they smile at the camera. My heart breaks when I see that they're both wearing fake smiles. I sniffle, whispering, "Thank you."

"Yeah. Now can you guys please get ready? We don't have much time," he pleads. I nod, dropping the duffle bag to the floor and kneel. I pull a hoodie out and slide it on, followed by socks, sweats and shoes. I rush over to Lore as she cries and stares down at her dad.

"Lore?" She stands there heaving, no response. "Fuck. I'm sorry." I bring my hand up and slap her in the face. She sucks in air and blinks, slowly staring at me. "I'm sorry. We have to go. Here." Tossing the hoodie up to her, I slide the socks and sweats on her and put the shoes in front of her. "Slide those on."

While she puts the shoes on, I watch as Sage pats Silas down. He reaches into one of his pockets and pulls out a set of keys, pocketing them. "Let's go." We both jump and hold onto each other, following behind him. I watch as he punches the code in the keypad and I choke. 0521. The day Aldo kidnapped me the first time. Mine and Rhydian's wedding anniversary. Trembling in anger, I walk over to the fallen metal rod and pick it up.

"Move."

Sage looks back, and Lore just steps aside. I scream and swing the rod down. The keypad shatters under the first blow, but I keep going.

"AHHHH!" Each scream rips from my throat as I slam the rod down, again and again. Pieces of plastic and metal fly off, clattering against the concrete.

Sage grabs the rod before I swing again and looks me in the eye. "Enough. We have to go." I pant for air and let go of the rod. "Both of you stay close. And for the love of everything, listen. If I say run, then run. If I say drop, then drop. Our lives depend on it."

Lore and I hold onto each other tight. We follow Sage up the metal stairs, dirt rains down on us as he pushes the hatch open above. He holds his hand up behind him, silently telling us to stop and looks around. He slowly steps out and walks away. "Okay, it's clear. Let's go."

Lore's shoulders bump against mine as we both step up and out of the stairwell. My body buzzes in anticipation, the fear of the unknown rolling through me. Walking through the door, I realize why it smelled like animal shit. We're in a barn, and the crunching beneath us was hay. Sage pushes the barn door open just enough to peek out and a chill hits my face. He looks out, sighing in relief. "We're good, come on. Run straight to the truck, okay?"

Lore and I both nod, our hold on each other getting tighter, the sleeves of our hoodies twisted in our grasp. He opens the door fully and the crisp air smacks me harder. My breath catches as I spot the truck just outside. We make a run for it. The loose gravel beneath us slows us down, our shoes sinking into it with each step.

I reach the truck first and yank on the door handle. "It's locked!" I shout to Sage. He nods and unlocks the truck on his side, jumping in. He reaches across and unlocks our door, shoving it open. I push Lore into the truck and scramble in behind her. He puts the key in the ignition and tries to turn it. The engine sputters, vibrating under us before stalling out completely.

"Come on, come on," he growls while turning the key and pumping the gas pedal. The sound of screeching tires and flying gravel gets our attention and we all look over. My heart is in my throat as headlights flash in the distance. Lore and I gasp, while Sage continues muttering, "Fuck, fuck, fuck, come on, come on," while trying to start the truck. Gravel sprays everywhere as a black SUV comes flying in and deep down, I know it's Aldo. The gravel drive is long, but not enough for us to sit here all day. They're closing in.

Please, no.

"Start it, start it, start it!" I beg.

"I'm trying!" Sage snaps. The truck roars to life and Sage quickly puts it in drive, gunning it. Gravel flies behind us and the truck shoots forward. The SUV clips the back end of the truck, making us fishtail. Sage corrects it and punches the gas harder. "Get down!" He demands.

Lore and I slide down so our heads aren't above the seat. I brace the jockey box in front of me with one hand and keep hold of Lore with the other. I watch as Sage checks the mirrors and shakes his head, muttering under his breath. The truck lurches forward with a crunch, Lore and I both scream. "Come on you piece of shit truck! MOVE!" Sage shouts and bangs on the steering wheel. The truck is shoved forward again with another hit from the back. We start to fishtail again and Sage grips the steering wheel tight.

"Fuck. HOLD ON, GIRLS!"

He yanks the steering wheel to the right and I slam into Lore as she slams into Sage. "I'm sorry, I'm sorry. Hold on!" He looks in the mirror again and slams on the brakes. "Out, out, out. Move it!"

He opens the truck door and jumps out, turning quickly to reach back for us. He glances over his shoulder, his face laced with fear, then back at us as we climb out of the truck. "See that hill? Run. Go down the hill and get in the river."

Lore and I instinctively reach out for each other and break into a run. The sound of screeching tires rings in my ears and I can't help but look over my shoulder. Sage is running behind us and the black SUV is right there. Oh god.

"GO!" Sage roars.

We reach the hill and start running down, the icy grass makes me slip and my feet fly out from under me. I slam onto my back hard and gasp for air. I cover my head as I tumble down the hill. I reach the bottom and hold my ribs, Lore slamming into me as she reaches the bottom as well.

"Ungh. Fuck."

"Sorry," she says breathlessly.

I scramble to my feet and whip around when I hear Aldo's voice. "GET THEM, FRATELLO!"

My eyes widen when I see Sage flying down the hill, tumbling with Alonzo as they grapple. They reach the bottom of the hill, still locked in a fight. I'm torn between watching them and watching Aldo at the top of the hill. He points at me with a cruel smile. Sage picks Alonzo up and holds him from behind in a chokehold. He looks over at us, his eyes blazing with urgency.

"GET IN THE FUCKING WATER!"

The river rages behind us and snowflakes kiss my face as they flutter around us. The setting would be peaceful under different circumstances.

"Ophelia, we're going to fucking freeze to death if we get in there. Or smash our heads against fucking rocks."

"We're dead either way, Lore. And honestly, I'd rather the river kill us than Aldo."

Just before stepping foot in the water, I hear Aldo's shout, "NO! FRATELLO, NO!" I look back and watch as Sage snaps Alonzo's neck and drops his lifeless body to the frozen ground. I watch in horror as Aldo pulls a gun out.

"SAGE! LOOK OUT!"

He looks back and notices the gun as well. Bullets fly, hitting the ground in different spots. Sage runs in a zig-zag towards us.

"Go! Go! Go!" I scream as I hear bullets whizzing past us. He slams into us from behind, pushing us into the water. I'm frozen in shock as I'm submerged in the icy water. I choke on water, coughing and blinking the water from my eyes. Every time I'm above water and look up, I see the snow falling upon us and the sway of tree branches. The raging, frothing waters quickly drags me down the river and I frantically search for Sage and Lore.

Every beginning has an end.

Is this mine?

"The woods are lovely, dark and deep, but I have promises to keep, and miles to go before I sleep, and miles to go before I sleep."
-Robert Frost

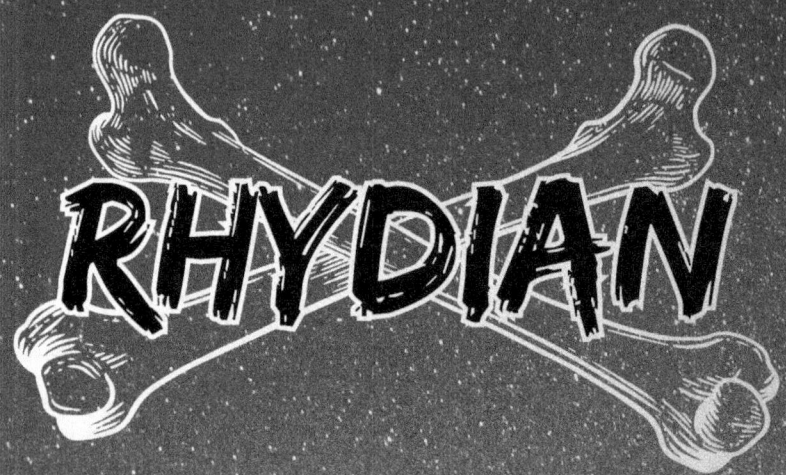

RHYDIAN

CHAPTER THIRTY-ONE

POSSIBILITY

Rhydian

Taking the ladder to the roof of *Vega Altair*, I prop the door open and walk to the edge. I sit down and let my legs dangle over the edge as I look across the valley. I absentmindedly spin my wedding ring and think of Ophelia. It's almost time to get my girl back and the anticipation is eating me alive. How much more of a monster will I need to become to rescue her this time? Will I be able to come back from it?

The distant sound of a train whistle pulls me from my thoughts, and I close my eyes remembering a happier time.

Ophelia has no idea where we're driving to. She put her trust in me and allowed me to blindfold her for the drive. I made her put her hand on my thigh to squeeze if she started feeling uneasy. Parking the car, I take a deep breath and look at the view, smiling. I take a moment to look at my beautiful bride. Fuck, she's beautiful.

"We're here. I'll help you out."

She nervously smiles and nods, "Okay."

I get out and walk around to her side, opening the door. Leaning closer, I bury my face in her hair and unbuckle her seat belt. She shivers, feeling my breath against her neck, and I smile.

"Come on, little raven," I murmur, taking her hand.

She grasps my hand tight as I help her out. My free hand hovers above her head to make sure she doesn't hit it. I shut the door and guide her, gravel crunching beneath us. I spin her in a circle, making her gasp and laugh, her hands reaching for me.

"Where are we, Bones?" I spin her once more and she throws her head back, smiling. Pulling her close, I bring her back to my chest, one arm around her waist. I use my other hand to gently pull away the blindfold.

"Last time we were here, we were just two orphans falling in love and dancing. Now, look at us."

She looks around and smiles, seeing the train tracks we danced next to and melts in my embrace. "You sang to me here."

"I guess we better keep that memory alive. I'm gonna sing a different song, though." She spins in my arms and wraps them around my neck, eyes sparkling as she smiles up at me. I pull her closer and we sway softly back and forth. I close my eyes and sing Daylily *by* Movements *to her, the lyrics floating in my head.*

I open my eyes, looking down at her as I continue to sing, the lyrics now dancing around her beautiful face. These are the moments I live and breathe for. I wish it would never end. As the song comes to an end, she stands on tiptoes, gently kissing my lips. The kiss lingers, as if we're breathing life into each other. Her lips brush against mine as she whispers, "Thank you for saving me, Bones."

My head shoots up, pulling me from the memory when the alarm system starts blaring. The flashing lights urge me to break into a run. I slam the door shut behind me and slide down the ladder. Over the intercom I can hear Mrs. Valour, "Conference room, now. Get to the conference room now."

My heart pounds in my chest, the sound of my boots on the floor matching the beat. Once I've made my way into the conference room, I see everyone is staring at the screens and watching a GPS locator. Cal is looking at his phone, pacing back and forth. "Something's wrong, something's wrong. This isn't right."

"What the fuck is going on? What's wrong?" I ask, short of breath.

"An alarm went off on his phone. I hacked it and put it up there. He keeps pacing saying something is wrong," Dorian says.

"CAL!" Rhys shouts.

Cal freezes and looks up, a panicked expression on his face and points to his phone. "Something's wrong."

I step forward. "Yeah, we got that, genius. What's wrong, though?"

He shakes his head, blinking his eyes to focus. "Right. Right. It's Sage. I have an alarm on my phone set to go off if he ever goes past a certain speed limit. Originally for if he was pushing it too far on his motorcycle. But then we figured it was a good idea for a regular vehicle. If he's in town and goes over 45, something is wrong. If he's travelling and goes over 90, same thing, something is wrong. I've been watching and his speed is erratic. It goes up really high, then slows down, goes up really high, then slows down. I think someone is chasing him."

"Can't you call him and see?" Rhyatt asks.

"That's just it. I've tried. No answer. Not even a quick answer to tell me to fuck off."

I feel little arms squeezing my leg and look down to see Rhayvin hugging me tight. I lean down and pick her up as she looks around the room and back at me. "Daddy?"

"What's up, little Rhay?"

"Did Mistuh Addo take Cal's famwee, too?"

I hug her tight, torn between telling her the truth or a lie. "I don't know, baby."

"We have to go!" Cal begs.

I kiss Rhayvin's head and whisper, "I love you, little Rhay."

"I wuv you, Daddy. Pwease get Mama." I put her down and she runs over to Nova and Theia.

Rhys spins his finger in the air and points towards the door, "Get your weapons and then we roll out! Let's move!"

Most of the crew runs to the armory while a few stay back. Some keeping Rhayvin occupied, others keeping an eye on the GPS and any surveillance they can. I throw the bag over my shoulder after grabbing everything I need and holster my gun. Rader, Fish and Sable jump in one of the unmarked vans. Rhyatt and I slide in next to Rhys in his truck. The back opens up; Viking, Muggzy and Cal hop in.

As Cal goes to close the back, V appears with a determined look on her face. "Darlin'?" Cal questions.

"I'm coming with." She starts to climb in and he reaches out to help her up. She swats at his hands and then sits in his lap. "Don't argue with me about this, cowboy."

"But-" She turns and glares at him, "I just said don't argue with me. I'm helping." She lifts her hoodie and shows a gun in a hip holster and pulls it out. She efficiently clears the chamber and slides the clip out. Quickly popping the clip back in place, checking that the safety is on and holsters it again.

Rhyatt throws his head back and laughs, "Yeah, you have fun with the spicy lady there, Cal. If you're not careful, she'll shoot you right in the ass cheek."

Cal wraps his arms around her and places his chin on her shoulder, pouting. He pulls his phone back out and says, "Head towards the fairgrounds."

Rhys nods, "Comms check." Everyone checks in and he starts driving.

As we get closer to the fairgrounds, Cal continues muttering under his breath. "Shit! Speed up. Head towards the park. Fuck, fuck, fuck."

I turn and shout, "What?!"

"He just took a corner at 60, and he's not even on a road now!"

"Where does it say he is?" Viking asks.

"The river," V whispers.

My eyes widen. "Is your cousin crazy enough to drive his ass into the river?" I ask.

He shakes his head. "Not unless he was forced to, and definitely not if he has your girls with him. He wouldn't risk it like that."

"Rhys?!" I say in a panic.

"I know, baby brother, I know." Rhys punches the gas, his tires squealing as he takes a sharp turn.

"We're close, the dot isn't moving anymore. Just a little further." Cal says.

I brace myself on the dash when Rhys slams on the brakes, shouting, "Fuck!"

"What, wha-" I look up and see why he stopped. Anger consumes me as I stare at Aldo through the windshield. He's standing on a gravel shoulder, his gaze bouncing between somewhere in the distance and us. He adjusts his cuffs, as we all jump out. The van speeds past us and turns around, tires squealing and smoke blowing. The sound of bullets being chambered echoes in the confines of Rhys' truck before we all hop out.

Aldo acts unphased, his own gun in hand, continuing to look off to the left of him. We close in around him, standing about twenty feet away, guns trained on him.

"WHERE ARE THEY?!" I roar. My body vibrates with restrained rage, and sweat drips down my temple.

"You hear that?" He says with a grin. The occasional bird chirps and the only other sound is the raging water of the river.

"Answer the question! Where are they?!"

He fully turns towards us, his hand with the gun twitches. He lifts his gun and we all take aim, firing. His body jolts with every bullet that impales him. Blood pours from the bullet holes and he bares his bloody teeth. Dropping to his knees and gasping for air, he looks at me as I walk up to him.

With a weak voice he rasps, "You're too late."

I raise my gun and shoot him between the eyes. Without thought, I drop my gun and run in the direction he was staring at. I slide down the icy hill and hit my knees once I reach the end. Alonzo lies dead with his head turned at an odd angle. I search up and down the river, screaming, "OPHELIA?!"

In the distance, I spot a log laying across the river, a dark object floating with it. I squint my eyes and run down the river bank. Everyone behind me is shouting and calling out their names. I run faster, throwing myself into the river. I fight the current and swim towards the log, shouting, "OPHELIA?!"

I grab hold of the log, my hands slipping. I grab at what looks like the hood of a sweatshirt and try to lift it. *Please, please, please.* I pull myself up onto the log. *Please be her. Please be alive.* I pull back the hood and scream in anguish, "NO!"

Tears blur my vision as I hold the torn, soaked hoodie to my chest and look down the river. My chest heaves, my body numb from the cold. *She's gone. My little raven is gone.*

"I miss her all the time. I know in my head that she has gone. The only difference is that I am getting used to the pain. It's like discovering a great hole in the ground. To begin with, you forget it's there and keep falling in. After a while, it's still there, but you learn to walk round it."
-Rachel Joyce

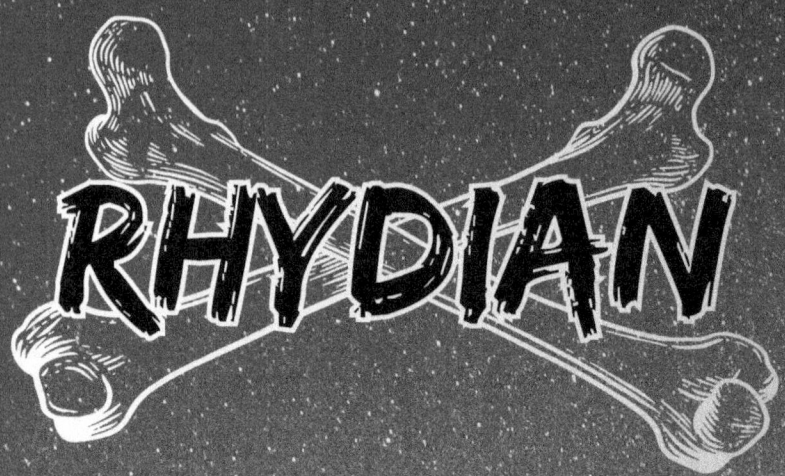

EPILOGUE

BAD MOON RISING

Rhydian

The group all sit around the private book nook at *Swan & Scribe*. We're all suffering. Grieving, but desperately grasping on to our last shreds of hope. Rhayvin is asleep in my arms. Ever since we came home without Ophelia, she only finds comfort in our arms. She'll hug one person and then move on to the next. I'm not sure if it's because she needs to feel everyone's love, or if she's trying to seek out the comfort she could only find with her mom.

I can feel my brother's pain, I need to find him. I hold onto Rhayvin and slowly stand up, looking around the room and back at the door. V walks over with her arms stretched out, whispering, "I'll take her. Go find him."

I carefully put her in V's arms, and hold my breath as Rhayvin stirs and whines in her sleep. If it's possible for my heart to break more, it does. Witnessing the pain of my daughter's loss is insurmountable. I turn towards the door, stopping when Dorian calls out to me.

"Rhydian. Um, you and Rhyatt are going to want to see this."

I drop my head and sigh. "See what?"

"I'll send it to your phone. Open it together after you check on him."

I nod as I open the door. "Thanks, man."

I feel the phone buzz in my pocket as I check the other book nooks. The only light in the room is that of a glowing laptop lighting up Rhyatt's forlorn face. I open the door just enough to squeeze through and quietly shut it behind me.

"Hey, Rhy," my voice cracks. He looks down, not saying a word. I walk around the table and stand next to him, looking down where he is. My eyes widen and I suck in a breath when I see what he's holding.

He holds up the ring box. "I was gonna propose to her," his voice breaks with a choked sob.

I sit down next to him and put my hand on his shoulder. "I swear you like it when that girl fights with you. Why would you propose to someone you're not even with and can't stand you?"

He sniffles with a sad smile, "She loves me. And we were together."

I blink in confusion. "What? No you weren't."

He looks up and a tear slides down his cheek "I've been with her since the beginning."

"Since the beginning of what?"

"That night she found us leaving and begged to come with us. After we got the motel room and you went off for the night to clear your head," he takes a shuddering breath, sniffling. "I held her in my arms all night as she cried, telling me about her life. Thanking me for saving her. I couldn't stand another second of just watching her from afar, and I kissed her. It was our first kiss, but man, did I kiss her like it would be the last one. Been together ever since."

"But-"

He nods with a sad laugh. "I know. My little succubus is feisty. It's all an act. She says what she says and acts like she can't stand me, but we really did fall in love. She was that last missing piece, like Ophie was for you."

"You hold onto that, okay? Cuz we're going to find them. I know it. We-" I growl in frustration to keep the tears at bay. "We have to. In the meantime, as usual, we have another problem to deal with. Dorian sent something to my phone that apparently we have to see."

Rhyatt carefully pockets the ring and turns towards me. I pull my phone out and unlock it, opening the article that Dorian sent. Rhyatt and I both look at it, the image and headline immediately catching our attention.

"Fuck," we exclaim at once.

NEWS

WORLD POLITICS BUSINESS SPORTS SCIENCE

Feb. 12, 2025   Damascus, OR

PATIENT BLAKE HANNIGER ESCAPES ST. JOHN'S DAMASCUS PSYCH WARD

The man, considered now armed and dangerous, escaped the infamous ward where the St. John Damascus Massacre occurred and left a note to the Gemini Slayers. Police believe Hanniger is

Why did Lore and Rhyatt keep their relationship a secret for so long? Will they have a chance at a full life together, or will it be cut in half?

Stay Tuned for…
Half Life
Coming Soon

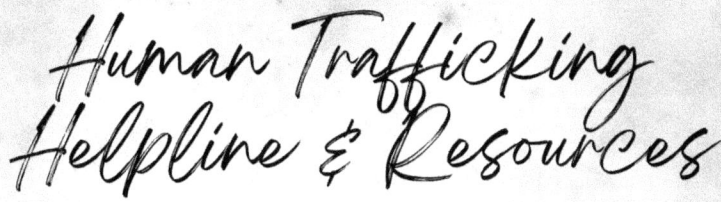

Human Trafficking Helpline & Resources

HUMANTRAFFICKINGHOTLINE.ORG

1-888-373-7888
TTY: 711
TEXT 233733

OFFICE FOR VICTIMS OF CRIME

HTTPS://OVC.OJP.GOV

VICTIM CONNECT

CALL OR TEXT
1-855-484-2846

Domestic Violence Helpline & Resources

NATIONAL DOMESTIC VIOLENCE HOTLINE

1-800-799-7233 | 1-800-787-3224

LOVE IS RESPECT
NATIONAL TEEN DATING ABUSE HELPLINE

1-866-331-9474 | 1-866-331-8453

RAPE, ABUSE, INCEST NATIONAL NETWORK

800-656-HOPE (4673) | RAINN.ORG

NATIONAL SEXUAL ASSAULT HOTLINE

1-800-656-4673

Substance Abuse Helpline & Resources

SAMHSA NATIONAL HELPLINE

1-800-662-4357

AMERICAN ADDICTION CENTERS

313-217-4572

OVERDOSE HOTLINE

FOR IMMEDIATE EMERGENCIES, CALL 911.
POISON CONTROL 1-800-222-1222

DRUGFREE.ORG

855-378-4373

DRUGABUSE.COM

888-969-7116

NATIONAL SUICIDE PREVENTION

1-800-273-8255

ALSO BY K. ILLER